Beata's Deliverance

By
Imogen Aldridge

WYNWORD
PRESS

WYNWORD PRESS

PO Box 557
Bonners Ferry, ID 83805
www.wynwordpress.com

Distributed 2018 by Wynword Press

Cover Art: David Meister

Printed in the USA

ISBN: 978-1-940638-04-1

This is a work of fiction and all characters are fictional. Any resemblance of the characters to persons living or dead is a coincidence.

❧ In loving memory of my dear son George ☙

You died too young, but before you went you taught me everything I know about unconditional love. I'm so looking forward to seeing you again some day. In the meantime, I celebrate the fact that you are finally happy in the arms of Jesus.

❧ BEATA ❦

Despite some evidence to the contrary, Beata considered herself a supremely ordinary woman. 50ish, divorced, one adult daughter, modestly successful at her career and as content as your average 50-year-old divorcee had any expectation of being, Beata ("Bee-AH-tah, as she continually corrected people who called her 'Beeta' and 'Bayta' and so on) lived a normal life. It was unfortunate, she thought, that "normal life" frequently seemed meaningless, that her job was boring and her daughter half a stranger, but Beata knew she had no real cause for complaint. Boredom and estrangement were a typical part of life, right? What was the sense in complaining about them? She complained anyway, but insisted it was a form of recreation, not to be taken seriously.

"I'm bored," she complained to her best friend, Gladys, over the phone one Saturday. "I want to retire."

"How is retirement going to fix boredom?" Gladys asked. "Retired people get bored all the time. From what I hear, retired people all want to go back to work."

"Well…those are the ones that don't play golf."

"*You* don't play golf," Gladys pointed out.

"Right, but I could learn. In fact, I have a hankering to redefine the game as a contact sport. You know…Power Golf. The way it is now, it's too civilized for me, not even worthy of being called a 'sport'. All that politeness, like yelling 'fore' and not making noise while other people are putting. Where's the competitive edge? In power golf, everybody wears body armor and hires a thug to be their caddy. When you're ready to go, you just whack the ball down the fairway and people can move or get cracked in the head. When it's time to putt, you fight for your turn like a hockey player instead of expecting everybody to back off like a bunch of wussies. No warnings. No Mr. Nice Guy. It's every man for himself."

"Sure," said Gladys. "Why not?" She seemed to think power golf was a grand idea. The two of them weren't strangers to redefining games. It had been Gladys and Beata who created No Rules Pool, a variant of pool in which nobody took turns, there was no cue ball, and it was acceptable to block the pockets to keep your opponent from scoring. Golf as a contact sport seemed a natural extension of the win-at-any-price philosophy.

"Or, if the golf thing doesn't work out," Beata continued, "maybe I could travel. I could go bungee-jumping at the Grand Canyon."

"Oh, the Grand Canyon," Gladys sighed. "I went there once. Actually, John and I went there together. It was probably beautiful, but I barely remember the scenery. What I *do* remember is the motel we stayed at in Las Vegas. It was kind of old and the rooms were small, but they had slot machines in the lobby and an outdoor swimming pool. John went out to the pool and left his cellphone in our room. So I picked it up and put it in my bag to carry it down to him because he was always paranoid about being without his cellphone."

Beata had heard the doleful tale of John and Gladys' divorce many times. However, having been Gladys' best friend for 12 years, she felt it was her duty to listen as Gladys went through it one more time.

"So his cellphone rang," Gladys continued, "and I thought John would want me to answer it. What a mistake *that* was."

"Who was the girlfriend, anyway?" Beata asked. "Didn't he run off with some doctor?"

"No, she was a chiropractor," Gladys said. "He'd been seeing her for months about a bad back. So I answered the phone and this woman's voice said 'Who *are* you? What are you doing with John's phone?' And I said 'I'm John's wife. Who are you?' And she said 'Well, I need to speak to John before I tell you anything.' So of course, I knew right away it had to be a girlfriend. And me completely clueless, thinking we were so happy together and everything was so great. After I took the call, or I should say after I recovered from the shock of taking the call, I looked at his text messages and found about a hundred of them, talking about all the fun they'd have after he cleaned out our bank account and deserted me. He was going to buy her a *fur coat*. And take her to *Maui*. So I confronted John about it, and he didn't even pretend to be sorry. He just shrugged and said 'You might as well know.'"

"What kind of a self-respecting chiropractor wears a fur coat?" Beata said. "I thought they were alternative. I thought they loved animals and advocated vegetarianism. Plus, what would you do with a fur coat in Maui?"

"I don't know…maybe she hated rodents," Gladys said. "Or she was just playing up to John. Nobody could mistake him for a vegetarian. I think the fur coat and Maui didn't really go together. John never had any sense about women's clothing. Or his own clothing, for that matter."

Gladys fell silent momentarily, but by the sound of open-mouth panting into the phone, Beata knew she was flossing between her back teeth. Her crippling experience with a philandering husband had not made her forget the importance of good dental hygiene.

"So what'd he say when you confronted him?" Beata prompted, knowing perfectly well what he had said.

"He said, 'It's about time you figured out what was going on.' Can you believe it? How cold can you get?"

"Okay," Beata said. "He leaves his cell phone sitting around with adulterous text messages on it, and then he calls *you* an idiot?"

"I think he subconsciously wanted me to know," Gladys said.

"I think he subcutaneously wanted you to know," Beata suggested.

Gladys giggled. "I think he subliminally wanted me to know."

"I think he sub-humanly wanted you to know."

"Well, it worked." said Gladys. "I found out."

"So you divorced him. Good riddance."

"I *did* divorce him," Gladys said. "But first, I threw his phone into the pool."

"I wonder which one upset him the most, losing his cell phone or losing his wife?"

"Actually, I think losing my half of the bank account hurt the most – the jerk."

Poor Gladys. She'd never quite recovered from her divorce. Unlike Beata, who'd not only recovered, but maintained a steely resolve not to get embroiled in another serious relationship ever again.

Oh, when she was young, she'd yearned to get married. Having a husband would make her feel lovable, she thought. She was an oddball: the prickly, sarcastic one who was always saying something mean when really she wanted to be funny and brilliant and charming. After 20 plus years of alienating practically everyone she met, she was desperate to find someone who would like her without her having to turn into a whole different person.

"The first time I saw you," Charlie said, "I knew you were the one I wanted."

Well…Beata just melted at that. Hadn't she been waiting all her life to hear someone say it? Finally she'd be cherished and necessary instead of repugnant and out-of-place. Finally there'd be someone who cared what she was really like under all the sarcasm.

But marriage to Charlie hadn't been quite the panacea she expected. For one thing, Charlie couldn't hold down a job, so Beata had to work like a maniac to pay the bills. Then, he exploded into irrational rages, which rained down on his family like a toxic firestorm. He smashed things to vent his fury, which, she figured, was better than hitting people, but still created an atmosphere of terror in which Beata and her daughter crept around trying to ward off the next outburst as long as possible.

Charlie didn't understand her, either, and he didn't want to. He was content as long as she paid the bills. Oh, he loved her after a fashion. At least he didn't betray her like John betrayed Gladys. He'd helped with the baby, and was kind when he wasn't lashing out in rage. What he *did* betray was her dream that, if only she could find someone that truly loved her, she wouldn't feel so hollow inside. Charlie hadn't filled the black hole in her chest. And being the only responsible one in the whole family made her feel like a pack mule under a backbreaking load.

The divorce hadn't been Charlie's fault. Sure, he had problems, but didn't everyone? The issue, she decided, was the notion that anyone's love could've saved her from herself. So she'd become militantly single, insisting that romantic love was nothing but a disguised hormone frenzy and preaching her Gospel of Self-Sufficiency to anyone who'd sit still and listen.

It was a testimony to Gladys' optimism that she rejected Beata's hormone theory, even in the wake of her own marital disaster. She refused to give up on love, maintaining unwavering confidence that she would eventually find the Mr. Right.

"Love has to be more than hormones," she told Beata time and again. "Being in love is beautiful. It makes people happy."

"But it's a lie," Beata would insist. "It doesn't last. Every time people fall out of love, they assume they must be with the wrong partner, so they dump that one and go looking for someone better. You, of all people, ought to know how painful that can be."

"Gee…thanks for reminding me."

"Oh, I'm sorry, Gladdie," she'd apologize. "Don't mind me. You know what a cynic I am."

"It's okay, hon. Anybody would probably feel like you if they'd never really been in love."

5

But that wasn't the point at all, Beata would silently protest. She'd been in love. It just hadn't produced the happiness Gladys said it would.

"Hey," Gladys was now asking her, "what are your plans for today…you doing anything? Why don't we get together for coffee this afternoon?"

"I can't," Beata said. "This is Daphne's week. I have to go grocery shopping and get the house in shape."

Daphne, Beata's daughter, was 26 years old and living with her boyfriend, Sean, on the other side of town. Beata suspected that if she saw Sean on the street without Daphne, she might not recognize him. All Daphe's boyfriends were carbon copies of each other. They seemed much older than they really were, besuited, dedicated to their careers, working diligently toward well-considered objectives such as a spacious house in the suburb, two cars (an SUV and a hybrid), and a couple of neatly pressed children whose science fair projects they would help build and whose teacher-parent conferences they would faithfully attend.

Daphne was a perfect match for these earnest young men; she shared their work ethic and their desire for a suburban lifestyle. Beata envisioned her happily toting their mounted bugs and home-made generators to the science fair, and accompanying them to the teacher conferences with a proud hand planted on their right shoulder.

"What a good boy Jason is," the teacher would marvel. "So studious and polite. I wish I had a whole class full of Jasons. You must be very proud." And Daphne would nod beatifically and rest the slender, manicured fingers of her free hand lightly on her husband's arm.

Daphne had a degree in Business Administration, which she had breezed through due to her rigorously organized study habits. She managed a small marketing department at…Beata couldn't remember where.

"Oh right," said Gladys. "You're having dinner with Daphne. Are you cooking?"

"Yep, I think I'll make a pot roast."

"That sounds yummy. Well, I'll let you get to it, then. I'll call you later, maybe tomorrow."

Beata hung up the phone and sighed as she surveyed the house. She had rented it many years ago, shortly after her divorce, and beyond slapping a coat of off-white paint over the interior walls, had done nothing to it. Its steeply sloping yard was surrounded by a chain-link fence. The fence's rusty decrepitude was concealed by a riot of Morning Glory vines whose pernicious fecundity threatened to engulf the entire yard. Early on, Beata had made a half-hearted attempt to root out the Morning Glory, but when this proved unsuccessful, she decided Morning Glory was superior to lawn, since it didn't require mowing, and let it grow as it would.

Beata thought she should fetch a chuck roast out of the freezer in the basement to prepare for tomorrow's dinner, but first went to the kitchen to refill her coffee cup. To her annoyance, there was no hazelnut creamer left. This reminded her she needed to make a grocery list, so she took her coffee (laced with 1% milk, a wholly unsatisfactory substitute for hazelnut creamer) into the living room and put it on the floor in front of the couch. She wandered into the office to look for a piece of paper. Sorting through the disorder on her desk but finding no paper, she unplugged her cell phone from its charger and returned to the couch.

"hazelnut creamER, TOILEt paper, carrots, s[omocj" she typed.

"Do I need onion?" she wondered aloud. This initiated another visit to the kitchen and an inventory of the vegetable drawer.

"Ugh," she said, fishing vegetables in various stages of decay from the drawer. "When did I buy this lettuce? Last week? Two weeks ago?"

She dropped the moldering vegetables into the garbage can and attacked the slimy residue they'd left in the drawer, making a mental note to add onion to her shopping list. After scrubbing the drawer out, she moved on to sorting and discarding decomposing leftovers and bleaching their ooze-covered containers, and then to scouring the dried-up meat juice off the bottom of the fridge, and then to washing all its shelves and walls.

The fridge-cleaning operation took an hour and a half, and by the time she finished it, her back ached. She cast a jaundiced eye over the floor, which now, in addition to the food crumbs that had been there previously, was covered with mashed vegetable bits and muddy footprints she'd tracked all over it in her numerous trips from refrigerator to sink. Instead of scrubbing it, which would've hurt her back even worse, she wetted a kitchen towel and scuffled it along the ground with one foot until the worst of the grime had either been wiped up or blended in with the rest of the dirt.

Mentally promising to tackle the dusting (just as soon as she gave her back a little rest), she plopped down on the couch for a few minutes with a book she'd read 50 times and could practically recite from memory. Her planned 20 minute break stretched into several hours. Every half-hour or so, she would glance up at the clock, note the time and remark to herself that she really needed to put the book down and start dusting.

At four o'clock, she threw the book down. She absolutely *had* to go grocery shopping. She carried the empty coffee cup to the sink and hunted for her purse, finding it, after an exhaustive search, tucked down between the bed and the wall. Before leaving, she carried a load of laundry downstairs to the washing machine. The stairs to the basement led out of the kitchen, bypassing the living room, so when she left, she left the cell phone, with its half-finished grocery list, sitting on the couch.

As she stopped on the back porch to lock the door, she thought she glimpsed a bulky, indeterminate shadow gliding across the sidewalk on the other side of the fence. As it reached the point directly across the fence from Beata, it paused for a heartbeat as if observing her turning her key in the deadbolt. She felt eyes boring into the back of her neck. Alarmed, she spun around to examine it straight on, but upon turning to face the street, could discern no shadow and no bulky form, only a few Morning Glory fronds stirring gently in the breeze.

Beata wasn't used to seeing things that weren't there. It was far more common for her to fail to see things that *were* there. She paused a moment and carefully scanned the street for signs of a voyeur, but saw nothing. She couldn't help feeling uneasy. She'd had such a strong impression of being watched, it seemed impossible it had been only her imagination. On the other hand, it also seemed impossible that someone could've vanished so completely, so quickly. Where would they have gone? The neat yards lining the street offered no cover. Only her own was unkempt and overgrown, and no one could have leapt over the fence and concealed himself in the yard without her seeing it. There couldn't have been a shadow. Like it or not, she must have imagined it.

***

The grocery store was a mile away, and it took Beata several minutes to get there in the late afternoon traffic. She parked her battered sedan, splotched with gray primer in several places where she'd gotten partial repairs for damage incurred by running into various stationary objects such as fence posts, garbage cans and the concrete posts that protect the pumps at gas stations from wayward motorists, at the farthest reaches of the parking lot. She hummed under her breath as she carried her homemade fabric shopping bags into the store.

"Hm, let's see," she mumbled as she strolled among the aisles. "Hazelnut creamer, toilet paper, carrots…what else do I need? I wonder if I have any laundry soap left? Ooo. This looks yummy." She paused in front of a chocolate cream pie. "How many calories do you suppose it has in it? 1200? 2000?"

Beata had a whole mouthful of sweet-teeth. She frequently resolved to cut back on her sugar intake, and carried out this resolution by not buying desserts and then, after dinner, running out for a sugar fix.

She escaped the store some time later with no chocolate pie, but $95 worth of other groceries that were not on her list. When she returned home and started putting the groceries away, she realized she had bought several duplicative items and neglected to buy others that she was out of. One of these was the onion, which she had been planning to use for the pot roast. Maybe Irene had an onion she could borrow, she thought. She'd run over and ask.

Irene was her next-door neighbor, a well-groomed woman 12 or 15 years Beata's junior. They weren't close friends (or any kind of friends, really, Beata thought). However, Beata never let not knowing a person stop her from jumping to conclusions about their private lives and motivations. Irene was always courteous, but slightly cold to Beata, and Beata knew exactly what she was thinking: Irene's principles dictated that she maintain a good relationship with her neighbors, so she was determined to be pleasant to Beata despite her disapproval of the way she kept her yard. She no doubt felt that allowances had to be made for Beata, who was old, and probably lonely with neither husband nor children to keep her busy.

Irene was always busy. Beata had decided that it was pathological…her ceaseless activity was supposed to demonstrate that she was important and necessary. She knew that Irene managed her home with ferocious competence. Not a speck of dust, not the tiniest hair, not even a germ defaced the spotless perfection of her domain. When she ran out of surfaces to polish and sterilize inside the house, she carried her maniacal crusade against filth into the yard. Although there were live plants growing in the yard, they were as symmetrical and bug-free as artificial ones. The fence she shared with Beata was the only portion of Beata's yard where the Morning Glory had been eradicated. Beata was convinced Irene had used Agent Orange on the Morning Glory, because there was still a strip of raw ground along the fence where nothing would grow.

Gladys pointed out to Beata that she might be projecting onto Irene some of her own guilt about being such a slob, but Beata knew that was completely untrue. And by the way, who was calling her a slob?

Gladys said *"You* call yourself a slob — you do it all the time."

Today, she interrupted Irene at the task of pruning her already perfectly shaped rose bushes. Beata wondered if she shouldn't, in compassion for Irene's poor roses, toss a few Morning Glory seeds over the fence to give Irene another focus for her maintenance obsession. If the roses took much more manicuring, there wouldn't be a leaf left on them. She could hear Irene's dogs yapping inside the house. It amazed her that an obsessive housekeeper like Irene could tolerate having dogs in the house, but Irene treated her dogs like children and did not begrudge the fact that eliminating their hair and dirt from the house forced her to vacuum and steam-clean her carpets multiple times a week.

Beata might berate herself for the sloppy condition of her yard, but she didn't see how Irene's family could stand living in this oppressively prim atmosphere. She glanced around the yard distastefully, thinking it exhibited a skewed value system.

"Hi there," said Beata.

"Hel-lo," Irene trilled, bestowing a bright smile upon her.

"Pruning roses?"

"Oh yes…It's long overdue, but I simply have not found the time."

"How's Ken?"

Ken was Irene's husband. Beata knew him mainly through Irene's reports, because she rarely saw him. Occasionally, they'd exchange waves when he was taking out the garbage or mowing the lawn, but he always seemed distracted, his mind full of more important things than socializing with the neighbors. Beata sympathized. If she had Irene standing over her with a "to do" list, she wouldn't be interested in the neighbors, either.

"Oh, he's doing wonderfully," Irene said. "He just got another promotion at work, and we are so proud of him."

"That's great," Beata said. "Listen, my daughter's coming over for dinner tomorrow. I want to make a pot roast for her, but I don't seem to have any onion. Do you have an onion I can borrow? I can return it by next Tuesday."

She had to be careful, she knew, about promising to return it. If she told Irene it would be back on Tuesday, it had better be Tuesday and not a moment later.

Irene frowned. "Um, let me see. Give me a moment to check."

She left Beata standing in the yard while she went to the kitchen to look for an onion.

Beata mumbled "Hmph." She was certain that Irene had an onion, but was reluctant to lend it...her meal plan might include a dish requiring onion sometime between now and Tuesday, and she might not be able to spare it that long. Irene did not keep extra onions, or extra anything else, in her house. Spare items took up valuable real-estate, and violated Irene's standards of efficiency. Plus, she could not approve of Beata deciding to make pot roast on the spur of the moment. Proper meal planning dictated that one choose dishes on the basis of available ingredients, not pull an idea randomly out of the air and then try to round up the necessary materials.

Beata had just finished working this scenario out in her head when Irene returned with an onion. Mercifully, it seemed it could be spared. She handed it to Beata a little nervously, emphasizing "I *do* need this back by Tuesday night."

"Sure," said Beata. "No problem. I'll pick one up on the way home from work."

By the time she returned home, it was well past six o'clock. She put the onion on the kitchen counter and mentally reviewed the uncompleted tasks on her list. She still hadn't washed the dishes, dusted, vacuumed, organized her desk or finished the laundry. In fact, what *had* she done? Grocery shopped and borrowed an onion. True, she'd cleaned out the refrigerator, but the freezer was still untouched and beginning to look like the next Ice Age.

Before she washed the dishes, though, she might as well make herself something to eat. There was no sense cleaning the kitchen and then getting it all dirty again. She put a pot on the stove to boil, unearthed a bag of angel hair pasta from a cupboard and found a half-eaten container of cottage cheese in the fridge. The water boiled and she threw in the pasta and a double handful of spinach. When the pasta and vegetables were done, she spooned the cottage cheese over it, added some crushed garlic from a jar and mixed it all up into a gooey green mess. She carried the bowl into the living room, and picked up her discarded book. When 10 pm rolled around, she was still sitting on the sofa, a dirty bowl at her feet and the book in her hand.

Daphne rang the doorbell late Sunday afternoon. Beata was still trying to finish her housework, which had transformed into a Medusa-like monster with every completed task spawning twelve more yet to be started. While she'd spent Saturday drifting blithely from one half-finished job to another, Sunday had settled into a grim battle against chaos that revealed itself in concentric and ever-worsening layers.

How was it, she wondered, that other people kept their houses clean? It didn't seem like it should be such a burden. Look at Irene – she had a husband and two dogs and she worked full-time, and her house was spotless. Beata was alone and had no pets, and her house was a mess. What was *wrong* with her?

At the instant at which the doorbell interrupted this meditation, Beata remembered that she had never taken the chuck roast out of the freezer. There would be no pot roast tonight. On the up side, she could return the onion to Irene and save herself the trouble of buying another one.

"Hi, honey," she greeted Daphne, kissing her on the cheek. Then, looking around for Daphne's boyfriend, she asked "Where's Sean?"

"Hi, Mom. He can't come today. He has to work."

"He's working on a Sunday? Shouldn't he get Sunday off?"

"I know, but they offered him some extra hours, and, since we're saving for a down payment we thought he should take advantage of it."

"Well, come on in, honey. You caught me trying to get my housework done."

Daphne's glance was devoid of interest. "House looks fine."

Daphne had inherited Beata's angular frame, but unlike Beata, who had padded hers with soft, aging flesh over the years, Daphne maintained a strict fitness regimen that kept her spare and lean. There was no running out for impromptu dessert at Daphne's house. Her hair was thick and wavy, like her father's, but she kept it in a severe, chin-length bob, which she sculpted with hair products each morning. She wore low-rise jeans and a stretchy, knit top.

"Honey, I'm ashamed to admit it, but I forgot to take the pot roast out of the freezer. We're going to have to pick up Chinese or something."

"That's okay, Mom, I don't really care what we eat. Pot roast is kind of heavy, anyway."

Daphne plopped down on the sofa. "Can I have some tea?"

"Sure, honey. Is that a new outfit?"

Daphne rolled her eyes. "Mom, you've asked me that the last three times you saw it. I've had this outfit for a year. In fact, I think I was wearing it last time you came over."

Beata shook her head as she walked to the kitchen to put the kettle on the stove. How could anyone tell what was new? All Daphne's clothes looked exactly the same. Admittedly, she was getting old and old people are always mystified by the fashions of youth. And admittedly, she couldn't tell one of Gladys' outfits from another, either, and Gladys didn't wear jeans and t-shirts.

"I guess I'm not a clothes person, honey," she apologized. "No, Mom, you dress like a bag lady." "I know, honey; I'm sorry I'm such a trial."

"I want Earl Grey, Mom, do you have Earl Grey?"

"Um, I don't know, dear. Let me see what's here." She rooted around in the cupboard, and came up with a cellophane bag of unlabeled tea bags.

"This's all I've got, honey," she said. "I'm not sure what it is. It *might* be Earl Grey."

Fortified with their respective beverages: tea for Daphne and coffee with hazelnut creamer for Beata, they sat beside each other on the couch and stared at the shrubbery that impeded their view from the front window.

"So, how's Sean?"

"He's fine."

(Interlude of sipping and staring.)

"How's work?"

"It's fine."

(More sipping and staring.)

"You guys are saving for a house?"

"Yeah."

"Where're you thinking about buying?"

Here, finally, was a topic Daphne could get her teeth into.

"We've been looking in Ballard and the U District, 'cause we love the charm of the older houses," she explained, "but we can't find anything even remotely affordable. We need something pretty sizable if we're going to start a family, at least three bedrooms and two or three baths. You know how hard it is to find an older house with three bathrooms. You only get them if the house has been remodeled, and those houses are expensive. So now we're thinking maybe we should go north, maybe to Everett. It's a long commute, but things are way cheaper up there."

"Honey, why don't you scale down your expectations some and stay closer to work?" Beata suggested.

"What exactly do you mean by 'scale down,' Mom?"

"Well, for example, what do you need three bathrooms for? There's only two of you. Aren't you going to share a bathroom anyway?"

Beata was somewhat fanatic on the subject of bathrooms. She and Daphne had shared a bathroom all through Daphne's childhood, and when she was married, she, Charlie and Daphne all shared. Sharing with Charlie was a real sacrifice, too, because Charlie tended to pee on the floor when he was groping around the bathroom in the dark. As with many of her personal choices, Beata put a moral spin on bathroom-sharing and felt that others should follow her example of frugality.

"Mom, that's not the point," said Daphne, all too familiar with Beata's point of view. "We're looking toward the future. We plan to have kids. We want a nice house in a nice neighborhood."

"Honey, I'm not saying you shouldn't have a nice house. I'm simply saying that 'nice' doesn't have to mean a hundred bathrooms. How much time do you plan on spending in the bathroom? Are you planning to throw parties in there? We shared a bathroom when you were a kid and it didn't kill us."

"Mom. I've heard all this before. I know you hate bathrooms, and you think modern conveniences are stupid."

"Daphne, I don't 'hate' bathrooms. I *have* a bathroom. And I don't think modern conveniences are stupid. I simply believe it's wasteful to spend money 'updating' things that are functioning perfectly well. In ten years, all those updates are going to be out of style, and everyone who spent thousands of dollars putting them in will just have to update them all over again. They'll rip out all the fancy granite countertops and bamboo floors that would've probably lasted for a hundred years and toss them in the landfill so they can make room for whatever the next latest and greatest fad is."

"Mom," Daphne sighed, "Sean and I are not you. We like what we like, and we happen to like bathrooms and modern kitchens. So will you stop trying to convince me we should buy the house you would buy?"

That was it in a nutshell, Beata thought. Of course she was trying to convince Daphne to buy the house she would buy. Wasn't she 24 years older than Daphne? Didn't she have 24 years of life wisdom to impart? She was a mother; that was her job. She didn't want Daphne to be stampeded into a materialistic frenzy just because she was dating a man who defined himself by the size of his wallet. Did she *know* that Daphne was being stampeded? No, but how could it be otherwise? How could a person raised under Beata's enlightened tutelage be so plugged into the typical consumerist mindset?

Although she never breathed a word to Daphne, Beata didn't really think Sean was right for her. He was so… conventional, so shallow. A good boy, plenty of ambition, a hard worker, but what did they have in common aside from a shared impulse to procreate and amass possessions? When the family was raised and the glow of romance was completely snuffed out by the tarnish of years, what would they have left? She didn't want Daphne to wake up at the age of 50 and think "What am I doing here? What does my life mean?"

"Why does everything have to *mean* something, Mom?" Daphne'd asked her once, exasperated when Beata was badgering her about – oh, she couldn't remember what. "People just *do* things. They live their lives. They do what needs to be done and don't agonize about it."

That was the difference between her and Daphne. She agonized about everything, and probed for meaning everywhere. In a proper world, she thought, life *would* be meaningful. She wouldn't wonder why she was doing things; they would all gather up like the swell of a giant wave moving toward the shore and carry her inexorably toward a glorious arrival at…somewhere. She wanted joy. She wanted happiness. She'd heard someone quote a Bible verse once about rivers of living water…that's what she wanted: rivers of living water flowing from her heart.

That was the reason, she supposed, that the New Age version of spirituality made so much sense to her. New Age people had a target: the beach called enlightenment. Or Oneness. She wasn't sure what those things meant (they sounded good), so she made them what she wanted them to be: a place where yearning dissolved into contentment and questioning became knowing.

Daphne seemed unconcerned with questions of meaning. She was content with Sean, as she had been with the Sean-clones she'd dated before him. She strode through life purposefully, aiming for a goal and then achieving it. She worked because people work, didn't ask "Where is this going?" She'd buy a house in the suburbs and deck it out with cherry cabinets and recessed light fixtures and never ask 'What does this mean in the greater scheme of things?'

Daphne didn't appreciate Beata's constant animadversions on consumerism. She didn't perceive any moral turpitude in buying cherry cabinets. "Not spending money doesn't help the starving children in Africa," she'd say when Beata was holding forth about wasteful spending habits. "What are *you* doing about it?"

Beata surfaced from these reflections to hear Daphne extolling the virtues of natural stone countertops, and sighed in defeat. Why fight superficiality? Like shallow water, it spreads far and wide across the whole landscape. When you try to dig beneath it, all you accomplish is to get muddy.

"Honey, I hope you two find what you're looking for," she blessed Daphne with deliberate vagueness. How would Daphne ever know she wasn't talking about a house?

"Thanks, Mom. Maybe we can take you along next time we go house-hunting."

"That sounds like fun, dear." She foresaw a tension-laden trip around Seattle, arguing about carpets and sizes of bedrooms. "So, what should we eat? Do you want to go to the Safeway deli and get Chinese?"

"Sure, that sounds good."

Beata was no cook, and during Daphne's teenage years, the two of them had relied heavily on fast food and the Safeway deli. Just as Beata was constantly resolving to keep her house in better order, she also was constantly resolving to cook things from scratch, and just as the house continued to be a mess despite her resolve, she also continued to eat from the deli.

Daphne had apparently absorbed Beata's aversion to cookery, so it came as a surprise when, on her way out the door later that evening, she invited Beata over for dinner in two weeks. "Why don't you come over to our place next time, Mom. I'll cook something," she said.

"Gosh, honey, are you sure? You never cook."

"I know," Daphne replied, "but next time I'm going to."

"What's the occasion?"

"There isn't one. I just figure it's time we had you over for a change."

"OK, honey, that would be lovely," Beata said. She suspected something was up, but she wasn't going to pry it out of Daphne. "What are we having?"

"I'll think of something," Daphne promised. "And Mom..."

"Yes, dear."

"Could you please wear something decent? So everyone in our building doesn't think you're a bum?"

"Daphne," reproved Beata, "what, exactly, do you mean by 'decent'?"

"Well, for starters, how about something that doesn't have holes in it?"

"Honey, my clothes don't have holes."

"The dress you have on right now has holes."

"There aren't any holes in this dress."

"Mom, what do you call these?" Daphne picked up the hem of Beata's voluminous dress, which almost brushed the floor, and indicated a spattering of small holes across the front.

"Oh, I think some bleach might have splattered on the skirt. They aren't really noticeable," Beata said.

"They are too noticeable; I noticed them. They're holes, Mom. Everyone sees them except you. Do you have a dress that doesn't have holes in it?"

"Of course I do, dear. I have any number of dresses without holes."

"Well, would you please wear one of them when you come over? Please?"

"Honey," said Beata, "I really don't think your neighbors could see these holes from their apartments unless they were looking out their windows with binoculars. If they spend their leisure hours examining other people's clothing with binoculars, they have to expect to be offended every now and then by finding some minor element that doesn't suit their taste. However," she held up her hand to ward off Daphne's reply, "I will find a dress without holes to wear to your house. Okay? Love you."

Daphne sighed. "Mom, you're weird. I love you, too."

Beata arrived in front of Daphne's apartment building punctually at 5:30 p.m. two Sundays hence. She was wearing a dress without holes, which had a large skirt gathered loosely under the bust so it swathed her form in tent-like comfort. She'd driven around the neighborhood several times, looking vainly for a parking place, and finally parked four blocks away with her front wheels encroaching two inches into someone's driveway and her rear bumper touching another car. The long walk to Daphne's building was no inconvenience due to her sensible choice of footgear: an old and comfortable pair of tennis shoes whose original color (possibly white) had long since been obscured by wear and dirt.

Daphne lived in an older neighborhood, and the streets were lined with ancient maple trees. The apartment building was set back from the street behind a small plot of grass. A paved walkway led to the front door, and this was bordered on both sides by a waist-high thicket of boxwood hedges. At the entrance to the sidewalk stood two large brick posts, each topped with a carriage lantern.

Beata reached the brick posts and paused for a moment before turning up the walkway. The lamps were not yet lit. Funny, she thought, how she'd felt almost *watched* as she'd walked those four blocks under the looming trees. Unlike Gladys, who was borderline psychic (or psycho, she joked) and sensed wraiths and "beings" on a regular basis, Beata never perceived anything insubstantial. There almost certainly were "beings," she conceded, but she, Beata, was not attuned to such things. She lived in an ordinary world, and the "beings" she perceived were embodied and solidly material: *human* beings. Yet, as she had walked to her daughter's apartment, she'd imagined a presence, like an invisible shadow, flitting from trunk to trunk behind her in the gloom of the maples.

She turned and examined the street carefully. There was nothing stirring but flickering sunlight filtered through the canopy of maple leaves and a couple of squirrels chasing each other up a tree trunk. She shrugged, and turned to go up the walkway to the door of the building. Ringing her daughter's bell, she announced "It's me," and was duly admitted.

* * *

Across the street, a man leaned against the side of a maple tree, rooted there as if he'd grown from the ground along with it. He was so still that he seemed to blend into the trunk of the tree, almost invisible in his worn khaki trousers and gray polo shirt. He looked across the street at the apartment building Beata had just entered, and then around the street, seeming to drink in the sparkle of late afternoon sunlight playing among the leaves. He did not move as minutes and hours ticked away. Passersby ignored him completely, perhaps didn't notice him, as Beata had not. He, on the other hand, seemed intensely aware of each one that walked by, watching them intently, like a personal friend waiting to be greeted.

Meanwhile, upstairs, Sean invited Beata in and returned her dry peck on the cheek with an uncomfortable half smile. Daphne was bustling around the kitchen, fussing over a chicken casserole. As Sean ushered Beata to the sofa, she called "Hi Mom! Do you want a glass of wine?"

Beata did not want a glass of wine, but she took one anyway. Perhaps it would make conversing with Sean a little easier, and even if it didn't, it would give her something to do while they stared at each other without talking.

Sean had never warmed up to Beata. She'd always been cordial to him in a stiff, overly-formal way founded not upon any specific aversion, but a general discomfort that arose from being thrust into closer relationship than their personalities could, without Daphne's mediating influence, sustain. Their interactions were always punctuated with

23

awkward silences, and, when they did converse, it was always on the most generic and impersonal of topics.

"I understand you guys are saving for a house," Beata remarked.

"Yeah," said Sean.

"Daphne tells me you are looking out in the Everett area."

"Maybe. We haven't done that yet, but we're talking about it."

"She also said that you're talking about starting a family."

Sean began to look nervous. "Uh, maybe."

"Don't you think it would be wise to get married before you buy a house together or start talking about a family?" The words were out of Beata's mouth before she realized how meddlesome they sounded. It was a bit premature, she thought, to become an interfering mother-in-law.

Sean shifted away from her on the couch, as if to deflect her prying comments, but said nothing. In for a penny, in for a pound, Beata thought, and plunged ahead with an explanation that she intended to be apologetic, but which came out sounding even more managing than before:

"I mean, when young people make such significant decisions without being married, it so often ends up backfiring if the relationship doesn't work out. For your own protection, your partnership should be formalized before you do things like that."

Sean gave her a resentful glance and rose from the couch to stand in the kitchen door. "Need any help?" he asked Daphne.

"No," she replied. "Mom, what are you hassling Sean about now?"

Beata gulped some wine, feeling inept. "Nothing, honey."

"She's telling me we ought to get married," Sean said.

"Mom, that's none of your business," Daphne said. "Stay out of it."

"Okay," Beata agreed meekly. "Sorry."

"Why don't you make yourself useful and set the table?"

"Sure, honey."

"You know where everything is, right? Sean, show Mom where the plates are."

"I know where they are," Beata said, and walked around Sean to retrieve three plates from the kitchen cupboard.

"No, we need four," said Daphne.

Beata's alert signal went off. "Four? Who else is coming?"

"Just someone I met through work," Daphne said.

"You invited someone from work to have dinner with us? Why?"

"No reason. We thought it might be nice to have a foursome."

A foursome? Now Beata was feeling really alarmed. "Daphne, I hope this isn't....this other person wouldn't be a man, would it?"

"Just relax, Mom. It's David's uncle – you know, David, who sits next to me at work. He's all alone and I thought he might enjoy sharing a family dinner."

Hot, accusatory comments bubbled to Beata's lips, but were forestalled by the ringing of the doorbell.

"There he is," said Daphne. "Please be nice, Mom."

"Daphne, I'm always nice. But I don't appreciate being ambushed like this."

"You're not always nice, Mom. You're intimidating."

Beata had no time for further recriminations, for Sean was now opening the door to admit the new guest. A gentleman of perhaps 58 or 60 years stood in the hallway, nervously combing his droopy white mustache with one hand. He was of medium height and slender build with a caved-in chest, ropy, sinuous arms and a demeanor that

25

suggested he preferred to fade into the background. His colorless eyes (could they be blue?) wandered aimlessly about the living room, touching Beata briefly and moving quickly on as if embarrassed.

Beata shot Daphne a murderous glance, which Daphne ignored. "Hi, Frank," she gushed, bustling out of the kitchen with a glass of wine in her hand. "Come in and have a glass of wine. Sean, honey, get out of his way."

Daphne ushered Frank to the couch and handed him the wine. "Do you like red? Let me introduce you to my mom. Mom, this is Frank; Frank, Beata."

"How do you do, Frank?" said Beata, offering him a firm handshake. "Daphne tells me you're not married."

Frank flushed and did not reply.

"Oh Mom," said Daphne with false heartiness, digging a warning elbow into Beata's ribs, "don't be rude."

Frank wiped his hand on his trousers as if to cleanse it of any microscopic organisms he might have picked up from Beata and unfurled a nervous smile. Beata sighed. After all, what harm was there in her daughter trying to fix her up with some co-worker's uncle? She was trapped here for the evening; she might as well go along with it.

"So," she forged ahead, "tell me about your nephew, David. Is he your sister's son, or your brother's? Are you two close?"

"Umm," he mumbled. This would be an uphill battle, she realized; Frank was not a conversationalist.

Beata sympathized. She hated small talk. Why was it so hard to find a topic a person could really get their teeth into? Weather, kids, work…not only were they boring, but they didn't last long enough. How could you get to know someone if you couldn't talk about anything important? She'd rather argue about politics or God than figure out what to say about the weather. She slogged along gamely, trying to draw Frank out, and from his monosyllabic replies to her increasingly desperate questions ascertained that he was a general contractor, owned his own business and had been divorced for three years.

Finally, after several false starts, she hit upon a topic Frank was enthusiastic about: recreational fishing. This was a perfect subject because Beata knew nothing about fishing, which enabled her keep the conversation going (when Frank ran out of stories) by asking a great many pointless questions about differentiating between fish species and the pros and cons of various types of equipment. When she ran out of technical questions, she requested detailed descriptions of all his favorite fishing spots including elevation, topography, flora and fauna present, and distance and direction from Seattle.

Even if Beata didn't care about fishing, it was better to be instructed in something she was completely ignorant about than to try to converse about something she understood but found boring. Plus, it enabled her to socialize without working too hard, an important consideration because she was naturally shy and, at the same time, reluctant that anyone should notice it. Her trick was to keep the other person talking as long as possible while nodding and smiling and asking enough questions to appear interested. The downside was that, by appearing interested, she created the false impression that she was interested enough to want to fish, herself.

She managed to prolong the fishing discussion until Daphne called them to the table. By this time, Beata was getting nervous, for it was sounding increasingly like Frank wanted to invite her on a fishing trip. Conversation was easier over dinner; they could alternate between chewing their food, commenting on how delicious the meal was, and marveling at Daphne's ability to produce such a gastronomic delicacy. Beata dawdled at the table as long as possible, and then, when she could not delay another moment, leapt up to help with the dishes.

"Mom," Daphne hissed as they collided at the sink with dirty plates in their hands, "go sit in the living room. I don't need your help to wash up a few plates."

"Daphne," Beata whispered, "you dragged me into this situation against my will and without my knowledge. If someone is going to be forced to sit in the living room and make small talk with a total stranger, it will be you and not me."

"But I have nothing to say to him! He's 30 years older than me!"

"You should've thought of that before you invited him over," Beata said, and refused to budge from the kitchen until the cleanup was done. It was completed in far too short a time, as Daphne, also, refused to leave and sped through the task with determined efficiency.

When Beata and Daphne returned to the living room, it didn't appear that Sean and Frank had found much to say to one another. They were sitting in chairs on opposite sides of the couch, staring blankly into space. Daphne took the end of the couch nearest to Sean and left Beata the position beside Frank. She then looked expectantly at Beata as if to say "Well...I've gotten you this far, now carry on."

Beata searched her mind wildly for an opening. Why, oh why had Daphne pitchforked her into this awkward situation? How could she be so mistaken in Beata's character as to suppose that she would welcome a blind date with – who cares who – any man with a pulse? Did her daughter really think her life was that pathetic?

* * *

Actually, Daphne did not think Beata's life pathetic. She hadn't meditated upon Beata's condition and found it pitiable; she'd simply reacted to a visceral assumption that her mom would be much better off with a man. Daphne thought Beata was unhappy, and she knew Beata was alone. Automatically drawing a cause-and-effect relationship between these facts, she figured duty compelled her to alleviate her mother's loneliness by hooking her up with someone. In choosing Frank, she hadn't presumed that Beata would grasp desperately at any man she could find; she had chosen Frank because he was the only man she could put her hands on that was the right age, and out of total ignorance about her mother's preferences. Like most children, she had no idea of her mother's inner workings. She expected Mom to gracefully smooth over all the rough spots that she couldn't figure out how to deal with. She was Mom. She would know how to act on a blind date. She would know how to draw Frank out.

* * *

Beata did not know how to draw Frank out. He sat in his chair like a sack full of inert gas. Beata wasn't sure he thought about anything, much less anything they could talk about.

She cravenly decided it was time to flee. Looking at her watch, she exclaimed in feigned surprise, "Oh my goodness! Just look at the time! I really must be getting home. I have work tomorrow, and there are so many things I have to do to get ready."

Daphne, trying to sound disappointed, made a half-hearted effort to convince her to stay a little longer, but was thwarted by Frank, who leapt up from his chair and announced that he would see her to her car.

"Oh, no, that's not necessary," she demurred. "I'm parked right down the street."

"It's no problem," Frank assured her. "I don't mind."

"Yes, Mom," Daphne chimed in, "it's dark outside. You really should let him walk you. Sean would do it, but since Frank is here..." she left the sentence dangling suggestively.

Beata chuckled to herself. Never in the whole course of their relationship had Sean displayed the level of chivalry that Daphne was now implying was an everyday event. But she wouldn't embarrass Daphne by pointing this out, so she meekly accepted Frank's offer, and left the building under his protective custody. Once out of Daphne's sight, she strode briskly down the walk as fast as her legs would carry her, while Frank trotted doggedly at her side.

"How about getting together for a movie?" he suggested.

The invitation shocked her. Surely this dinner had not been such a success that Frank wanted to repeat it. For herself, she was relieved it was over, and wanted nothing more than to forget about it as soon as possible.

"Um, gosh, thanks. It sounds great, but it's hard to say when I would be free," she stalled, hoping he would withdraw the invitation gracefully.

"We could do it next weekend," he suggested.

* * *

Involved in this exchange, neither of them observed the man standing beside the tree on the other side of the street. He hadn't stirred since Beata entered Daphne's apartment hours earlier, but Frank and Beata seemed to arouse his interest. As they came down the walkway and passed between the brick columns, he straightened up and watched them intently. After they'd taken a few steps down the sidewalk toward Beata's car, he crossed the street and walked behind them. He made no effort to avoid their notice, but moved so silently that they didn't realize he was there. When they stopped at Beata's car, he stopped as well, standing a few feet away under the trees, not hiding but indistinct in the deep evening shadows.

Beata, relieved to be so close to freedom, fished her keys out of her purse and turned to Frank. "It was lovely meeting you," she said with artificial heartiness, and climbed into the car.

"What about that movie?" he persisted.

"Um, well, maybe," she said, "Why don't you call me?"

This prompted some fumbling for paper and pencil, followed by an exchange of telephone numbers. As they talked, the man watching them seemed to fade gradually into the dark, starting at the top, as if someone were pouring water over him and washing him away. By the time Beata started her car, his shoes where barely visible. By the time she'd locked her doors and pulled out into the street, there was nothing left of him.

The next morning, Beata woke before the alarm went off. She set the alarm for form's sake, as she rarely slept in long enough to be wakened by it.

"Wouldn't it be nice," she commented as she trailed into the bathroom, "to feel some sense of anticipation on Monday morning? Some excitement about the week ahead?"

But the coming week held no appeal. On the contrary, she felt gloomily that she knew exactly what to expect, and none of it was good.

"Monday, Monday," she sang as the warm water from the shower poured over her face, "so good to me. Monday Monday, la la la la."

Beata never remembered more than the first half-line of any song, though she remembered hundreds of them. She also could not carry a tune, but delighted in belting out the words she remembered and braying tunelessly along with the rest as random snatches of music played in her head. Sometimes she forgot which song was which and stitched together two different ones. It was one of the benefits of living alone, she figured, being able to sing in the shower without her husband making her a laughing stock at cocktail parties.

Although she usually worked from home, today, she had to go into the office, so she put aside her bag-lady dress in favor of a cashmere sweater, blazer and slacks. Her mania for good grooming extended only as far as her clothes. Nothing, not even going to the office, could motivate Beata to do anything with her hair. Her mom used to say she had "bad hair," and indeed she did: thin, fly-away, shapeless and now, more than half gray. Once every three or four months, Beata had it streaked blond to conceal the gray and cut in a low-maintenance style, pointless because no style was low maintenance enough to overcome her lack of skill in styling it. In fact, she did not own either a blow dryer or a curling iron, so her hair always looked frizzy and ragged.

Today, Beata put it, wet, into a ponytail so it would dry into some sort of orderly form, and went to the kitchen to make coffee. She was something of a coffee snob, always drinking either espresso or French press. Since she was going downtown, she would have espresso later, but for now, she made a pot of French press to jump-start her circulation, lacing it with a hefty dollop of hazelnut creamer.

She brought the coffee with her into the front yard as she went to retrieve the morning paper. She could not immediately find it. She reconnoitered the perimeter of the yard, and finally sighted it half-buried in Morning Glory at the base of the fence. "How on earth did they get it in there?" she wondered. "I couldn't throw a paper like that if my life depended on it. Do they get out of their car and come inside the fence to bury it under the leaves on purpose?"

Bending to retrieve it, her hair caught in the green tangle on the fence and she tussled with it briefly. It was an even match: the Morning Glory pulled about as much hair out of her pony tail as she pulled Morning Glory off the fence. As she straightened, picking leaves out of her hair, a man walking by on the street turned to look at her, then smiled and waved. Beata wondered who he was. It was kind of early for people to be out walking unless they had a dog. And she didn't recognize him from the neighborhood. She waved back.

"He doesn't look dangerous," she decided, "but why's he staring at me? And why'd he smile and wave like I'm supposed to know who he is?" Maybe she *was* supposed to know him. Perhaps they'd met before and she had forgotten him – such things had happened to her before.

He stayed in place, still watching as she retreated into the house, locked the door behind her and closed the front blinds before sitting on the couch to scan the paper. She waited a moment, then got up and peered through the blinds. He was still there. She was beginning to feel uneasy. It was creepy to be watched by a stranger.

"Go away," she willed silently. She felt too nervous to sit in the living room, exposed to the street. She took her coffee to the dining room, which had no window, and sat there to read the paper.

To Beata's relief, the man was gone by the time she left the house to catch the 7:08 bus a block from her house, and she quickly banished the unpleasant incident from her mind. The bus delivered her downtown, right in front of work, but before badging in she walked an extra block to the closest espresso cart and fortified herself with a triple latte. As she rode the elevator to the 11th floor, she was still humming "Monday, Monday" under her breath.

Beata strode purposefully to her cube, ignoring coworkers already sitting in their cubicles with their backs to the door openings. She didn't cultivate acquaintances at work. Oh, she was cordial. She'd go out for a beer with someone every now and then, but usually couldn't find much to talk about. Beata felt that her mind was too full of weighty matters, like the Meaning of Life and the Nature of God, to relate to people who seemed to think only of their children's grades and the next mortgage payment.

She turned her computer on, first addressing herself to the hundred or so emails that had collected over the weekend, and then to analyzing network packet captures. In contrast to the haphazard way she meandered through her personal life, she excelled at a highly technical job. Somehow, she could produce analyses of network and software performance that were masterpieces of acuity and sharply-honed logic, but could not keep track of her own shoes.

As the morning wore on, Beata's blood pressure rose. She did not understand how a person could be simultaneously bored and stressed out, but apparently it was possible. As she opened file after file and completed her assessment documents, she kept glancing at her watch.

She was supposed to finish twelve of these by 5:00 and had over half to go. She could've done this at home, and would have preferred it, but she had promised to meet Gladys for lunch at 12:30.

"Oh no," she moaned, "What is this?"

Three of the network trace files, which were supposed to be identical, bore no discernible resemblance to each other.

"How will I ever get this done by five?" she muttered, Googling madly, hoping against hope she'd find something that would magically resolve the inconsistencies. After a couple of hours, she put them aside. She would finish all the rest and come back to these last.

Beata had a love-hate relationship with her job. On the love side, she earned a good income and was able to work from home most of the time. On the hate side, she'd been in the IT field so long she was burnt-out and perpetually bored. She'd stopped wanting to advance…at this point, she just wanted to cling to the paycheck as long as she could. Her company went through periodic layoffs as they "down-sized" and then "right-sized," and each time, Beata bit her fingernails and teetered along the edge of anxiety, expecting disaster.

"They're going through another resource action," she'd tell Gladys. "I hope they keep me."

"Beata," Gladys would point out, "You've been saying this for ten years. You're always expecting to lose your job and you never do."

"But I could this time," she'd say.

When she'd first joined the company, she'd been proud of her career. She'd pursued success relentlessly, eager to take on new tasks and learn new skills. She wasn't sure where all that enthusiasm had gone. When had it morphed into this grim determination to hang on as long as she could, doing as little as she could get away with? With an attitude like this, would it be any wonder if they fired her? But she couldn't change her attitude. She was tired of the job; it added nothing to her life except a paycheck.

Ironically, as money became her only reward, she made more and more of it. Despite her high income, she clung to her lower-income lifestyle, determined to prepare against the day when she'd lose her cushy job. She bought a car and drove it until it disintegrated. She refused to buy a house, fearful that she'd be stuck with an expensive mortgage and no job. She wouldn't even buy her own computer – she used the one provided by the company and figured she'd simply give it up when they wanted it back.

If Charlie hadn't left her with an avalanche of debt, she would've amassed a huge savings account by now, but it had taken a decade to dig herself out of the hole he'd sunk them in. Now, try as she might, she couldn't accumulate enough money to feel secure against the day (inevitable, she felt) when she would fall off the gravy train.

At 12:15, Gladys called.

"I'm right outside," she said. "Can you come down?"

"Be right there," Beata said.

"Hey. Having a good time at the office today?" Gladys called, waving as Beata opened the door onto the street. Despite the lunchtime crowd, Beata had no trouble finding Gladys. Gladys did not blend. She wore flamingo pink pants, a violently flowered blouse and a large silk hibiscus in her upswept locks.

Gladys, the same age as Beata, had once had light blond hair, but this had faded early to a pure snowy white. She was a head shorter than Beata but weighed the same. On Gladys, the extra weight didn't look like fat. She looked like a little, round fertility goddess. Gladys loved decoration of every kind. She always wore a generous quantity of makeup, and usually one or more quirky accessories. Today it was the hibiscus.

"I'm too old for this grind," Beata whined. "I want to retire."

"There you go again with retirement. You can't retire," Gladys said. "You have to work hard so you can support *me*."

"Well, I'll get a nice cardboard box from the appliance store, and you can share it with me," Beata promised. "Which bridge should we put it under?

Gladys pretended to consider this question. "I think we should find a nice, central location." They were walking toward the waterfront, and she waved at a dank corner under a concrete overpass. "Like that, for instance."

"Well…it certainly *is* convenient. But it doesn't get much sun, and who knows about the drainage; it smells like urine. No, I really think we can do better. Let's find a nice park somewhere with a mountain view. The good news is, no matter where we put it, we can always move if we change our minds," said Beata. "It's one of the benefits of mobile living."

"Good point," said Gladys, losing interest in the box. "Hey listen. I'm going to Aberdeen this weekend for the Psychic Fair. Want to come?"

"Oh….gosh, I don't know. What time do you have to leave?"

"It starts at 10, but we can go anytime. We can have lunch, see the sights, go to the fair. C'mon, it'll be fun."

"See the sights? In broad daylight?"

A few years ago, Gladys and Beata had begun taking driving trips into the countryside. Their work schedules, combined with Gladys' incurable tendency to procrastinate, usually caused them to leave late in the evening, always caught by darkness long before they returned home. So they began referring to these as sightseeing trips and spent much of the time peering out the car windows guessing at the terrain as they passed by.

"I think I see water over there," Beata would announce.

"Where?"

"Right there, through the trees. See how the lights are glimmering like reflections on water? Is there a river around here?"

"I think it's a lake," Gladys would say.

"Why do you say that?"

"Because. It looks like there might be a bunch of houses back there on the other side. Wait, here's a clear spot coming up. See how far back those lights are? It looks like a whole subdivision back there on the water."

"Oh yeah. I think you're right. It *is* a lake. Too wide for a river. And behind that, I think there's a mountain, see where the lights just stop abruptly?"

"No, that's a clump of trees."

And so on. It had become a private joke, and at the suggestion that they do some sightseeing during daylight hours, they would react as if such a commonplace activity was too crude to suit their fastidious taste.

"I know it's not ideal," Gladys apologized, "but if we delay long enough, it might be dark on the way home."

"If you think we might get back after dark, I guess it's okay," Beata decided. "Say, where are we going for lunch, anyway? Do we have a goal, or are we just wandering around here?"

"Let's go to the Crumpet Shop."

They went to the Crumpet Shop, where Gladys ordered a watercress, cream cheese and tomato crumpet, and Beata had one with Nutella.

"That doesn't look very nutritious," Gladys scolded, eying Beata's crumpet.

"It's nutty," defended Beata. "Nuts have protein."

"It looks like mostly sugar to me."

"It is mostly sugar, I think," Beata admitted, "but it's high-protein sugar. If we stop for a latte on the way back, I can get high-protein caffeine, too, and then I can pretend I've had a decent lunch."

They stopped for a latte, and Beata walked Gladys to her car, parked in a garage close to Beata's work. By the time she returned to her cube, over an hour had flown away. Hoping she had somehow miscounted the number of documents remaining, she went through them again. No, there were still four left. They seemed to accuse her of squandering her time on fripperies such as food while vital work remained unfinished. She now attacked them vigorously to atone for her weakness in making them second to her bodily requirements. At 5:27, with only the problematic traces unfinished, she attached the remainder to an email, clicked the "send" button and collapsed in her chair, limp and depleted as boiled lettuce.

"What an awful day," she muttered. "All that craziness and I still didn't make my deadline."

By now, she had missed the 5:35 bus, and had to choose between the 5:45 and the 6:05 express, both of which were scheduled to arrive at the corner near her house at the exact same moment. The 5:45 local would be less crowded, she decided, and she might as well spend the time sitting on the bus as waiting at a bus stop. The local didn't leave from the stop in front of her building, so she had to walk three blocks to catch it. Sure enough, it was less than half full, and she found an empty seat and settled comfortably in.

Two stops up the street, someone sat down beside her. It was a man of indeterminate age somewhere between 35 and 50. His hair was dark, streaked with tiny threads of gray at the temples. His khakis and polo shirt were worn, stretched out of shape and blotted with stains, but washed to within an inch of their lives. Following standard public transportation etiquette, Beata ignored him.

Without visibly encroaching onto her side of the seat, he seemed to expand to fill the entire bus. He exuded confidence. "Hi," he said, fixing her with a friendly smile.

Beata eyed him hostilely, responded with an indistinct grunt and turned her shoulder toward him. What was he doing? This was not a tour bus.

He seemed not to notice her animosity. "How you doing?" he said.

Beata turned even further away. She gazed out the window as if fascinated by the commuters ambulating mechanically up the street. She fumbled through her laptop bag. Finding there a sheaf of papers that belonged to a project completed three weeks ago, she extracted it and pretended to study them. "Fine," she mumbled, flipping over the top page and plunging into the next. Out of the corner of her eye, she thought she saw him glancing at the papers.

"Ahem," she coughed, hunching over the papers so he couldn't see them and focusing her eyes on them as if to burn a hole through the whole stack. She fished a pen out of her bag and mumbled to herself as she made irrelevant notes. The man sat and watched her quietly.

"Working?" he inquired pleasantly.

"Hmm," she mumbled, glancing up momentarily and then returning studiously to the papers as if to emphasize she was concentrating on important matters of business.

"Isn't it quitting time?" he persisted.

For a moment, Beata considered changing seats, or even getting off the bus. But he seemed harmless enough, nothing threatening in his manner, so she barricaded herself behind her spurious notes and waited for him to leave. The busier stops closer to downtown came and went, but her seat-mate stayed put. He continued to look at her affably, waiting for a response to his friendly overtures, oblivious to her determination to ignore him. His eyes did not waver from her face, and she began to wonder, uncomfortably, if she had met him somewhere and forgotten about it. She shifted in her seat, but could not glance at him for fear of meeting that bright, inquiring gaze.

Finally, as the bus pulled up to her stop and she stuffed her notes back into her bag, he stood. He allowed her to pass first, then exited the bus behind her.

"Is he going to follow me home?" she wondered, but instead he stood at the stop after the bus went on, looking in her direction (was he watching her?) with an interested air.

He looked vaguely familiar. Suddenly, she remembered the man she'd seen on the street that morning, and wondered if it could be he...did they look the same? She couldn't tell. It'd been so dark this morning that she hadn't really noticed what the man looked like.

Since her back door was visible from the bus stop, she pretended to walk further down the street so he wouldn't know where she lived, and then slipped around the far side of the house, down the alleyway and through the yard to the front door. She unlocked the door, dropped her laptop in the crowded foyer, kicked off her shoes and went to the bedroom to change into one of her house dresses. Then, keeping out of sight of the window, she slunk into the kitchen and looked over at the bus stop. Whew! He was nowhere in sight.

"That's a relief," she said to herself. "What a strange guy. I guess he must live around here. Funny I've never seen him on the bus before."

She grabbed a container of cold, leftover Chinese food from the refrigerator and picked up her book, still unfinished from the weekend.

The psychic fair in Aberdeen was held in a large hall at the civic center, and because the weather was fine, booths spilled out into the parking lot. The fair had attracted hundreds of New Age seekers who flocked there to purchase every service and product imaginable.

Beata was a hanger-on; she flirted with the New Age without embracing it fully. She liked its mysticism and openness to diverse ideas. She also liked the thought that she was living on the edge of a transcendental reality that, while largely unseen, gave meaning and significance to her mundane life of work and home. There has to be something more than this, she thought, and the New Age had a thousand ideas about what that "something more" might be.

At the same time, the movement's credulity bothered her. It seemed that anything that *said* it was supernatural had carte blanche to dispense advice and wisdom. How was she to know she could trust these beings they supposedly channeled and the visions they supposedly saw? Thus, she adopted an attitude of skepticism that hoped for miracles while secretly fearing most of these people were deluded.

Today, she resolved to suspend her distrust and enjoy the happy cacophony of the fair. She and Gladys wandered among the booths, sniffing essential oils, ringing chimes, listening to snatches of Native American flute music, and sampling the various kinds of readings.

Gladys decided to have her aura photographed, and Beata had a chakra reading. The booth she'd chosen was draped with oceans of white tulle studded with small round mirrors, which created the illusion of privacy while obscuring neither vision nor sound. At the back, on a curtain of heavier white fabric, a poster hung showing a silhouette of the human body. Down the front of the figure ran a series of colored blobs. These started at the crotch with a red blob, and ended at the top of the head in purple. Scientific looking arrows pointed to each chakra, indicating their names and functions in text too small to be read from the front of the booth. The whole effect, Beata decided, put her in mind of a circus tent decorated for a wedding with a surgical theme.

The reader, a woman with hair dyed flat black and wearing a flowing white caftan with scarlet accents at the hem and wrists, invited her to sit at a table. She emitted a faint jingling noise when she walked, and Beata realized that she was wearing a bracelet of bells around her ankle. With no words of introduction, the caftan woman plunged straight into the reading.

"What is all this change I see around you?" she asked.

"I don't know," Beata said. "As far as I can tell there *is* no change. My life is pretty much the same old same old. In fact, it would be nice if there *were* some change." Then, recollecting the blind date with Frank she added, "My daughter did introduce me to a guy the other night."

"Hmm," the reader said. "Tell me about this guy.""He's okay," Beata said. "He's a few years older than me, divorced. He seems a little lonely. I didn't connect with him all that well. Besides, I don't want a relationship. I'm happy being alone."

"You're happy being alone?" The reader's air suggested that she was determined to suspend judgment, but nevertheless found Beata's statement suspicious.

"Yes, I am," Beata insisted. "Men are okay. But every time I try to get into a relationship, I end up changing my routine, trying to get interested in what my partner's thinking. I start doing the little things women do to try and show their appreciation for men, and then I get fed up and bored and I just want to be alone again. Romance doesn't *fit* in my life. It's like a disease…your whole system rises up to cast it out and you can't be well until you get rid of it."

"You think relationship is like a *disease*?" the reader sounded appalled.

"Okay, maybe not a disease," Beata conceded, "say it's a foreign object. Like a splinter in your finger, or maybe

43

an extra organ, like a second gall bladder. The point is that it's unnatural. Honestly, it seems to me there's not much give and take in most relationships. Everyone is really in it to gratify their own needs. 'You give me what I need and I'll give you what you need'. And the problem with that is, what do I need? Even if they were asking, which they aren't, I wouldn't know. So I end up getting nothing out of the deal, and I don't think they get much, either. Whatever they want, it doesn't have anything to do with who *I* am. Any available woman would do just as well."

The reader was looking stunned. "Um, have you had counseling?" she asked.

"Lots of it," Beata assured her. "Why do you ask? Is it inherently sick to not want a relationship? Am I so much more twisted than the thousands of people mooning around looking for Mr. Right? They're all happy and fulfilled, and I'm a bitter, empty old woman? I'll tell you what, I felt a whole lot emptier back when I was yearning for the Perfect Relationship than I do right now."

At this point, Gladys, having finished with her aura photograph, had strolled up to the booth and caught the last part of Beata's diatribe. Pulling up a third chair, she dug her elbow into Beata's side.

"Are you harassing the psychics now?" she inquired, "Can't I ever trust you on your own?" Turning to the reader, she advised "Just ignore my friend here. She's always getting on her soapbox whenever you mention the 'L' word."

"She didn't mention the 'L' word," said Beata, "it was the 'R' word. No, wait, *I* was the one who mentioned the 'R' word. She mentioned the 'M' word, didn't you? What word *did* you say that got us off on this track?"

The reader frowned and tapped one of her long fingernails on the glass tabletop. She glowered at Beata without responding.

"Anyway, I think we're getting sidetracked here," said Beata. "Can we move on? I don't need anyone to validate my views on romance; I just want a chakra reading."

For a moment, it seemed the reader might refuse. Shifting back in her chair, she raked the two of them with a challenging glare. She seemed to be searching her mind for a scathing retort that would awaken them to a sensibility of the crime they had committed in making a joke of what she took seriously, but finding none, and loathe to forfeit her fee of $50, she gathered up the shreds of her dignity and continued.

She closed her eyes and meditated silently for several minutes, as if to emphasize the awesome sanctity of the psychic process. Then, opening her eyes again, and after another moment of pregnant silence, she began: "I see the picture of a knife in your second chakra. The color associated with this chakra is orange, but yours is a muddy color, indicating blockage. The knife shows that you've been wounded in this chakra, which is the seat of emotions, so it shows emotional wounding. There is also a chain of this muddy color connecting the third chakra, the seat of personal power, to the second. This shows that your personal power is controlled or imprisoned by the wounding experience. The heart chakra, which is the seat of love, is green, but the energy is moving inward instead of exploding out. This shows that even though you feel love, you are not expressing it to others. The heart chakra and the throat chakra are indistinct. This indicates that there are general communication problems here. You don't express yourself freely, and you particularly don't express love freely."

Well, this wasn't exactly news, Beata thought. She didn't express love freely? She wondered if the psychic would've said this if she hadn't had the benefit of listening to Beata's diatribe against relationships. And what was all this about emotional wounding? That was safely generic. She'd never met anyone who wasn't wounded by *something* in their past.

45

The reader had paused again, whether for effect or because she was contemplating another image, Beata could not tell.

"Hovering over your right shoulder, I see a blinding white light, so pure it cuts like a knife," she continued. "It's approaching you slowly, from the rear, which signifies it is coming from your past. Something from your past is getting ready to overtake you."

This was a little more promising. Maybe the woman really was psychic, after all.

"What is it?" Beata asked.

"It's very old," said the reader, dodging the question. "From a past life, maybe. The whiteness of it means that it's spiritual. It can give you wisdom and healing."

Beata wasn't sure she'd had any past lives.

"Couldn't it be from this life?" she asked.

The reader considered this. "It could be," she said. "But the point is, you're driving it away with your skepticism. You have to believe and stop doubting. Don't resist. Welcome the change. Let in the new."

"But what *is* it?" Beata asked. "Can't you say any more except that it's old?"

The reader didn't answer, just rose to her feet and picked up the check Beata had left on the table before the reading began. Her ten minutes were up.

"Um, thank you," she said to the reader. The reader flounced to the back of the booth, turned her back and began fiddling with a metal cash box, pointedly ignoring Beata and Gladys. Apparently, they had not been forgiven for getting the reading off to a rocky start.

"Ooo," Beata said to Gladys, "I think we need to get out of here. We are persona non grata. Or at least I am."

"As well you should be," Gladys said, following their private code of loyalty, which dictated that each should exaggerate, and even if necessary manufacture, faults on the part of the other.

The two women rose and left the booth, brushing against the tulle bunting and causing some of the round mirrors to flutter wildly.

"You heard the reading," Beata said to Gladys, "what did you think? Are you any clearer on what this influence from the past is than I am? She said 'don't be skeptical,' like that's a problem that's standing in the way of whatever it is I'm supposed to be doing. What am I skeptical about?"

"You're skeptical about *everything*," Gladys said.

"Yeah, but is that a bad thing? It's not like I can't be convinced. I'm willing to change my views if the arguments are good. Besides, if I'm skeptical about everything, how do I know which of the things I'm being skeptical about is the important one?"

"Maybe you should get another reading and see if they can give you more information about it," Gladys suggested. "Here's a Spirit Guides booth, why don't you ask them?"

Gladys indicated a booth decorated in a wolf motif with painted drums, antlers and indigo hues designed to evoke the eerie mystery of a moonlit night.

"I don't know about this 'spirit guide' thing," said Beata. "Who are these guides, anyway? Do we know their credentials for giving people advice? Why would I assume that a dead person knows more than a living one? I could be getting advice from the Village Idiot, who set himself up as a 'guide' just because he's dead. It doesn't make sense to me."

Gladys rolled her eyes. "Is that...could that possibly be *skepticism* I hear? How come it's ok to get advice from cards and psychics and not dead people?"

That was a darn good question, Beata had to admit. She had the vague belief, she supposed, that God, Himself, manipulated the stars and cards or gave visions to the psychic. Why God didn't speak directly to Beata, she didn't know. He probably had better things to do than worry about her silly little problems. God, in Beata's mind, sat above the cosmos like a giant miasma of love and wisdom, radiating benevolently down upon His creation, and sucking everything inexorably upward into the vortex of Godlike perfection.

It was up to us, Beata felt, to cooperate with God's sucking program by working our way up the ladder of spiritual evolution until we were attuned enough to hear His voice, or perhaps ultimately to merge with Him in some mystical way. His job was to sit there being God, and our job was to strain with utmost persistence and sincerity to ascertain His will for us.

"I don't trust their motives," she concluded to Gladys. "At least when you get advice from an embodied being, you can look at their face and get some idea what kind of a rube you're listening to."

Gladys was not attached to the spirit guides. "Well then," she offered, "how 'bout that Tarot reader over in the corner. She looks okay."

Gladys pointed toward a small, plain booth at the very edge of the floor. It was constructed from a canopy such as you might buy from Wal Mart to put up over a picnic table. The canopy was dusty blue with white stripes. Fastened to its edge was a string of white Christmas tree lights, and a sign that said "Wisdom from Medicine Woman Tarot". The reader sat inside, at a table covered by a silk scarf over a blue and white checkered tablecloth, laying out and gathering up her cards. Every finger on both hands was clad with one or more silver rings decorated with cabochon stones. When she tired of laying out and gathering up cards, she played with her rings. She looked bored.

She looked up hopefully as Beata approached. The movement made her earrings, woven of intricate silver wires, dance in the light.

"How's business?" Beata said. This corner of the fair looked as barren as the Mohave. "Bad location?"

The reader, correctly divining that admitting business was bad would be the kiss of death to any remaining chance of financial success, denied it vigorously.

"Oh, *no*," she said, smiling brightly. "It's a little slow now, but that's all to the good. You can get in with no waiting."

"My lucky day," Beata said.

"Are you enjoying the fair?"

"Yes, I am," Beata said. "There's quite an impressive crowd here for such a small town. It kind of surprised me."

She sat down on the opposite side of the flimsy table, and sent it flying when she pulled in her chair. The reader grabbed it, adroitly righting it and adjusting the tablecloth, which had been knocked askew, while, at the same time, pretending nothing had happened.

"Sorry," Beata mumbled.

"So," asked the reader, shuffling her cards, "what is your question today?"

"I just had a chakra reading," Beata explained, "and she told me that there was a significant change coming into my life. She said I had to embrace this change, but I'm not sure what kind of change it is and what 'embracing' it really means. I'm a practical person, and I get frustrated when someone tells me I should take action but don't have a clue what, specifically, I'm supposed to be doing. I was hoping you could tell me more about it."

"Okay," said the young woman, handing Beata an awkwardly large deck of cards, "Think about your question and shuffle the cards."

Beata shuffled the cards and thought about her question. She felt, rather than heard, someone come quietly up behind her.

Gladys must be done with her healing stone reading already, she thought, and handed the cards back to the reader. The reader laid them out in a circle, face down.

"The first card," she began, reaching for the card on the far left of the circle, "shows influences over your question from the past." This was promising. Perhaps it would tell Beata something about the blinding white light the other reader had seen over her left shoulder. She held her breath as the reader flipped over the card…it was white, with no picture.

"Aren't there supposed to be pictures on these cards?" she asked the reader. The reader stared at the card.

"Uh," she said. "This is strange. Hold on, let's move to the next card."

"But I want to know about the past influences," Beata protested. "This is important to my question."

Ignoring her, the reader flipped over the next card. It, too, was blank.

"Hey!" the reader gasped. She flipped over another card, and another. Her face blanched as white as the cards winking up at her from the table.

"What's going on here?" she demanded of Beata.

"I – what do you mean?" faltered Beata. "I haven't done anything."

The reader gathered up the cards furiously. "You have bad energy," she announced. "This is not nice and it's not funny. I am here trying to help people."

"But seriously; I promise," Beata pleaded, "I didn't do anything to your cards. I wouldn't play a joke like that."

The reader pivoted on her heel, marched out of her booth and over to one of her neighbors. Beata saw her whispering, rifling through the cards and gesticulating in her direction. She rose from the table and turned to leave, plowing right into the man standing behind her.

"Hi," said the man.

Beata was too agitated to wonder what he was doing there, and too agitated to figure out why his dark eyes and olive skin looked vaguely familiar.

"Did you see that?" she demanded.

"Yes," he replied.

"What happened?"

The man said nothing.

"I have to find my friend," Beata said, scanning the crowd for Gladys.

"You look upset," the man said. "Why don't we have a cup of coffee and talk about it?"

"No, I don't want a cup of coffee. I need to find my friend."

The man put his hands in the pockets of his khaki trousers. "Okay," he said, stepping back to let Beata go by.

Beata raced through the room looking for the healing stones booth. By the time she found Gladys, she was feeling calmer. She told her the story, omitting the part about the strange man, who had hardly made an impression on her in the agitation following the blank card debacle.

"Weird," commented Gladys.

"What do you think happened?"

"Bea, I really don't know. Maybe the reader was playing a trick on you. Those cards had to be blank in the first place. Did you ever see them face up before she laid them out?"

"No, actually I didn't. She sure didn't act like she was in on the joke, though."

"Maybe embodied beings aren't as reliable as you thought," Gladys joked.

"Maybe not."

"Why don't you try someone else?"

"Y'know, I think I've had enough of psychic readings for one day," Beata said. "My old heart can only take so much. How was your healing stone thing, anyway?"

"It was great," Gladys said. "She warmed up these stones and placed them on my chakras one by one. It was relaxing."

"Were they just regular stones, or what?"

"They were like river stones, with runes or something painted on."

"So did she say anything, or just put them on your body?"

"No, she said stuff, too. She told me I was really psychic."

"You're psychic?"

"That's what she told me. She also felt that I was going to meet someone, you know, like relationship-wise."

"Oh Gladys," Beata groaned, "Not *that* again."

Gladys was offended. "Just because *you* don't want a relationship doesn't mean I shouldn't have one," she pointed out. "You don't know what it's like to be with someone truly compatible and then lose them."

"Yeah, but that 'true compatibility' didn't last, did it?"

"That's not fair," said Gladys. "It *could* have lasted. It would have lasted, but John changed, his priorities changed. When the kids were little, he was devoted to us. He was so good with the kids, so involved. I don't just mean fishing and Little League, either. When John, Jr. was a baby, he had ear infections all the time. He would wake up at night screaming his head off. His father would get up and walk the floor with him so I could sleep, or take him out driving in the car. He was a good father."

"Okay," Beata replied. "I guess I just don't understand what basis you have for building another relationship like that at your time of life. You are done with the kids and family. They're raised. You don't need a good father anymore."

"Yes, but I need to be appreciated," Gladys said. "I want someone to cherish me. I want to have someone I can do things for. I like taking care of someone, cooking dinner for them and such."

Beata was mystified by this attitude. 'Taking care of someone', to her, sounded like a thankless burden, not a delightful addition to daily life. The only person she didn't resent taking care of was Daphne, darling Daphne, whose departure from home at the age of 20 had just about ripped her heart in half. Of course, Daphne had started leaving long before that, getting more remote as she'd progressed through her adolescent years. Beata understood this intellectually, but grieved about it privately, agonizing over every independent decision Daphne made and smothering her with advice she rejected with increasing hostility.

In the end, Daphne had turned out all right, she grudgingly admitted. She'd pried Beata's fingernails out of her flesh and struck out on her own, and no great disaster had ensued. She made a success out of her job; Sean was a nice enough boy, and one day soon, Beata supposed, she would start her own family. But children were different. They needed to be taken care of. That was a mother's job. Men were supposed to be adults; they should take care of themselves.

Gladys was lucky. She'd had a husband who, for many years, at least, had truly partnered with her. She saw him as a support rather than a liability, someone she could depend on to do the things she couldn't. Beata's husband had never been like that. He'd hung around her neck like a millstone, and getting rid of him made her life easier, not harder. So it was natural, she thought, for her to be cynical about relationships.

"So, did she tell you anything more about this guy you're supposed to be meeting?" she asked.

"No," said Gladys, "just that we would be together for the rest of our lives. Unlike John. And that he would love me for who I really am."

"Well...good luck with that," said Beata. "I hope she's right. Hey, at least you *have* a future. Apparently mine is blank."

"No, actually, I don't think it is," said Gladys. She stopped walking and closed her eyes, intoning, "I see a booth surrounded by a large crowd of people. You are standing beside me with an object in your hand....it is small and rounded...yes, I believe it is half of a pita bread. I sense – I sense that you will be eating lunch in the very near future."

The young man in the closest booth, which displayed a banner saying "Intuitive Energy Readings", gave them a dirty look.

"That person has no sense of humor at all," said Beata, taking Gladys by the arm and steering her away. "Let's go eat some falafel."

As they munched on their falafel and wiped dribbles of yogurt sauce off their shirts, Beata suddenly remembered the man she'd run into at the Tarot booth.

"Hey I forgot to tell you about another strange thing that happened at that Tarot booth," she told Gladys. "I ran into this man, and I mean literally ran into him, on my way out of the booth. I was too flustered to realize it until I walked away, but I've seen him before. I saw him on the bus on the way home the other day. He sat down on the seat beside me and tried to strike up a conversation."

Gladys cocked an interested eyebrow at Beata. "Really? What's he like?"

"Oh, you have love on the brain," said Beata. "It's nothing like that. He's younger than me as far as I can tell, but not a lot younger, maybe a few years. He's sort of Mediterranean looking, has olive skin and dark hair. His clothes are a little on the shabby side, not dirty, exactly, but kind of faded and stained looking like they're worn out."

"Is he good looking?"

"I don't know. Not really."

"Oh," said Gladys, sounding disappointed. "Still, at our age we can't be too picky."

"On the contrary," said Beata, "we can be very picky at our age. I'm so picky that I wouldn't have the man if he looked like Paul Newman."

Gladys giggled. "You're showing your age," she said, tossing the last of her falafel into a nearby garbage can. "Paul Newman is way old now. You should have said Brad Pitt, or someone else born in the last half century."

"*I* wasn't born in the last half century," said Beata, "and, oh, by the way, neither were you."

"Rub it in," said Gladys. At this moment, her attention was distracted by a pink chiffon scarf printed with silver moons and stars, and scattered round the hem with bells. "Oooo, look at this," she squealed, pulling it from the display rack and winding it around her head.

"Very exotic," approved Beata. "It matches your outfit."

"It matches all my outfits," said Gladys, which was quite true. Gladys was a lover of pink, and wore it so often that her prematurely white hair had taken on a subtle pink glow that reflected in her rosy cheeks and set off her china-blue eyes. She looked like a little tuft of cotton candy, Beata reflected. It would be no wonder if Gladys found a man who would welcome the nurturing embrace of her soft, wistful arms, ample bosom and pinkly glowing complexion.

All that feminine pliability, however, camouflaged an intelligent wit that blended happily with Beata's sharper one. They abused each other gleefully, often raising the eyebrows of casual onlookers who thought their humor too pointed for comfort. When push came to shove, though, each flew instantly to the other's defense, and had more than once been mistaken for blood relations despite the complete lack of physical resemblance between them.

"I may not want a relationship with a man," Beata had sometimes thought, "But I sure am glad I know Gladys."

Gladys, coquetting with herself in the mirror the vendor had hung thoughtfully from the frame of the booth, had decided to buy the scarf.

"I don't really have the money for this," she confided to Beata, "but I can't pass it up."

Gladys never had the money for anything, because money ran through her fingers like water through a sieve. Beata had no idea where it all went. Gladys made a good salary and lived modestly, but she certainly never had any money to spare.

"I like the scarf," she said cautiously, "but are you sure you need it?"

"Do I need it?" repeated Gladys. "Of course not. But look how pretty it is. I could never find anything like this in the city."

"Gladys. You find things like that in the city all the time. Leave it be," advised Beata. "Your credit card is probably going to melt if you use it any more today. In fact, I know your card will melt, because I have a propane torch in my purse that I'm going to pull out and attack it with if I hear one more word about buying that scarf. Here, let me adjust it for you."

Beata wound the scarf closer around Gladys' face, covering her eyes, and pretended to make a grab for Gladys' purse.

The booth owner looked daggers at Beata. Great. Now she had antagonized three readers and a store clerk, and the day was little more than half over. What else could possibly go wrong before this debacle ended? If she kept on as she was going, she would get them thrown out of the fair by a mob of angry vendors and banned from all future fairs as scoffers, troublemakers and looky-loos.

The feared expulsion did not come to pass. Although Beata stuck to her decision to have no further readings, she waited patiently while Gladys had three, craving enlightenment on various points of interest regarding the man supposedly coming into her life. The readings paid off with information galore. Gladys' suitor would be a tall man of medium height with dark, sandy, blonde hair. He would be a wealthy, professional blue-collar laborer of modest means, pale black, of young middle age just over sixty, and would have (apparently) three eyes of different colors. Gladys' sanguine temperament dismissed these contradictions as extraneous details, and she looked forward happily to the promised advent of True Love.

Futilely, Beata tried to convince her she was being gullible. She didn't think it was a good idea for Gladys pin her hopes on a man that, let's face it, could be just about anyone, or a hundred different someones. Didn't she think that, just maybe, the psychics were playing along with her because she obviously wanted a man? They were promising her she'd get what they already knew she wanted? No, Gladys did not think that. Beata always thought the worst about people, she said.

"I don't think the worst about people. I just try to be realistic," Beata defended.

"Well, why does your realisticness always come out sounding like negativity?"

"Because reality *is* negative," she protested. "Most of the time."

"Even if that were true, it still doesn't mean that nothing good will ever happen," Gladys said.

Gladys was right. Beata never expected anything good to happen. She always knew calamity was lurking right around the corner. Oh, sure, everything seemed okay *now*. But what fresh disaster was brewing, waiting to pounce on her the minute she dropped her guard and admitted maybe things weren't so bad?

"Isn't it better," she said, "to expect the worst? That way you'll be prepared for disappointment. It won't sting so badly."

"It always stings anyway," Gladys pointed out. "The only thing you accomplish that way is to miss out on the good things that are happening right now."

Beata couldn't agree. She was convinced it would be devastating to be taken by misfortune unaware, ambushed by expecting good and getting served up a nasty plate full of evil instead. She felt she should talk Gladys out of this ingenuous notion that good was just as probable as evil, like you had a 50-50 shot at getting one vs. the other. The chances were 90-10, she believed, that Gladys would meet nobody. Or that she would meet someone, but he would be a bigamist or an axe murderer, or just a selfish jerk who would break her heart.

Gladys would not be convinced. She just laughed at Beata's pessimism. Looking forward to her promised relationship made her almost as happy as actually having it. Gladys pulled up to the side of Beata's house at twilight. It wasn't nearly dark enough for sight-seeing but dark enough to make it difficult to pick out the man resting his elbows on Beata's fence near the front gate.

"Look!" Beata said, clutching Gladys' arm. "Look at that man right over there."

"Where?" said Gladys.

"Right there by the mailbox. There's a man skulking around my yard."

"I don't see any man."

"Gladys, he's right there, leaning on the fence in plain view."

Gladys peered at the front yard. "I don't see anyone."

The man straightened up and lifted a hand. "He's waving at me," Beata said.

Gladys shook her head. "You're seeing things."

"I can't believe you don't see him. He's staring straight at us. Drive me away from here. I don't want to get out."

Gladys started the car. "You really are losing it," she said, turning the corner. "How far are we going?"

"Just drive me around the block."

Gladys drove around the block. When they returned to Beata's house, the man appeared to be gone.

"I'm still nervous," she said. "Walk me in."

Gladys frowned. "Beata, this isn't like you. You're worrying me."

"Gladys, I swear there was a man standing right there," Beata said, pointing to where she'd seen the man. "He was leaning both elbows on the fence, and when we pulled in, he stood up and waved."

Beata wouldn't go into the house until they'd walked the perimeter of the yard, poking around the bushes and Morning Glory to make sure no one was hiding there. They went in the back door, and Beata made Gladys walk through the entire house with her.

"He's not here," Gladys said when they finished looking through the basement. "Everything's fine. Just lock your doors, and if you see anyone, call the police."

"Sorry," Beata said, accompanying Gladys to the back door. "I don't know what came over me. Am I going crazy?"

Gladys raised her eyebrows. "*Going* crazy? That's impossible. You've been crazy for a long time."

Beata laughed. She could always count on Gladys to make her feel better. "Thanks," she said. "I'd like to remind you that means your best friend is a crazy woman. What does that say about *you*?"

"It says I'm a deeply compassionate person," Gladys said.

Beata was not certain she'd enjoy her upcoming date with Frank. She was nervous, and it made her preparations both lengthy and chaotic. She paced back and forth between the closet and the full-length mirror hanging in the hallway, scowling as she examined and rejected one article of clothing after another. Most of her dresses were of similar pattern, dark colored, loose and somewhat faded from hard wear. The challenge was to pick one that had no obvious structural issues such as split seams, tears, or bits of unraveling hem. Having once become fond of a garment, Beata never stopped wearing it, and was blind to its gradual deterioration. The small flaws she was unaccustomed to noticing seemed to have spread through her closet like hookworm to every dress she owned. No sooner would she seize upon a dress with a relieved sigh than closer examination would reveal irregular silver glints where she'd stapled a seam shut, or subtle yellow stains where she'd slopped mustard on herself a few months back.

When she finally found a serviceable dress, she had to decide on shoes, and this was even more difficult. Beata's shoe wardrobe included two extreme options: high-heeled pumps procured for days of sitting at the desk or conference table, never used to walk farther than 50 feet at a stretch, and ragged tennis shoes. Either one would look ridiculous with her dress, and the pumps would not only look silly, but massacre her feet as well. Finally, almost driven to contemplate an emergency trip to the shoe store, she unearthed a pair of rubber flip-flops buried at the back of her closet that would do nicely, being neither snobbishly formal nor offensively tattered.

Now her attention turned to her hair. This was easier, as some semblance of neatness was all she could hope for. She'd already washed it and put it in a ponytail, and she now extracted it and smoothed it down with a brush. The application of the brush generated enough static electricity to cause a few fine hairs to fly up randomly around her face. "I look like a fright," she commented, pawing at it despairingly. While rooting through her rarely-used dressing table for some hairspray to cement it down, she heard the Irene's dogs raising the alarm that a stranger was in the vicinity. She abandoned her search and went to the front window.

"Aaaugh," she said, espying Frank approaching the front fence. "It's later than I thought."

As arranged, Frank had come by at 6:00 to pick her up. He drove a tiny, dilapidated yellow pickup whose tailgate had been replaced with a sky-blue one from the junkyard. Its previous owner, a youthful hipster in the style of the 1990's, had, before totaling his truck, obliterated from the tailgate all but the letters 'YO', giving it an air of outdated modishness.

Frank searched the front of the house for an address. Surely this untamed jungle of a yard could not belong to Beata. But the tarnished brass numbers on the house verified that it did, so he approached the fence looking for ingress. Here, he paused in confusion, for the pernicious Morning Glory had so overrun the fence that the location of the gate was undetectable. He had placed one hand casually in the pocket of his faded Dockers, and now he jingled his keys with it as he pawed ineffectually at the Morning Glory with the other hand.

Beata hastened outside to rescue him. "Here," she called, directing him to the opposite end of the fence. She hurried up the walk and dug through the tenacious riot of vines to wrest open the gate.

"I usually use the back gate," she explained. Her house was situated on a corner lot, so the back gate was at the side of the house, convenient to a set of concrete steps and a door leading into the kitchen. "You can see I don't get much company."

Frank glanced uncertainly around the yard. Was he nervous, or did his glance mean to convey disapproval over the condition of her property? Beata could not tell. His eyes rested briefly upon a jumble of two-by-fours half-concealed by the overgrown lawn, a partially-framed, never-erected shed that Beata had started, with the help of Sean, to house her lawnmower and various other barely-used gardening tools.

"Would you like to come in for a few minutes?" she invited.

"Um, sure," mumbled Frank, following her up to the front door and into the small foyer. This was crowded with umbrellas, fleece vests and jackets hanging on hooks, and winter footwear. Beata kicked a pair of boots further out of the way and led him into the living room.

"Please have a seat," she offered, indicating the sofa, which sat against the back wall facing the large window that opened onto the yard. "Can I get you something to drink? Soda? Tea? Juice? Coffee?"

Frank perched uncomfortably on the very edge of the sofa. "No, thanks," he said.

Beata sat in an overstuffed chair at right angles to the couch. Frank's refusal to take refreshment created an awkward interlude, she reflected, as she couldn't very well sit there guzzling beverages while he stared out the window. She smoothed her dress carefully over her knees, attempting to project an air of social ease that was foreign to her nature.

"It's nice to see you again," she said, and clasped her hands in her lap. "How are you doing?"

"Okay," said Frank.

"Have you done any fishing lately?"

"Naw. Too busy at work."

"Oh, I can imagine," she said, "this must be a busy season for construction."

"Yeah," he agreed.

"Is that a four-wheel drive you have?"

"Naw."

Beata settled back in her chair and tucked her feet up on the seat, hoping to encourage Frank to occupy something more than a scant two inches of sofa. They sat silent for a moment as she frantically searched her mind for an opener that might awaken Frank from his monosyllabic stupor. Presently, he rescued her by offering one of his own:

"What's up with the wood in your front yard?" he asked.

"Oh *that*," she said, leaning forward to denote her eagerness to engage in meaningful conversation, "that's a tool shed I've been building with my daughter's boyfriend. We haven't made much progress on it because we're both so busy, but we hope to finish it before this winter. I don't have a garage, and I can't very well haul the lawnmower up and down the basement stairs, so the tools all sit outside, and they're rusting in the rain. I throw a tarp over them, of course, but it doesn't really keep out the damp."

"I could finish it for you," Frank offered, looking hopeful at the prospect of having found a task that was within his masculine domain of usefulness.

"Well…gosh," floundered Beata, startled at this sudden display of personal interest, "I couldn't ask you… that is, I really don't know…I don't expect…I mean, that's really nice of you."

"No problem," said Frank. This was comfortable ground, and having found it, Frank expanded like a thirsty sponge drinking up water. He settled back, crossed an ankle over his knee and draped his arm across the back of the sofa.

"I'll bring some of my guys out next week and take a look at it," he promised. "We can put it together in no time. You're looking at, what, an 8x10? Metal roof? You got the siding already?"

"Um, no," said Beata, "What do you recommend?"

Frank nodded contentedly. Tool sheds, siding and roofing were his turf, and by taking responsibility for these worrisome details off of Beata's frail shoulders, he was fulfilling his duty as a man. She could leave the whole thing in his capable hands.

Beata, who didn't consider tool shed construction to be as incomprehensible to the female mind as Frank apparently did, still was content to let Frank run with the project. It would be one less unfinished task she could accuse herself of neglecting. Her only hesitation was that it implied a shift from casual acquaintanceship to a deeper level of mutual obligation. She was a little worried about being beholden to him. She dismissed this thought sternly, remembering the reading she'd received at the psychic fair. Be open, she reminded herself.

"I thought we'd catch the 7:15 show at the Cinerama," he suggested.

Beata had scanned the movie listings in the paper that afternoon, and immediately recalled the special effects extravaganza playing at the Cinerama. Her interest in this film was one degree above absolute zero, but there was nothing else she wanted to see, anyway.

"Won't parking downtown be a pain?" she demurred.

Frank waved off this objection without comment. She was not to worry her head with logistical difficulties. He had matters well in hand.

"We'd better get going, then," she advised, "I'll just run and get my purse."

The purse having been duly retrieved, she accompanied Frank to his truck. Its floor was stained with oily residue, but the seat glowed baldly as if recently shaved of a scruffy beard of many years' standing. She had no doubt that, could she have seen it on an ordinary day, it would have been cluttered with tools, car parts and construction debris, but Frank had polished it up for this special occasion.

"A working truck," Beata approved.

Frank looked slightly offended. It was not polite, the set of his chin implied, to make any but the most flattering remarks about a man's wheels.

Frank and Beata sat through the movie in silence sharing a bucket of popcorn, specks of which Frank

64

occasionally had to brush from his mustache, and sipping sodas. Going to the movies with Frank was very different from going with Gladys, Beata reflected. Unless the movie was unassailably excellent, she and Gladys maintained a running commentary on its implausible plot twists and idiotic characters which, although conducted in low whispers, usually drew glares from the surrounding audience. Tired of exciting public censure, they had taken to renting movies and watched them at home where their nit-picking could not be an irritant to other viewers. Frank, by contrast, absorbed the movie with uncritical solemnity, and afterward made no comments about its quality.

"Um, that was okay," offered Beata, hesitant to begin her usual slash tactics until she knew how much Frank had liked it.

"Yeah," he said. He didn't sound overly enthusiastic, so Beata felt safe in going a little further.

"The special effects were good. But I have to say it always annoys me when they cast a block-buster star that's pushing 60 with a 22 year old girl as the romantic interest. Are we supposed to pretend this guy is in his first blush of youth? He's probably half bald under his toupee, or weave, or whatever it is, and you could actually see his little paunch when he turned the wrong way during the action scenes. Why is it that men never age but women are old hags at the age of 35?"

"She was hot," Frank objected. He felt vaguely disturbed at the hint of outrage in her voice. Was she now going to devolve into a raving feminist lunatic? Who on earth would go to the movies to watch some old broad prance around in a skintight leather jumpsuit?

"Right," she pursued. "That's the point. Why does she have to be 'hot' when he's a balding, paunchy old man?"

This wasn't working, she realized. Why was she always criticizing things? Couldn't she accept *anything* the way it was, even the financial realities of the movie industry, which had to pander to our penchant for young, beautiful women while still needing an established star to draw the moviegoers to the box office? She had violated Frank's comfort zone, although she wasn't sure whether it was the charge of ageism or the crime of criticizing a movie he liked that was bothering him. She offered no further comment on the movie, and, after a several minutes of companionable silence, was rewarded with an invitation to stop for a beer on the way home.

They stopped at a dingy, narrow tavern that barely accommodated three pool tables end-to-end while still leaving enough room for the patrons sitting at the bar. Beata, although a horrible pool player, enjoyed playing and would have challenged Frank to a game except that the tables were all occupied by men who took their billiards seriously. Money was exchanging hands, tension was palpable and concentration fierce, and when one man lost, there was already another who had anted up to play the winner. This bar had no room for dilettantes.

They settled at the far end of the bar. Frank ordered a draft: some pale, insignificant American lager that Beata found indistinguishable from every other pale, insignificant American lager. Beata preferred only stout, porter and other dark beers, but the selection in this working man's bar was not extensive. They catered to a crowd that could put back six beers and still drive home in a straight line rather than the seven dollar, microbrew-sipping, crowd that Beata was accustomed to. After requesting (and being denied) Negra Modelo and Black Butte Porter, she settled on Guinness, not her favorite but the one dark beer available in almost every tavern.

"You were married before, right?" Beata asked.

"Yeah."

"What happened with that?"

Frank pulled at his beer and stared at the wall above the bar as if examining the labels of the bottles there displayed. "Aw, she was always bitching about something.

She wanted me to do this and buy that. Want, want, want."
He cleared his throat and smoothed his mustache.

"How long did it last?" Beata probed.

"Seven years." He glanced surreptitiously at Beata from the corner of his eye, perhaps suspecting that he was making himself appear pathetic by admitting, at his age, to having been attached for so few years. So he added: "Then after that I hooked up with someone else for a long time, but she wanted to get married and I didn't."

"I was married for ten," Beata said. "We had money issues – namely, he didn't make any, just spent it. If I wouldn't let him buy something he wanted, he would just get a credit card and buy it anyway. Every year I made more money and every year we got further in debt. Finally, I couldn't even afford the minimum payments on everything and we started falling behind. The credit card companies started calling me at work, so I went to one of these places that helps you pay off all your credit cards, and they set up a whole payment system with reduced interest rates and so on. Three months into it I found out my husband had opened up another credit card account and charged up five thousand more dollars. That was the last straw. Here I was trying to get on top of things and he was stabbing me in the back. So I told him to move out."

"Deadbeat," said Frank.

"Well, that's what *I* thought. And to add insult to injury, I had to pay him $20,000 in spousal support. The man ruins me and I have to pay him for the privilege."

"Tough," Frank sympathized.

"Did you have to pay?" she asked.

"Paid seven years."

"I'm surprised it was only seven. Didn't you guys have kids?"

"Naw. She didn't want 'em."

"That's too bad," Beata said, "I can't even imagine life without my daughter. She is the dearest person I know."

"You want to listen to some music?" Frank asked, nodding toward a battered jukebox standing near the front door.

"Okay," Beata said.

Frank shuffled past the pool players and stood examining the jukebox for several minutes. He fished some change from his pocket, fed it into the machine and punched a few buttons. The jukebox began emitting strains of a country ballad unknown to Beata, which tangled with the staccato bursts of drunken laughter and the terse remarks of the pool players to create a muddy cacophony of indistinguishable noises that broke upon Beata's ears like surf rhythmically surging and receding on the beach. Frank made his way back down the bar.

"Do you like to dance?" he asked, settling onto his stool.

"Well...no," said Beata. "I really can't dance. In my day, people didn't dance *with* each other; they danced *in front of* each other. I can do the type of dancing where you don't have to touch each other; you just writhe in time to the music."

"I could teach you," he offered.

"It wouldn't be the first time someone tried," she said. "I have no aptitude for it."

"We should go out dancing sometime," Frank insisted.

"Maybe. We'll have to see," said Beata. She hated country music and danced like a mongoloid elephant. No way was she going dancing with Frank. She turned the conversation into safer channels. "How long have you lived in Seattle?" she asked.

"Born and raised here," said Frank, "at least, born and raised in Tacoma. My daddy was a contractor and he got me into the business when I got out of high school. He died a few years back, but Momma and her husband still live down there."

"Do you see them often?"

"Naw. Me and the husband don't get along."

At this moment, a loud group of merry-makers entered the bar: two men and two women affecting a raw, biker-chic image. Denim and tattoos were plentiful among them, but, due to the lack of "colors," Beata guessed they were weekend pretenders rather than genuine outlaws. Authentic or not, they were getting into their roles with gusto. The two brawny men, in sleeveless denim jackets, projected a taciturn, aggressive attitude as they strode in the door and muscled up to the bar, ignoring both their women and everyone else in the place. It was the women who generated all the noise, guffawing, elbowing each other and rasping crude remarks as their heavy boots thundered across the floor. They paused by the jukebox, and presently the country whining was replaced by a raucous, screaming heavy metal band.

"Move over, honey," one of them commanded Beata, who obligingly rose from her stool and retreated to the furthermost seat on the other side of Frank. Frank clenched his jaw, unhappy with their high-handed displacement of his date.

"There's plenty of room down there," he said, indicating other vacant stools closer to the door.

"Fuck off," the woman advised. This epithet awoke the biker chick's gallant swain from his brooding, hostile stupor. He glared dangerously at Frank, whom he obviously considered an upstart old pussy, inviting disaster by challenging their right to take whatever seat in the bar might strike their fancy.

Frank was caught in a lose-lose situation. Unless he could provoke the biker chick's companion to challenge him openly, he had two untenable choices: he could either back down, thus surrendering every shred of his masculine self-respect, or he could fight with a woman, a prospect even more appalling than the first. For a moment, it seemed he *would* provoke the biker. He locked eyes with him and moved slightly forward on his seat to suggest he was ready to attack at the first hint of open aggression. The biker, too, straightened, flexed his shoulders and swiveled to face Frank. It seemed he was about to speak when the bartender, attuned through long experience to the signals of a nascent fight, quashed it authoritatively.

"Don't start nothing," he ordered, "or I'm calling the cops. As of right now, I ain't serving none of you, so get out." Without taking his eyes off them, a slight motion of his head indicated a sign hanging behind the bar: 'We reserve the right to refuse service to anyone'.

Any self-respecting outlaw, Beata thought, would have ignored the craven suggestion he should fear the police, and promptly launched into all-out war. But this guy didn't want to spend the night in jail, probably had to get up and go to work in the morning, and was content to leave with no more than the threat of a stomping hanging thickly in the air. So, under the stern eye of the bartender, both parties left the tavern, Frank and Beata first, followed by the four biker wannabees.

"And don't start nothing outside, either," the bartender hollered as they passed through the door. "The cops are right down the street."

"Asshole," Frank muttered under his breath.

"Fuckwad," Beata heard drifting over from the other party.

Beata's heart was pounding and her palms were sweaty. She clutched at Frank's arm. Despite the fact that just one of the two bikers weighed as much at two Franks, he wasn't frightened at all, just fighting mad. He would have taken them both on, even if they pounded him to dust.

"Now, now," he said, patting her hand. "Don't get upset. It's no big deal."

By the time they'd made their way down the block to Frank's truck, her fear was subsiding and her sense of humor reasserted itself. "You sure know how to show a gal a good time," she giggled. "That's the first time I've ever been thrown out of a bar. What's next? Shall we roll a drunk? Break into a store? Go home and cook some meth?"

"Mmm," said Frank. He was still angry and adrenaline-charged and did not approve of Beata's levity.

They drove to Beata's house in silence. When they arrived, Frank parked in front of the house and shut off the engine. He appeared to be turning something over in his mind.

"So," he finally said, "about that shed. I'll be over to check it out, maybe on Wednesday."

"I'm working from home this week," Beata said. "Any day works for me."

"Wednesday morning," he concluded.

"Sure, that'd be great."

Frank stretched his arm along the top of the bench seat. Although he didn't touch her, his sleeve was close enough to brush the collar of her dress. She felt awkward and a bit panicky, not wanting to invite further intimacy, but also not wanting to offend him by being stand-offish. This balancing act was the worst part of meeting new people -- new men, she should say. Women were easy...you were either compatible or you weren't; you liked each other or you didn't. There wasn't any agonizing over whether you liked someone *enough* to have sex, or how long you should wait to have sex, or whether he felt the same about having sex with you as you did about having sex with him. This whole sex thing complicated everything, and perhaps was made worse instead of better by their age. At least when you were young, you had a clear picture of your overall objective: find a suitable mate and raise a family. But at her age, raising a family was no longer the goal. What was she looking for? If she didn't know, how could she possibly decide whether Frank was It?

In the handful of relationships she'd had since her divorce, Beata had never resolved this question. She had drifted passively into each one, carried along by the agenda of whatever man seemed interested in her. Soon feeling

71

bored and impinged upon, she would never continue more than a few weeks. If the man refused to fade gracefully into the sunset, she dumped him. She always felt bad about it, because she realized she had misled him into believing she actively desired the relationship, when in fact she had never felt anything more than lukewarm ambivalence toward any of them.

Beata knew this pattern demonstrated a shameful lack of accountability. She had no right to drift and lie and act like a jerk. On some level, though, she felt *she* was the victim. Had she created this muck in her own character? Had it not been visited upon her by circumstances beyond her control? Certainly, she comforted herself, she *intended* to be a good person. Was it not up to the Universe (or God, which in Beata's mind was the same thing), to reward her good intentions with opportunities, advice, and support from whatever cosmic forces or beings drift around in the heavens assisting good people to bootstrap themselves ever upward on the ladder of spiritual evolution? Shouldn't doors be opening in front of her and paths be smoothed? Beata was doing *her* part. She asked for direction (case in point, the psychic fair she'd recently attended). She faithfully participated in hundreds of hours of counseling. She did her work. Where was the payoff? Was she expected to spend the rest of her life playing hide-and-seek with God? If God wanted her to do something, why didn't He (or She) just march right up and say so? Why all these hints and obscure messages, why all this uncertainty about whether she was getting a for-real message from God or a load of gibberish from some deluded shill who thought she was channeling an ascended master?

How had her uncertainty about whether to encourage Frank's apparent desire to move their relationship to a more intimate footing turned into a diatribe against God? Beata was momentarily lost in the maze of her own thoughts. Besides, it didn't seem like Frank was offering to go to bed with her. He was still sitting quietly with his arm behind her neck, as if he had placed it there to ease a cramp in his shoulder rather than signal a desire to touch her. Beata felt relieved. The choice, if there was one, need not be made tonight.

"Thank you, Frank, I had a good time," she said, opening the door.

"See you Wednesday," he said.

****

The next morning, Gladys dropped by for coffee. She demanded that Beata recount every detail of the bar expulsion, agog with excitement about Frank's heroic refusal to back down in the face of a brute twice his size.

"Men," she sighed. "I *love* that about men. Their adrenaline gets going and they lose all sense of self-preservation."

"Is that a good thing?" Beata asked.

"Well *yeah*. What, you would rather face those people by yourself?"

"No, of course not. I wanted to run screaming from the bar the moment they set foot in the door. I don't want *anyone* to have to face them. And I don't want to be in the middle of a brawl, either. I would've been happy to skulk away at the first sign of trouble."

"Not me," Gladys sighed. "I would love to have a man stand up for me like that."

"Maybe I should introduce you to Frank then."

"I don't think he's my type," Gladys giggled, "too skinny."

"I'm trying to put you together with your knight in shining armor and you're complaining about his physique? What's wrong with you?"

"I'm shallow."

"Obviously."

"Now that we have that settled, tell me what happened afterward. Did he kiss you goodnight?"

"No, Gladys, he did not kiss me good night. In fact, for a minute I was paranoid he was going to try, but he didn't. So apparently, I'm not *his* type."

"Maybe you scared him."

"That sounds likely. I scared a man who, a half hour earlier, was ready to take on two bruisers that outweighed him by 400 pounds. Of course he would be utterly terrified of me. I'll tell you what, though. He *is* going to build me a tool shed from all that wood piled in the front yard."

"He's going to build your tool shed?" Gladys squealed in delight.

"Don't start planning the wedding yet," Beata said. "It's only a tool shed, not the Taj Mahal. The man is a contractor. Building a tool shed is not that big of a deal. It's like the Roto Rooter guy snaking out your drains or the lawn guy pruning your roses. Let's not embroider on it too much."

"I think it's very promising," Gladys said. "He'll try to kiss you yet, just wait and see."

"I'll kiss the tool shed," said Beata.

At that moment, the doorbell rang. Before answering it, Beata crept to the front window, which yielded an oblique view of the front porch, and stood half-hidden behind the curtain. All this talk of Frank was making her nervous, and she wanted to see who was there before she answered. It was not Frank. It was a dark-haired, olive-skinned man wearing khaki trousers. Her heart started pounding, and she ducked hastily back away from the window.

"Gladys," she hissed, "c'mere."

"What," said Gladys, loathe to abandon her comfy place on the sofa.

"*Come – here*," Beata commanded. "The guy at the door is the same one I ran into at the psychic fair, and the same one that sat beside me on the bus. I think it's the same guy that was lurking around my yard. That same guy is at my *door*. What should I do?"

74

Gladys' curiosity was aroused, so she joined Beata at the window to peer at the stranger. "How do you know it's him?" she asked. "How could you tell him apart from any other guy wearing khakis?"

"Because I know," insisted Beata. "I've seen him three times, for crying out loud."

Gladys was unconvinced. She had known Beata to meet people three, and even four times without remembering them. And those were people she'd looked in the face, shaken hands with and called by name! How likely was it she would remember a stranger she'd glanced at on the bus, particularly one as unremarkable as this?

"Maybe," she said.

"What's he doing at my house?" Beata demanded in an agitated whisper.

Gladys shrugged and backed away from the window. "Why don't you answer the door and find out?"

"I can't. I'm freaked out."

"Oh, for crying out loud," said the exasperated Gladys. "Do you want to know who it is or don't you?"

"I do, but what if he's an axe murderer?"

"I've had enough of this," said Gladys. She marched over to the door and yanked it open. The doorstep was vacant. Beata, who'd taken cover behind her as best she could given the fact that Gladys was six inches shorter than she, now peered over her head, trying to catch sight of the man walking away from the door, but there was no sign of him. Nothing stirred in the front yard, on the sidewalk or in the street; the man had vanished. There was a piece of white cardboard fluttering from the doorknob, which Gladys removed and examined.

"What's this?" she said. She turned the cardboard over and read "THE KINGDOM OF GOD IS NEAR".

"Oh for crying out loud," said Gladys. "It's the Jehovah's Witnesses. That wasn't your stalker, you nut; it was a Jehovah's Witness."

Beata felt embarrassed. What an idiot! She was getting jumpy. Was she going to start accusing every dark-haired man wearing khakis of following her around town? She took the piece of cardboard from Gladys.

The message was emblazoned in large, primitive letters that might have been written by hand with a red crayon. "I thought the Jehovah's Witnesses handed out the *Watchtower* magazine", she said, turning it over and over.

The kingdom of God is near. Usually people who said that meant to warn you: the kingdom is coming soon! Repent now, before it's too late! But didn't 'near' really mean something different – right next door, right around the corner, just across the street? Perhaps this piece of cardboard was meant to point out something obvious, like 'the sun rises in the morning' or 'your fence is covered with Morning Glory'. Any minute now you'll stumble and break into the Kingdom like falling through a plate-glass window.

"Stop being so paranoid," Gladys said.

On Wednesday morning, Frank arrived as promised, and caught Beata preparing to take the neighbor's dogs for a walk. Irene had asked Beata to babysit her dogs for ten days while she and her husband were on vacation. Their dogs, a hyperkinetic Jack Russell terrier and a Corgi, could not be left at the kennel because, Irene confided, they were too high-strung. The terrier had given one of the kennel staff a teeny nip the last time they'd boarded there, and they were now banned from the only kennel Irene felt she could really trust. None of the other kennels seemed to have adequate facilities for the pampered pair. Most didn't even offer their canine boarders a TV set, much less daily massages and organized social activities. Beata had agreed, but not without reservations.

"I can't offer them organized social activities, either," she cautioned Irene. "And I'm not doing any massages."

"Just leave the TV on for them," Irene said, "and take them to the off-leash area twice a day. Besides that, all they need are their blankies and their food. Isn't that right, pumpkin," she cooed to the terrier, "We need our num-nums evewy day."

"Uh, where are the num-nums?" Beata asked.

"Right here in the cupboard. These are for Grover," she said, nodding at the terrier, "and these over here are for Cleveland. Cleveland won't touch chicken or fish, so don't get them mixed up. He gets a large can of beef twice a day. Grover gets the smaller can of chicken, and twice a week I feed him the salmon. I have a schedule written down so you don't forget. She showed Beata a paper taped to the inside of the cupboard door, which read

"Monday – chicken
Tuesday – salmon
Wednesday – chicken
Thursday – chicken
Friday – salmon

Saturday – chicken
Sunday – chicken"

"But Cleveland gets beef every day?" Beata asked.

"Right. He gets the big cans of beef. This is his dish, and over beside the fridge is Grover's. Be sure not to mix those up, either. Cleveland mustn't eat out of Grover's bowl because it has nasty fish smell in it. He's very sensitive. Cleveland, Cleeeeeveland! Come to Mommy," she sang. "Come meet Miss Beata, who's going to take care of you while Mommy is away." Cleveland was sleeping on the couch in the living room. When Irene opened the cupboard, he raised an exhausted eyelid and cocked one ear, clearly at the uttermost limits of his strength, yet ready to leap up if she made a move to open a can. When he heard the cupboard door shut, though, his head flopped back down on the couch and he ignored her.

"Why don't you feed Grover beef? If he likes it, wouldn't it make everything simpler?"

"Oh, I couldn't do that," said Irene. "It upsets his little tummy. Doesn't it upset your wittle tummy-wummy?" she cooed to Grover, who bared his teeth at her affectionately. "He must never, ever have the beef," she said, "and that's why you always have to be here when they are eating. Grover is a bad boy, and he will run over and steal Cleveland's food, and then he barfs on the floor."

"Delightful," said Beata.

She'd gone next door early that morning and, after feeding the dogs, brought them to her own house. They seemed to take the change in good part, lolling about on the living room floor because she wouldn't allow them on the couch. As Frank drove up, she was trying to determine which leash was Grover's and which was Cleveland's because, Irene cautioned her, they got very nervous if they didn't have their own leashes on. The sorting was made difficult by the fact that the two leashes looked identical, as far as Beata could tell. She had just finished attaching a leash to each dog and was headed for the back door when

Frank and his crew pulled up in front. When the dogs heard the sound of Frank's truck, they began yapping hysterically. Grover ran between Beata's legs, wrapping his leash around her ankle, and Cleveland charged the front door.

"Ouch!" Beata said, as Grover's leash bit into her ankle. Cleveland had pulled his leash out of her hand and was now bashing himself against the door in a frenzy. "Grover! Quiet! Cleveland! Back!"

They ignored her. Cleveland caught sight of Frank through the front window, and his barking rose to an ear-splitting pitch. Grover extricated himself from Beata's leg and joined Cleveland at the door, bouncing up and down with each yap as if to get his whole body weight behind it.

Beata stood in the midst of the pandemonium in momentary confusion. She didn't dare open the door. The dogs sounded like they wanted to tear Frank to bloody shreds. Divide and conquer, she decided. She grabbed Grover's leash and tried to drag him back from the door. He resisted with every shred of determination in his small body. He wheezed and gagged as the collar bit into his neck. His claws scrabbled against the floor. Foam bubbled from his mouth. Beata feared he would have an apoplexy…how would she explain that to Irene? Finally, she reached down, scooped him up by his little round belly and carried him off to the bedroom. As she backed away, she could see a white nose poking under the door as he tried to wriggle under it head-first.

She went to retrieve Cleveland, who'd by now started digging at the bottom of the front door. His stubby legs paddled furiously as she picked him up and his beady eyes burned wrathfully at the intruder behind the door. She shut him up in the bathroom, where he plopped down on his haunches and started to howl.

She returned to the front door and found Frank on the front steps looking dazed.

"Hi," she shouted above the yapping and howling, "I'm babysitting my neighbor's dogs. Do you...can I get you some coffee?"

"Uh, no thanks," said Frank.

"What?"

"NO, THANKS," he shouted. "I CAME BY TO LOOK AT THAT SHED."

"OH, GREAT! THANKS A LOT. LISTEN, I HAVE TO TAKE THESE DOGS TO THE OFF-LEASH PARK RIGHT NOW, AND THEN I'LL TAKE THEM BACK TO IRENE'S. CAN YOU CARRY ON WITHOUT ME, OR IS THERE SOMETHING WE NEED TO TALK ABOUT FIRST?"

"Naw. If it's okay with you, we'll just get started."

"What?"

"WE'LL JUST GET STARTED," he bellowed.

"SURE, FINE, FINE. SEE YOU LATER." As she closed the door, she muttered to herself, "Whew. Those are some good watch dogs, I'll say that for 'em."

She'd planned to walk to the off leash park, which was only a few blocks from her house, but she quailed at the thought of getting the dogs past Frank and his crew. She decided to load them into the car and drive. As soon as she opened the bathroom door, Cleveland came barreling out like an exploding mortar shell. The retractable leash's handle, still hanging from his collar, ricocheted wildly off the door frame and cracked against one of Beata's kneecaps.

"Oof," she said, grabbing her knee and hopping up and down. Cleveland bounced off her shin, knocking her into the wall, and tore back to the front door, where he resumed trying to excavate under it.

"I outweigh these critters by a hundred pounds," Beata told herself, "There is no way I'm going to let a couple of itty bitty dogs push me around." She hobbled to the door, snatched Cleveland up off the floor, tucked him firmly under her left arm, and carried him out the back door to her car. Grover was smaller and therefore harder to catch, but once caught, he was easier to hang on to. She hauled him to the car, too, and then made a third trip for her purse.

The off-leash park was a long, narrow strip of ground on a hill overlooking the Puget Sound. At one end, there was a parking lot, and beside this, a grassy area the approximate size and shape of a football field surrounded by a chain link fence with gates randomly placed on three of its four sides and a few picnic tables arranged along the back. The fourth side bordered on a busy street. Beyond the grassy area was an acre or so of sprawling coastal forest criss-crossed by trails.

It was early, but there were a number of dog owners already at the park. Most of them had ranged themselves along the fence where they could watch their dogs without exerting too much effort. Beata, half afraid Grover and Cleveland would run off and suspecting they would pay little heed to her commands, followed them inside the fence and across the field. She unsnapped their leashes and they attached themselves to a group of five or six other dogs who were taking turns sniffing the ground, peeing on trees, and chasing each other around.

They seemed content to pal around with the other dogs and made no move to run away. Beata began to relax. Suddenly, an English Bulldog and a Lab mix who had been sniffing each other warily with tails high and stiff, began to bristle and growl. The excitable Grover promptly jumped in on the Lab's side and ran around behind the bulldog, yapping and feinting at its heels. His barking seemed to push the two larger dogs over the edge, and they sprang on each other snarling, salivating and grabbing for each others' throats.

"Grover!" Beata shouted, snatching helplessly at his collar as he darted around the two fighting dogs, jumping, snapping and egging them on with his maniacal yapping. "Grover, stop! Leave it! Bad dog!" she screamed. She chased him to one side of the fight and then the other, never able to reach him before he leapt to some new vantage point.

A man sitting at one of the picnic tables at the back of the field rose to his feet and strode purposefully toward the fighting dogs. At almost the same instant, the dogs' owners, who'd been standing on the other side of the fence chatting with other dog owners, realized what was happening and started running toward their dogs, shouting and waving leashes.

The man from the picnic table reached the dog fight first. He leaped straight into the mad tangle of writhing dog, but neither spoke nor touched them. The dogs stopped fighting instantly, as if hit by a shot from a tranquilizer gun. They released whichever of their opponent's body parts they were ripping at, stood up, shook themselves, sniffed at each other amiably, and walked away. Grover, too, fell silent. He watched the departing dogs for a second, then turned, trotted over to the man and sat down on his foot. He gazed up at him adoringly and wagged his tail. The man chuckled, reached down and stroked Grover's head, while Grover, beside himself with joy, tried to lick the man's hand and face at the same time.

"You're a good dog," the man assured Grover soothingly. Cleveland, who had stood aloof from the fight, now came up to the man as well, flattening his ears submissively, bouncing a little on his stubby front legs and fixing his eyes on the man's face. "Pet me, pet me," he seemed to be saying. "I'm a good dog, too." The man obligingly patted Cleveland's head. He set his fat haunches down right beside Grover's, and the two of them almost moaned in ecstasy as the man scratched behind their ears.

"Thank you," panted Beata. "You saved my life. These aren't my dogs, and I don't know what I would've done if one of them had gotten hurt. I can't believe how you stopped that fight. Are you the Dog Whisperer or something?"

"No," the man said. He straightened up and fixed his dark eyes on her face. He put his hands in the pockets of his threadbare khaki trousers, and looked at her silently. Beata's mouth dropped open. She was frozen in shock, finally recognizing him as the man on the bus, the man at the fair and the man who'd left the leaflet at her door.

"Have – have we met before?" she said.

"Several times," he said. He extended his right hand and came toward her. "Joshua," he added.

"Beata," she replied, automatically shaking the proffered hand.

"Beata," he said. "That means 'blessed', doesn't it?"

She didn't answer. Her mind was a jumble. She didn't feel blessed; she felt panicky. She wanted to run home to the safety of her quiet house. He withdrew his hand and put it back in his pocket. He stood and watched her, rocking back and forth very slightly in his worn huaraches. He seemed utterly comfortable, as if he'd grown out of that spot of ground like a tree and occupied it for the last hundred years. Beata noticed several pinholes in his faded blue polo shirt. She backed away nervously. She worried he was going to start haranguing her about the Kingdom of God. Why did he keep following her around?

"Can – can I take my dogs now?"

"Of course," he said.

Grover and Cleveland sat quietly while Beata snapped their leashes on. As she walked toward the car, one of the fighting dog's owners came hurrying up to her.

"Wow," he said. "How'd you get those dogs apart?"

"Me?" said Beata. "I didn't stop the fight. He did." She turned and pointed to the spot where Joshua had been standing, but he was gone again.

"I didn't see anyone else," the man said.

"Well, anyway, there was another guy there. He stopped the fight."

Grover and Cleveland walked beside her all the way to the car, one on her left and one on her right. She drove back home, parked in the alley and put the dogs in Irene's house, turning on Animal Planet before she left. She went home and, too upset to start work right away, stood watching Frank from the front window. He and his crew had already sorted through the jumble of materials she and Sean had left piled in the yard, and Frank was directing people here and there. He'd apparently already selected the spot where the shed should be, at the side of the house, accessible from either the front or the back but out of view from the street, and men were carrying tools and supplies around to this spot. He caught sight of her through the window, and moments later knocked on the door.

"Hi," he said when she answered. "We're going to frame it up today, and I'll pick up the siding and roofing later this afternoon. I have some left over from another job. Would it be okay if we used that? I've got light brown vinyl siding, and green steel for the roof."

"Sure," Beata said. "How much is it going to cost me?"

Frank looked insulted. "Nothing," he frowned. "It's left over."

Beata was uncomfortable about incurring an obligation to Frank. "Are you sure?"

"I'll have to pick up some OSB and a door," he said. "We can't use what you've got here; it's been sitting out in the weather and it's rotten. It shouldn't run more than 200 bucks. Is that okay?"

"Sure," said Beata, "$200 is fine."

"We'll spend another hour or so here, then we have to get over to another job. We'll be back tomorrow."

"That's fine," said Beata, "I really appreciate this, Frank."

"No problem," he said, turning to rejoin the crew.

Over the next few days, the shed took shape. Frank never worked on it more than an hour at a stretch, sometimes in the early morning and sometimes in the evening, once with a crew but usually by himself. Gladys suggested that he was dragging it out so he could be there every day, but Beata pooh-poohed the idea.

"He has to work the paying jobs first," she explained. "He doesn't want to pay his crew to work on a freebie."

"Maybe," said Gladys, "but I think he's sweet on you."

"Eh," said Beata noncommittally, but privately she was alarmed. She wanted to keep Frank at arm's length, and feared the whole tool shed thing was not only putting her in debt to him, but also implying a closer relationship than she had any intention of having.

Each morning and evening, she took Grover and Cleveland to the off leash park. The evening of the first day, she'd walked the dogs around the neighborhood rather than taking them to the park, fearful that she would encounter Joshua again. Walking the dogs on leash was a pain, because they crossed from one side of Beata to the other, now lagging behind, now tearing ahead, and tied their leashes together in knots. They raised Cain with other neighborhood dogs and tried to burrow under their fences, charged at people who were out watering their lawns, and generally made themselves obnoxious.

So the second morning she returned to the park, determined to ignore Joshua if he was there. The dogs immediately frustrated her intention by making a bee line for the table where he'd been sitting the previous morning, and spent several minutes sniffing the legs and staring mournfully into empty space. Finally, they were distracted by other dogs and abandoned the empty table, but they returned to it wistfully every morning and evening as if hoping to meet him there.

Gradually, as the days passed and he didn't return, Beata's discomfort faded. Probably, their meetings had been coincidental. No reason to embroider on them. He seemed normal enough; there had been no threat in his manner when he'd introduced himself. Maybe he was dropping religious tracts off at every house in the neighborhood. It didn't have to mean he had any special interest in *her*.

85

The ten days of Irene's vacation passed, and Beata looked forward with relief to her return. She'd become fond of Grover and Cleveland, but her life was busy enough without the added responsibility of the dogs. She'd taken to bringing them home with her for most of the day, as it was easier to let them in and out in her yard than to walk over to Irene's four or five times.

They'd become accustomed to Frank's arrivals and departures, and after a few moments of hysteria each time he came, they lay around on the floor like a couple of throw rugs and watched him through the window as he worked. They swapped food companionably, and Grover had thrown up on the floor only once. Cleveland seemed to have forgotten his aversion to fish, and was as content to eat out of Grover's bowl as his own. Beata's only concern was that she had mixed up the food schedule and had several extra cans of salmon left, so for the last couple of days, she'd had to feed Grover fish every day.

"It's a good thing you can't rat me out," she told Grover on the tenth evening as she spooned a can of salmon into his dish. "Your mom would never forgive me."

Grover cocked his head intelligently and wagged his tail. His eyes were fixed anxiously on the bowl.

"Let's eat, boys," said Beata, putting the bowls on the floor. The dogs attacked the bowls ravenously, eyeing each other over the rims to see if the other had gotten something better, but loathe to leave their own bowls until they had polished them clean of every speck of food.

"Okay, time for walksies," she announced, and fetched their leashes from the dining room table. She'd even picked up Irene's habit of cooing at them in baby-talk, she realized disgustedly. She snapped on their leashes and walked them out the back door. They no longer drove the car down to the park. It was ridiculous, Beata thought, to drive four blocks when the dogs needed exercise. By the time they arrived, their leashes would be so snarled that Beata could spend 20 minutes disentangling them while the dogs ran around on the lawn. It gave her something to do besides chatting with the other dog owners.

The evening shadows were getting long as they reached the park that day. Beata caught glimpses of the lowering sun through the branches of the firs as it dipped down behind the peaks of the Olympic mountains across the sound, painting a mosaic of light and dark on the grass. She let Grover and Cleveland go, and they tore across the lawn to the picnic table, as usual, hoping to find Joshua. There was no one there. In fact, the park was quiet today, with only two other dogs roaming around the field. Beata didn't see their owner. She crossed to a picnic table close to the parking lot and sat down to reorganize the leashes.

She'd been picking at the knot for several minutes when a shadow loomed suddenly behind her, and she turned to see someone silhouetted against the setting sun. Was it Joshua? The man walked round the table to stand before her. It was not Joshua, but a much burlier, unkempt man wearing torn jeans. His belly bulged under his thin t-shirt.

"Those yer dogs?" he said, pointing at Grover and Cleveland, who were now at the far end of the field.

"No," said Beata, "but I'm watching them for their owner."

"Well one of 'em bit me the other day," he said, putting one foot on the bench and pulling up his pant leg to reveal a faint mark on his calf.

"Are you sure you have the right dogs? I've been here with them every day," Beata said, "and I've never seen them bite anyone. I've never even seen them come close to anyone."

"You calling me a liar?" said the man, dropping his pant leg, putting his foot back on the ground and straightening up. He seemed to swell larger beneath his clothes as he came a step closer. "I've got medical bills," he said. "Who's gonna pay for 'em? You think you can just let yer animals run around biting people and not pay for it?"

He eyed her purse. Beata's thoughts were racing, but she could not squeeze a word from between her paralyzed lips. What was this guy after? Was he going to beat her up? Grab her purse? Beata snatched up her purse and rose to her feet as quickly as her trembling knees would allow. "Grover, Cleveland," she warbled weakly."

"Yer not blowing me off," the man said. "Them dogs is a menace, and yer responsible for 'em."

Beata sidled along the bench, trying to get to a position where she didn't have the table behind her so she could back away. The man stepped right along with her. As she reached the end of the table, she sensed another person coming up behind her. Oh, no. He had an accomplice. Tears of panic started in her eyes.

"Trouble?" said a calm voice behind her.

She whirled around, and found Joshua standing there, hands in pockets, gazing pacifically at the outraged thug.

"Joshua!" Beata cried, as the tears spilled out of her eyes and made tracks down her cheeks.

"This ain't no concern of yers, asshole," said the thug.

Joshua pierced him with an inquiring gaze, and the thug froze. They stood that way for interminable minutes, Joshua looking at the thug, the thug glaring at Beata and Beata watching Joshua. Beata expected that, at any moment, the thug would spring on Joshua and beat him to a pulp, but Joshua didn't appear worried. He barely seemed to notice the thug's hostility, and stood looking at him exactly the same way he'd looked at Beata the morning they'd first met.

After an eternity, Joshua shifted his eyes to Beata. "Walk you home?" he offered.

"Yes," she gasped. "Yes, please."

"Let's go," he said. He turned and began walking toward the gate. Beata wobbled after him obediently, and Grover and Cleveland, materializing out of nowhere, fell in behind her. The thug seemed still glued to the spot near the table. He neither spoke nor moved until they passed through the gate and headed across the parking lot. Then he called "Don't think yer gettin' away with this, lady. You owe me."

It was several minutes before Beata could speak. She hadn't put Grover and Cleveland on leash, but they'd stayed at her heels all the way down the busy street.
Finally, Beata gasped "Do you think he's going to sue me? Honestly, I have no idea what he's talking about. I could swear Grover and Cleveland never bit anyone at that park. They don't even let other people get near them. Except for you."

"I wouldn't worry about it," he said.

They had just reached the corner where Beata's house stood when she grabbed Joshua's arm and said, "Thank you. Thank you. I've never been so scared in my life." The effort caused her eyes to spill over again.

"It's okay," he said, patting her shoulder. Embarrassed, she looked away, her eyes wandering across the street to her own yard. Frank was standing in the middle of the front lawn, hands on hips, glaring indignantly at Beata and Joshua's display of apparent intimacy.

"Oh, brother," she thought. "It isn't enough to get mugged in the park and rescued by a stalker, now I have to deal with an outraged boyfriend."

"Joshua," she said, fighting to pull herself together, "I can't thank you enough, but I have to go. I hope some time I can thank you properly."

"It's okay," he said again, dropping his hand from her shoulder. He smiled and stepped back. Beata hurried across the street to her house, not noticing when or where he went. Frank had turned his back and was now snatching tools and bags of screws up off the lawn in front of the completed shed.

Beata entered the house, gathered up Grover and Cleveland's food bowls and other paraphernalia, and carried it all back over to Irene's. It took her several minutes to return everything to its proper place, shake out and refold the dogs' blankies, and turn the TV on. By the time she returned home, Frank had left. Beata was not sorry. The last thing she felt capable of doing was pandering to Frank's wounded ego. Her nerves were raw and she felt fragile and exhausted. Frank would just have to mother himself; Beata was not going to do it.

Frank ignored her for an entire week. Beata relaxed back into her solitary life without suffering any heartburn over his absence. Aside from occasional pangs of remorse each time she saw the tool shed, she forgot his existence entirely. To assuage her guilt, she decided not to use the tool shed, so she left it vacant and parked the lawnmower and all the gardening tools under its eaves. They were partially protected from the rain, but not enough to keep them from rusting, and this would be her penance for accepting a gift from a man she barely knew.

Gladys and Daphne were vocal in their disapproval, both of her decision not to use the shed and her acceptance of Frank's disappearance. Daphne asked frequently about the progress of Frank and Beata's relationship, and was palpably dissatisfied when she heard that Beata had allowed Frank to drop out of sight.

"Call him," she advised. "Explain what happened. He can't blame you for getting mugged, for crying out loud."

"Why?" Beata asked. "I'm just leaving well enough alone. There's no sense in leading him on any further. I feel bad enough about letting him build me a tool shed."

"What do you mean there's no sense in leading him on? Do you want to be alone for the rest of your life? Frank's a nice guy. What's wrong with him?"

"Nothing," Beata said. "There're worse things than being alone. Like being with someone who makes you *wish* you were alone."

"You make him sound like a monster."

"No...he's not a monster. I just...I don't love him, honey." There. That ought to keep Daphne off her back.

"Not *yet*," Daphne said. "Give him a chance. You might love him if you tried."

"Honey, I seriously doubt I'm ever going to love Frank. We don't have that much in common."

"Nothing in common? You have tons of things in common. You're the same age. You're both divorced. You've both been single for a long time. You aren't on the rebound. You have lots of time on your hands. *Call* him."

Beata didn't want to argue, so she pretended to give in. "I'll think about it," she said.

Gladys was harder to put off.

"Why are these tools sitting around in the yard?" she demanded. "Put them in the tool shed; that's why you built it."

"I didn't build it. Frank built it."

"You built it, Frank built it, who cares who built it? It's a shed for tools, and your tools are rusting in the yard."

"I know, Gladys, but I feel badly about using it. I shouldn't have let Frank build it for me."

"It's already built. Do you really think you're atoning for something by not using it?"

"Yes," Beata said.

"Well then, instead of letting all your tools rust, why don't you atone in a way that actually does some good? Why don't you apologize?"

"You think I should apologize for letting him build me the shed?"

"No, you moron. I think you should apologize for hanging all over another man when you're supposed to be dating Frank."

"To begin with," Beata said, "I was *not* hanging all over another man. I was, very naturally, thanking someone who just practically saved my life. And to end with, I am not 'dating' Frank."

"Not now," Gladys said. "But you were. You went out with him, didn't you? And Frank doesn't know you weren't hanging all over another man. That's what it looked like to him. He doesn't know you were almost attacked in the park. If he knew, he would have rushed to your defense, not stomped off in a huff."

"I didn't need him to rush to my defense. The incident was already over," Beata protested. "Besides, I only went out with him one time. It's not like we were engaged."

"Look, you hurt his feelings," Gladys said. "There's nothing wrong with apologizing for hurting someone's feelings."

"But they shouldn't have been hurt," Beata pointed out. "He had no right to get his feelings hurt. It's not fair."

"People do weird things when they're in love with someone."

"Gladys, Frank is *not* in love with me. Please, please don't say that again."

"Well, he likes you enough to get jealous when you're hanging on another man's arm.

"That's not love, Gladys. It's pride."

"Whatever. You're so stiff-necked. Can't you give a little?"

"All right, all right," she said. "I'll call him."

But she put it off day after day, dreading talking to him again, not sure how to start and what to say. Finally, he beat her to it, showing up at her door one Saturday afternoon.

"I need that $200 for the shed," he said.

"Oh, right," said Beata, flustered, "Let me write you a check. Would you like to come in?"

"Naw," he said, stepping inside the foyer but not coming into the living room. "I gotta go."

He stood tensely near the door as she ransacked her bedroom looking for the purse, then sat down at the table to write the check.

"Can I offer you some water?" she asked.

"Naw," he said again. "I just came by for a minute."

"Well, I'm glad you did," she babbled. "I'm so sorry I haven't called you; I've been meaning to apologize for the other night. I was really freaked out. I almost got mugged at the dog park. That guy you saw me with rescued me and walked me home."

"Mugged?" Frank looked dubious, suspecting that Beata was trying to put something over on him.

"Yeah, mugged. This guy accosted me and accused me of letting Irene's dogs bite him. He wanted money, I guess, and was acting really threatening."

"Uh huh," said Frank. "So, who is he?"

"I don't know. Some thug that gets rich shaking down old ladies, I guess."

"Not him, the guy you were with."

"Oh, him. He's just a guy that came to my rescue. I've seen him here and there, but I don't really know him. His name's Joshua."

"You looked pretty close," Frank said curtly.

"No, we aren't close. I barely know his name. I only met him the other day. It's just that I was in trouble, and he helped me out. I was grateful. I haven't set eyes on him since that evening."

Frank seemed uncertain whether to believe her story or not. He pondered this for a while, then asked "How's the shed working out?"

No way was Beata going to tell him about the tools piled under the eaves. "Just great," she chirped. "It's wonderful."

"Door working okay? Sometimes they stick when the weather gets damp."

"Oh, no, it never sticks" she lied, having no idea whether the door stuck, since she had never set foot in the shed.

"Good," he said. He seemed to have decided to forgive her. He moved into the front room and stared out the window at the shed. Beata gave silent thanks that the tools were around back where they could not be seen from the front window.

"So, what about getting some dinner?" he suggested.

Beata's heart fell. "I knew this would happen," she scolded Gladys in her mind. "I can't say sorry without raising expectations. Now I'm back in the same predicament I was before."

"You have to take responsibility for your decisions," the imaginary Gladys argued back. "If you want to stop seeing someone, you have to step up and tell them so, not depend on circumstances to remove them neatly from your life with no effort on your part. What are you, a baby?"

Yes, she admitted, sighing and turning back to Frank. I guess I am.

"Dinner sounds great," she said.

Frank came back by Beata's house three hours later to pick her up. He'd gone home to change, and Beata, too, had showered, redone her ponytail, dug her flip flops out of the closet and had a nice long chat with Gladys. After all this, she'd just had time to load all the tools into the tool shed. It was roomy and clean and smelled of fresh-cut wood. She was tempted to leave the tools outside and put her desk in there, but things would look different, she assumed, on a gloomy, winter day than they did with an idyllic summer breeze wafting through the open door. Her initial panic about reconciling with Frank was over. She'd concluded, with Gladys' help, that she had a commitment phobia. A glass of wine mellowed her feelings still further, and by the time he arrived she was legitimately happy to see him.

"Where are we going?" she asked as she climbed into the truck.

Frank named a middle-of-the road steakhouse in Burien, south of the industrial district.

"Oh, good," Beata said, "I could use a nice steak."

Frank patted her knee paternally. They had little conversation during the half-hour it took them to reach the restaurant, but Beata didn't care. The silence wasn't awkward. She looked out the window and thought about Grover and Cleveland, whom she hadn't seen since Irene came home. She thought she might get a dog of her own. Or maybe she'd start small and get a cat. They pulled up to the steak house. Since they had no reservations, they waited for a half-hour in the bar for a table. Frank had two beers and Beata had a martini. By the time they were shown to their table, she was feeling tipsy and, as a result voluble.

"What kind of steak do they have?" she said, opening the menu. "I hope they have rib eye; I love rib eye."

They had rib eye, so she ordered it. Frank requested the 16 ounce t-bone.

"Wine?" he suggested.

"Oh…gosh, I really shouldn't," Beata said.

"A bottle of Merlot," he told the waiter.

While they waited for dinner, Beata consumed another glass of wine and regaled Frank with meandering and pointless tales about the antics of Grover and Cleveland. She giggled a lot, which made her feel silly, but Frank seemed to like it. His usually vacuous blue eyes became warmer as the evening wore on, and he kept adjusting himself in his chair to reduce the space between them.

By the time they finished dinner and the wine, Beata could hardly find her way to the Ladies' Room. She reeled out the door of the restaurant and clutched at Frank's arm as the curb loomed threateningly before her unsteady feet. He obligingly put his arm around her waist and assisted her to the truck. He deposited her inside and went around to the driver's side, then sat staring ahead without starting the car. After a moment, he put his arm along the back of the seat, as he had the first night they'd gone out, only this time he dropped it onto her shoulders, and then lower, to her waist, pulled her along the seat, leaned over and kissed her. His mustache tickled her upper lip, and she giggled again. He moved his other hand to the back of her neck and crushed his mouth on hers. She tasted wine on his breath. She closed her eyes and imagined barefooted peasants tromping up and down in a vat full of grapes.

He let her go and started the truck, still without speaking. He drove back to the city, not to Beata's house, but to a neighborhood she wasn't familiar with. They stopped in front of an apartment building.

"Where are we?" Beata asked.

"My house," he said, getting out of the car and opening Beata's door. As she climbed out of the car, he put his arm around her waist again, and slid it now higher, now back and lower, feeling her butt, guiding her in the front door, up the dark, musty stairs, through his apartment and into his bedroom. Beata paid little attention to her surroundings; she was falling-down drunk. The world was spinning madly, and it seemed good to her to be naked in a strange man's bed.

* * *

She awoke early the next morning. With the return of the light and some semblance of sobriety, her normal state of mind reasserted itself.

"Where am I?" she wondered, climbing out of bed. "I'm naked. I need to get some clothes on."

She grabbed her tent-dress and slipped it over her head, then, properly clad, she wandered through the apartment. It was small, old and utilitarian, with a moderately sized front room that served as both living and dining room, a small kitchen with an old gas stove and stained porcelain sink, and a tiny bathroom. The only other room was Frank's bedroom, which Beata did not want to go back into. The apartment was on the second floor, and from the windows she could see a busy street, a bus stop and several other apartment buildings. In the kitchen, the microwave oven had a clock, and she noted that it was only 6:30. She rooted through Frank's cupboard looking for coffee and the equipment to make it, but couldn't find everything she needed. There was a Mr. Coffee but no carafe, and a rusty can of ancient coffee but no filters.

Giving up on making coffee, she thought "This is Seattle. There's bound to be an espresso stand within a few blocks." Where was her purse? She had no recollection of carrying it up last night. Finally, creeping back into Frank's room, she found it sitting on his dresser, and snatched it up along with her underwear and flip flops. Frank rolled over and sighed without waking up.

In the early morning light, he looked older and more beaten down that usual. His mouth sagged open and his mustache drooped untidily from his upper lip, fluttering in and out of his mouth as he breathed. What kind of madness had she succumbed to last night to go to bed with this alien, this stranger?

97

She tiptoed out of the apartment, locking the door as she left. She crept down the stairs and out the front door before stopping to put on her flip flops. Her underwear she stuffed into her purse...she could not bear putting on dirty underwear.

There were two shallow steps leading from the apartment building down to the sidewalk, and Beata sat down on one of these to reflect upon her situation. Obviously she had two logistical problems; these were most critical. She needed coffee and she needed to get home, and getting home would be difficult because she had no idea where she was. There was a bus stop right before her, but she was not familiar with the route numbers posted on it, and there was no schedule or map. The second problem would be easier; there was bound to be coffee available within a few blocks, but which direction should she go? As she pondered this, other issues, the ones she had resolved to put out of her mind, kept intruding on her thoughts.

She was ashamed; that was the long and the short of it. She was burning with shame, and the fact that nobody else knew about it did not lessen her discomfort one bit. What had she been thinking? How could she be so foolish as to act like a hormone-crazed teenager out on her first date? She was a mature, experienced woman. She should be above this kind of behavior.

Equally uncomfortable was the thought of having, in essence, lied to Frank. She didn't dislike him, of course, but going to bed with him implied more than mere liking. It implied that he was in some way special to her: especially loved, especially attractive, especially close, especially valued...if he was none of these things (and she knew he wasn't), she had no business implying that he was.

She couldn't even muster the feeble justification of believing that he'd fulfilled a need she had but didn't recognize, for she was unaware of any need that their drunken encounter could satisfy. Their sham intimacy made no more of a dent in her emotional being than bumping into a street sweeper. No, her whole motivation for sleeping with Frank could be summed up in two words: pride and indifference. She was proud that he found her attractive enough to sleep with and not interested enough in him as a person to either offer or demand sincerity or real feeling or, indeed, anything beyond the grossest superficiality.

Having concluded she had once again fallen prey to the less admirable aspects of her nature, Beata now had to face another thorny problem: what was she going to do about it? Not the specific problem of Frank; her ponderings had distracted her from that. She was wrestling with issues of character.

"I can't stand myself when I act this way", she thought, "I hate being like this. How can I be different? If scorn, disgust and self-hatred were going to do the job, I would have changed long before now."

It was a problem Beata often faced. Her shortcomings didn't escape her, but they seemed wired into her being in a way that defied change. She'd been raised to "do the right thing whether you want to or not", and she obediently applied that philosophy to these ugly character traits. She hid them as much as possible and tried to act as if she were a better person than she actually was. This approach had not produced much real change, and it discouraged her.

Beata scowled, wrapped her arms around her legs and propped her chin on her knees. She brooded gloomily at the bus stop. Presently, a man came into view, walking down the sidewalk from the right. He whistled quietly to himself. As he drew near, he glanced at Beata, who didn't notice him. He sat down next to her on the stoop, and startled her out of her reverie.

"Hi," he said.

Beata was dumbfounded. "Joshua?"

"Yes."

"What are you doing here? Do you live around here?"

"Sort of."

Beata searched for something to say, some explanation of her predicament that wouldn't make her look like a tart. Even worse than *being* a tart was having everyone *know* she was a tart. "Uh – I'm trying to find my way home, but I'm not familiar with this neighborhood," she said carefully. "If you live around here, would you happen to know anything about the bus schedules?"

His eyes twinkled at her. "I sure would," he said. "I'm waiting for the downtown bus myself."

"Oh!" she exclaimed. "I'm glad you came along, then. When does the downtown bus come?"

"In about 20 minutes."

"Well, is there any place close by that I can get a cup of coffee?" she asked.

Joshua nodded toward the intersection to their left. "Down that street to the right about two blocks, there's an espresso stand," he said. "Across the street from the espresso stand is a stop where you can catch the bus downtown, the same bus that stops here, the 56."

Beata rose from the stoop and clutched her purse. "I think I'll go get some coffee, then," she said.

"I'll join you," said Joshua, "if you don't mind."

Beata did mind. She was still embarrassed, light-headed and queasy-stomached from the extraordinary quantity of alcohol she'd consumed the night before, and wanted to be alone with her thoughts. It would be rude, though, to brush off Joshua when he'd been so helpful. It wasn't his fault she'd acted like a jack-ass.

"Um, ok," she agreed. "I'll warn you though, I'm not very good company this morning. Not feeling too well."

Beata couldn't read his response: he merely said, "Okay." Did he suspect she was hung over? She felt too miserable to sort through her anxiety about the impression she was making on top of all her regrets about last night, so she let the matter drop. She would worry about it later when she could talk the whole thing over with Gladys. Gladys would help her dissect every nuance of his tone and facial expression, and she would then have ample time to agonize over the further idiocies she was no doubt committing at this very moment.

She tagged along at his side as he walked to the espresso stand, slowing his steps to match her somewhat faltering progress. They reached the stand, and she ordered a quadruple latte. Perhaps a mega dose of caffeine would help clear her head. He ordered a small cappuccino, and they waited in silence while the drinks were made. Beata reached into her purse to extract her wallet, and out tumbled the crumpled underwear. Her face burned bright red as she quickly stooped to snatch it up and stuff it back into the purse.

Curse her addled brain! She'd forgotten all about that stupid underwear! Everyone knows what it means when a woman shows up in the morning with dirty underwear in her purse.

She wished she could vanish into the ground like water into sand. She stole a glance at Joshua from the corner of her eye. Perhaps he hadn't noticed exactly what it was she'd dropped? He was facing her full-on, an interested but non-committal expression on his face. Obviously, nothing had escaped his notice. He knew perfectly well what had fallen from her purse.

He didn't seem worried by the discovery that Beata was a wanton floozy stuck in a strange neighborhood after a drunken night on the town. His manner toward her didn't change in the slightest; it was as if he had known all along what she had been doing last night. He paid for his coffee and escorted her to the bus stop.

When Beata finally reached home, she felt wrung out and battered. She closed the door, groped her way to the couch and, falling down on it, burst into tears. She had a good, long cry, but it didn't make her feel any better. It was all well and fine, she thought, mopping her swollen eyes and slimy nose with a limp Kleenex, to weep and wail and indulge in self-recrimination, but it changed nothing that she had done, and did nothing to expiate her guilt. When all the weeping was done, she still had to face the fact that she'd acted wrongly and then followed it up by making a fool of herself.

She spent the rest of the day skulking in the house, talking only to Gladys, who, after dissecting every moment of her encounters with Frank and Joshua, expressed the opinion that she was making too much of the whole affair. She certainly shared Beata's embarrassment over throwing her dirty underwear in the street, but, as she advised Beata, "Who cares? This Joshua person isn't a friend of yours and you aren't trying to impress him. Are you?"

Beata assured her that she was not.

"I swear, Beata, you are the strangest person I know. Men have sex with perfect strangers at the drop of a hat, and then high-five each other about it afterward, like it makes them more of a stud. You go to bed with someone you don't love and you're ready to slit your wrists on the bathroom floor."

"I know," Beata responded, "but I don't *approve* of men having sex with strangers at the drop of a hat and high-fiving each other about it afterward. That sort of behavior isn't okay with me. So it's disturbing when I find myself doing the exact same thing. I suppose I like to think of myself as having more integrity than that. It's humiliating to realize you aren't the person you pretend to be, or that you thought you were."

"There's nothing you can do about it now," said Gladys. "What's done is done."

"But what am I going to say to Frank?"

"Haven't you talked to him yet? Didn't you see him this morning?"

"No. I sneaked out without waking him up, and I haven't answered the phone all day."

"Coward," Gladys scolded. "You know you're going to have to face him eventually. Why not just get it over with?"

"Well," said Beata hopefully, "maybe it was a one-night stand. Maybe I won't have to face him at all. Maybe he won't call."

"Okay, then," Gladys said. "If he doesn't call, woo-hoo, problem solved. If he does, you'll have to play it by ear depending on what he says."

"But what if he asks me out again?"

Gladys pretended to consider this. "Well, let's see," she said. "You could tell him that your cat died and you're in mourning. You could tell him you're entering a convent. You could tell him the whole lower half of your body has been consumed by a deadly disease."

"Wait," Beata said. "I'm taking notes. Which disease should I say?"

"The point is, it isn't worth all this agony," Gladys said. "You have to make up your mind so you're prepared, but this business of going over and over what you did or should have done or shouldn't have done isn't getting you anywhere."

Gladys was right; it *wasn't* worth all this agony. Why was she agonizing? Because, she thought, she knew herself too well. Chances were that if Frank called and asked for another date, she would go because she didn't like saying "no." On the other hand, she didn't know how many more dates with Frank she could handle. Besides, she liked occupying the moral high ground. She was hoping that, if she thought about it long enough, she could figure out a way to frame this up so she didn't feel like such a heel.

Beata continued to agonize for the rest of the evening and throughout the next morning. While pretending to watch TV and read, she ran through countless imaginary conversations in her head, taking Frank's part as well as her own. After reiterating each of these several hundred times, she felt almost as if they'd actually talked, an illusion which gave her a sense of comfort and finality.

It was several days before Frank called. By this time, Beata had pushed him to the back of her mind. She figured his experience must have been similar to her own: their brief foray into intimacy had satisfied whatever curiosity or appetite he had and the relationship was now over. Still, each time the phone rang, she checked the caller ID nervously, hoping it wouldn't be Frank. As day followed day and no call came, she became more and more comfortable in this idea: it had been a near miss, but no harm, no foul.

Thus, when the phone rang and the caller ID showed his name, she was overcome with panic.

"*Hi* Frank," she burbled with artificial happiness. "How *are* you?"

"Good. How are you?"

"Oh...*great*."

"Uh huh. How's that shed doing?"

Beata didn't know how the shed was doing because she hadn't set foot in it since the day she piled the tools inside, but she immediately lied, "It's doing great, really good. It's so nice to have some place to store everything out of the weather. I am so happy you put it up for me."

"That's good. So listen, what are you doing this weekend?"

Beata thought, "I can't believe this. Doesn't he have anything to say about me sneaking out of his apartment without saying so much as 'see you later'? Is this his way of carrying on a relationship? Hi, want to come over and sleep with me again?"

"Oh gosh," she said, frantically searching her brain for a plausible excuse, "I think I have to work."

"Well, I thought maybe you'd like to go out for a drink."

"A drink," she thought. "Like I need more drinks. Last time we had drinks, a complete disaster ensued." But apparently it was not a complete disaster in Frank's mind. He seemed utterly content with the situation, as if getting drunk and sleeping with strangers and then not talking to them for a week afterward was a great way of getting to know someone.

"Oh...gosh, Frank, I don't know. It sounds tempting, but if I'm working I really don't think I'll be up for staying out late. You know how it is."

"We could do it Saturday night after you're done at work. I'll meet you downtown."

"Well..." Beata was out of excuses. It would have to be either yes or no. Cravenly, she decided she couldn't face telling him no, with all that it implied about the irresponsibility of her conduct the other night, so she acceded.

"Okay," she said.

They made arrangements to meet downtown at 5:00 on Saturday -- now Beata would have to drive down there and pretend she had been at work all day, adding deception to her other crimes. How much worse could this thing get? As soon as she got off the phone with Frank, she dialed Gladys' number.

"Gladdie, I'm really upset. Frank just called."

"Really? It's about time. I wonder where he's been for the last week. What'd you tell him?"

"That's why I'm upset...I told him I would go out for a drink with him on Saturday night."

"Go out for a drink? Does that mean have sex with him again?"

"I suppose."

"Don't sound so enthusiastic about it. If you didn't want to have sex why'd you say yes? Wasn't that kind of self-defeating?"

"Yes, Gladys, I know it was self-defeating. I'm a chicken. I didn't want to admit I had sex the first time when I didn't really like him all that much."

"Didn't you plan out what you were going to tell him when he called?"

"Yes, but as soon as the phone rang my brain turned to jelly and I forgot everything."

"Yeah, that happens to me too. Maybe you should write something out and post it by the phone so you don't do it again."

"I guess I could try that. I feel kinda stupid saying no after I already said yes."

"Right," Gladys said. "But you've backed yourself into a corner here. Listen, why are you so opposed to going out with him? He sounds like a decent guy."

"I don't know," said Beata. "He *is* a decent guy. But he's boring."

"Boring?"

"Yeah. We don't like the same things at all."

"Well, just set him down in front of the TV to watch a basketball game and go do something else."

"I don't want him sitting around my house gathering dust. I have enough furniture already. Besides, he's got expectations. Like this business about sex: once you have it, he expects you to keep on having it every time you go out. What if I don't like that? What if I don't want to?"

"Well, he's not going to know that if you don't tell him."

"I know it sounds simple, Gladys. I know it *is* simple. But the fact is, I've already said yes. I've already had sex. At this point it would sound silly to get all prim and say I just want to be friends. Besides, I *don't* just want to be friends. The reason we drink and have sex is that we have nothing else to do. If we didn't drink and have sex, we'd sit like rocks and grow moss. I'd rather have a good cup of coffee and read a book. Do you have any idea how guilty that makes me feel? To realize that I only think people are only worthwhile if they *give* me something?"

"Maybe," said Gladys cautiously, knowing she was treading on dangerous ground, "you just haven't met the right guy."

"Oh…the right guy," Beata groaned. "Maybe there *is* no right guy. Maybe all guys are like this."

Gladys giggled. "If you can't have Mr. Right, you might as well have Mr. Right Around the Corner. I read that in a newspaper article."

"Say," said Beata, having a brainstorm, "how about if you dress up like me and go out with Frank yourself? I'm sure one of those people at the psychic fair must have described someone that looks like Frank as the love of your life."

"You don't think he'd notice you'd gotten six inches shorter?"

"Oh, maybe. But he wouldn't care."

"You don't know that. He might actually *like* you."

"I doubt it," she said. "Maybe I'm crazy, but I swear he doesn't know me from Adam. I don't know why he's going out with me."

"Such a pessimist," Gladys clucked.

Beata hung up the phone and sat brooding on the couch. It was early twilight. The sun had disappeared below the horizon but darkness had yet to settle in. The front yard, with its hedge of Morning Glory and tangle of overgrown shrubs, began to take on the mystery of an Amazon jungle.

The phone rang again...sometimes, Beata felt, she didn't do anything but talk on the phone. This time it was Irene with another plea for Beata's dog-sitting services.

"I know this is the last minute," she apologized, "but my grandmother passed away this morning and Ken and I have to drive to California to take care of her affairs."

"Oh, Irene, I'm so sorry to hear that."

"I'm completely stressed out about leaving so soon, but obviously we have to get down there right away." The petulance in Irene's voice brought a wry smile to Beata's face...the death of a relative would be nothing to Irene compared with the affront of disarranging her carefully crafted schedule.

"So can you do it?"

"Sure," Beata said. "How long do you plan to be gone?"

"We're not sure. Probably no more than a couple of weeks. Can we call you from California and let you know?"

"Yeah, no problem."

"I dashed out this evening to make sure we have at least four weeks' worth of food," Irene continued, "so all I need to do is drop off the key. Can I leave it in your mailbox tomorrow morning?"

"Sure. Don't worry, Irene. The dogs will be fine."

Beata heard Irene put her hand over the receiver. "Gwover! Cwevewand!" she cooed, "Auntie Beata is going to wook after the babies for a few days...are woo happy? Woo wove Auntie Beata, don't woo?" Beata heard kissing sounds as Irene smacked the air above the dogs' heads. "We're leaving early, at 5:00, so they'll need to come out in the morning," she said, turning back to the phone.

"Okay, Irene, no worries."

"I didn't have time to make a list. Don't forget, beef for Cleveland and salmon for Grover on Tuesday and Friday, otherwise, chicken. Are you writing this down?"

Beata was not writing it down. She could see that the death of a family member was not momentous enough to justify disrupting Grover's diet and the commensurate risk to his delicate digestive system, but she didn't have a paper and pencil near the phone. Irene would never understand this, she decided. Irene would never be caught without a paper and pencil by the phone.

"Yes," she lied, "salmon on Tuesday and Friday, right?"

"Right," said Irene, sounding relieved. "And don't forget about not mixing up the leashes.

"Got it," Beata said briskly. "Don't mix up the leashes; don't mix up the bowls. We'll be fine."

"Okay," said Irene. "Thank you. You're a life-saver."

Watching the dogs would be fun, Beata decided. Apart from their neurotic mom, Grover and Cleveland were a pleasant influence. She looked forward to their exuberance. They would break her out of her routine and give her something to worry about besides Frank.

"Zzzzzzzzzzzzzzzzzzzzzzzz!!"

Beata jumped at the sound of the doorbell, and leapt up from the couch. By now, it was dark enough outside so the window was reflecting back a faint, glassy image of her living room; she could not see the front porch. She opened the door. Joshua was standing there.

"J-Joshua?"

"Hi," he said. "Can I come in?"

"Uh," she said, wondering frantically whether it was safe to let a stranger into her home and suspecting it wasn't, "um, yeah, I guess so. Come in."

She backed away far enough to make room for him on the doormat, but still block his way into the rest of the house. They stood looking at each other for a moment, and then he said "Walk down to the dog park with me?"

"I don't have the dogs tonight," she explained. "Those were my neighbor's dogs."

"Uh huh," he said, oblivious to her discomfort and seeming to take her consent for granted.

"It's almost dark," she pointed out.

"Right," he agreed.

Joshua was the most persistent person, Beata thought. The night he'd rescued her from the thug, she'd stopped being afraid of him. He wasn't the sort of person you could be afraid of when you actually met him. But this walk idea was simply crazy. Who knocks on someone's door and asks them for a walk in the dark?

"My jacket's in the other room. I don't even know where it is."

"You said you wanted to thank me properly," he said.

"Right, but...I didn't mean going for a walk in the dark."

"What *did* you mean?"

"Well, I meant I'd like to be able to return the favor."

"Okay," he said. "You can return the favor by walking down to the park with me."

He put his hands in his pockets and blinked at her, standing comfortably on the doormat as if willing to take up residence there. She sighed and went into the bedroom to retrieve her jacket. He was still standing in front of the door when she returned. As she was preparing to open the door, he said, "Do you have any food?"

"Food?" she repeated stupidly.

"Anything to eat," he clarified.

Beata was stabbed by sudden embarrassment, then swiftly on its heels, by anger. Was this man asking her to feed him? Was he standing here in her house *panhandling*?

"I don't think so," she responded coldly.

"Really?" he said, "Nothing? You don't even have a can of chili or some string beans or applesauce?"

She opened her lips to say "no" and order him out of the house, but was abruptly silenced by the memory of going through her cupboard not two weeks ago wondering why it was full of food she'd had for months and never used. Chili, string beans and applesauce were the very items she'd puzzled over, wondering why she was enticed to purchase things she never ate just because they were on sale. She'd told herself that she really ought to take them down to the food bank, but couldn't be bothered with it at the time and so had thrust the cans back in the cupboard and forgotten all about them. Now, here was Joshua practically reading her a grocery list of the spare items in her cupboard as if he'd made an inventory.

"Uh, maybe," she said.

"Bring them along," he ordered, and waited in the foyer as she dug several cans out of the cupboard and put them in a paper shopping bag.

"Good," he said, taking the bag from her, rolling up the top and tucking it under his arm. He held the door open and waited for her to go out before him, then clicked it gently shut and preceded her down the walk. He went straight to the gate, not confounded by the wall of Morning Glory that made it blend into a seamless whole with the rest of the fence, and opened the latch without a fumble. The gate swung shut, and the Morning Glory swallowed it back up again.

"How does he do that?" she wondered. "Even *I* can't find that gate in the dark."

They walked to the corner of the main road in the gathering dark. The streetlights were just coming on, making a chain of luminous stepping-stones along the river of sidewalk which led to the park. The alternating ambience of harsh, mechanical light and soft darkness cast a dreamlike quality over the moment. As they walked, they exchanged sporadic conversation.

"I wanted to introduce you to a friend of mine," Joshua said.

"You have a friend at the dog park?"

"That's right."

"Isn't it kind of late for someone to be at the dog park?"

"She lives there," he said, as if living at the park were the most natural and obvious thing in the world.

A woman? He was introducing her to a woman? Beata said nothing, but she was uncomfortable. Who was this bizarre person that lived in the park? Why did Joshua want her to meet her?

"Her name is Mary," he finished.

The parking lot was brightly lit. Joshua moved through it toward the fenced-in field, which was, in contrast, pitch black. He didn't go through the gate, but instead turned and walked along the fence toward the wooded area in the back. Nervously, Beata remembered thug. Hadn't he come from back here in the woods?

They reached the woods, and Joshua walked straight in. There was a ledge of level ground about 20 feet wide beyond the parking lot, and then the earth dove steeply down toward the rocky beach at the edge of the sound.

Joshua continued down for several feet, and Beata's nervousness increased. It was dark and isolated here, a perfect spot for an ambush. Plus, she was beginning to have trouble finding her footing on the sloping ground, and the darkness was so heavy under the trees that she couldn't avoid the roots and twigs that kept threatening to send her head first down the hill. Just as she was making up her mind to turn back, Joshua turned sharply to the left into a bare, hollow spot hidden amidst a clump of trees.

"Hi," he said. Someone turned on a flashlight and shined it in Joshua's face, then Beata's. She put her hand up to her eyes to cover them.

"Joshua?" said a gravelly female voice, "Is that you?"

"Yes," said Joshua. The light went out, and another light came on, this time a fluorescent electric camping lantern. In its sickly, blue light, Beata made out a rough shelter lashed together out of tarps, sheets of plastic and duct tape. There was an untidy bedroll under the tarps, and a dented aluminum pot next to a can of Sterno. Standing in front of this homey scene was a woman so thin her cheek bones jutted out of her face like hatchet blades. Her hair hung lank and dirty on her shoulders from under an unraveling knitted hat. Her clothing was torn, stained and of different sizes. It looked like she had unearthed it from a dumpster. She had the beaten-down look of a 30-something-year-old whose hard life had prematurely aged her, and there were scabs on her face and hands.

"Beata," said Joshua, "this is Mary. Mary's a special friend of mine. Mary, this is Beata. She lives up the street."

Silently calling down curses on Joshua for telling this (obviously homeless) woman where she lived, Beata reached out to shake Mary's hand. Mary stared down at the hand stupidly, and made no move to take it. Beata put it in her jacket pocket, feeling strangely embarrassed that someone so desperate should reject her magnanimous overtures of friendship.

"We brought dinner," said Joshua, proffering the shopping bag.

"Huh," said Mary, grabbing the bag and rootling through it.

"Let's eat," he suggested.

"I don't need no company," she said, scowling at Beata.

"I'll cook," he offered. He took the bag back from Mary and started pulling things out of it: three cans of chili, a can of green beans and two of applesauce, some paper plates and plastic spoons. Beata was startled...she hadn't put all those things in the bag. When had Joshua added plates and spoons? Hadn't she been walking beside him the whole way to the park? Hadn't he had that bag rolled up and tucked under his arm the whole time?

Joshua pulled out a tiny, one-burner propane camp stove and a box of matches. Ignoring Beata, who was craning her neck to get a glimpse inside the bag without grabbing it, and Mary, who was glaring at both of them as if to drive them away with the sheer force of her antagonism; he squatted on the ground and started the camp stove. Pulling a can opener from the bag, he opened the cans of chili, dumped them into Mary's aluminum pot and placed the pot on the stove. The chili began to bubble. Joshua stirred it, and the aroma of chili filled the air.

"Mary, open this," he directed, handing her the can opener and the can of beans. She had her arms folded across her skinny chest, and it seemed for a moment that she would refuse. His calm assumption of authority had the same effect on Mary as it'd had earlier on Beata: Mary shrugged, took the can, sat down beside Joshua and began to open it.

Beata wasn't sure what she should do. Clearly, Mary didn't want her there, and she had never felt so awkward in her life. Just as she was getting ready to mumble an excuse and flee, Joshua said "We need some plates," and nodded at the stack.

She sat down.

"Mmm-mmm," said Joshua, stirring the chili. "Pass me those plates. While we're eating this, I'll get the beans on."

The cheap plate sagged as he loaded it with chili, so he supported it by cradling it in his hand like a tortilla and kept on spooning in beans. When it was threatening to spill out the ends of the paper taco shell, he handed it to Mary and began spooning up one for Beata.

Mary dug into the chili like a starving wolf, and Joshua handed Beata the second plate. Before she'd daintily nibbled the first exploratory morsel off the spoon, Mary had gobbled down half her plate. Meanwhile, Joshua was still fussing over the pot. He put his plate on the ground and emptied the rest of the chili onto it. Then, he grabbed a battered gallon milk jug full of water from Mary's supplies, poured a slug of it into the pan, sluiced it around, dumped it out, and then upended the can of string beans into the cleanish pot. He glanced first at Mary and then Beata, and remarked conversationally, "Father, thank you for this food and bless it to our bodies." Then he picked up his plate and began to eat.

Beata froze with her spoon half way to her mouth. She hadn't expected him to say grace, and felt uncouth about starting before he had said it. Weren't you supposed to make a warning announcement about grace before you blurted it out? Give people a chance to organize themselves? Weren't you supposed to bow your head and fold your hands? What was the deal with just throwing it into the conversation like a bomb?

Neither Joshua nor Mary paid any attention to Beata's discomfort; Mary was too busy vacuuming the last specks of food off her plate and Joshua had started engulfing his chili like a force of nature. His arm stroked down to the plate and back up to his mouth like a metronome…she could have played a march to its regular beat. Beata unfroze and nibbled another half bean from her spoon. Really, she had lost her appetite in the face of their ravenous hunger.

"You want the rest of that?" Joshua asked, eyeing her almost full plate hungrily. His own was empty, and Mary had practically scraped a hole through hers.

"Um, no thanks. I'm done." Beata offered him the plate. He shoveled two-thirds of it onto Mary's and dug into the rest himself.

Beata shifted uncomfortably on the cold, damp ground, trying to move her weight around on the twigs and pebbles that were digging into her behind, as Joshua and Mary finished the chili, devoured the string beans and then switched to clean plates and slurped up the applesauce.

"That really hit the spot," Joshua sighed. "Let's get some water on for coffee."

"I got no coffee," Mary said.

"There's some in here," he replied, and sure enough, reached into the bag and pulled out a jar of instant.

"Listen, I better get going," Beata said.

"Why?" Mary growled, "Too good for your company?"

"Well...n-no, of course not," Beata stammered, taken aback by her bluntness.

"Mary, when did you last see Fanny and the kids?" Joshua interrupted, settling back against a tree and looking as comfortable as a cat on a down pillow.

Mary snorted. "The court won't let me see 'em without supervised visitation. Not since the last time I got busted."

"I'm sorry to hear that. You'll be glad to know they're doing pretty well. They miss you, though. Zack's grades are starting to come up again, and Tia's made a new friend at school. Fanny's arthritis is bothering her, but it's not too bad."

"Yeah, well..." Mary stared off into the darkness. "I could care less about that bitch's arthritis. That Fanny, she never liked me. She doesn't never tell them CPS people nothing good about me. I'll prolly never see them kids again."

"Not so," Joshua said. "Fanny is worried about you. She wonders if you're still clean. She doesn't want the kids to know you're homeless so she's told them you're working out of town."

"They might as well know the worst," Mary said flatly. "As for being clean, it ain't none of her business and it ain't none of yours."

Beata wanted to strangle Joshua. What was he doing to her? Now he had her sipping coffee with a drug addict.

"Maybe they don't want to know the worst," he pointed out. "If they knew you were around and weren't seeing them, what would they think?"

"They would think their mom is a loser. Which is true."

"But they might also think she doesn't love them, which is *not* true."

"Love," she said, with a humorless laugh. "Yeah, I love them so much I left them at home alone to go out tweaking with some asshole. I love them so much I spent their food money on shit to put up my arm. This kinda love they're better off without. And I don't know what you're staring at," she rounded on Beata. "I guess your shit don't stink Miss Perfect. You can take your give-away chili beans and cheap-ass coffee and stick them up your ass. You think I'm falling all over myself thanking you for a couple cans of beans?"

"The cheap-ass coffee came from me," Joshua explained.

"Get the hell outta here, both of you."

Beata rose to her feet. She didn't have to be invited twice. Mary's hostility was boiling over, and Beata feared she might slash her throat with the dull kitchen knife and pick her pockets clean. What had Joshua been talking about a 'special friend'? She couldn't imagine behavior less friendly than Mary's. She didn't seem to like him any better than she liked Beata.

Joshua, too, stood up.

"Listen Mary, we'll see you again soon," he promised. "Enjoy the coffee." Mary turned her back and ignored them.

Beata stumbled back up the hill toward the lighted parking lot with Joshua following silently in her wake. As soon as they were out of earshot of Mary, she turned on him furiously.

"What on earth were you thinking?" she demanded. "Who *was* that woman? And don't tell me she's a friend of yours because she sounds like she hates you. Where do you get off dragging me around in the middle of the night to meet homeless drug addicts who would just as soon steal my money as look at me?"

Joshua blinked at her. "Didn't you like her?" he asked.

"NO, I didn't like her. Are you crazy? What's there to like?"

"Oh, I don't know. There's just something special about her. I think you have more in common than you realize."

"You're insane," she announced, whirling away and beginning to march across the parking lot. "We have absolutely nothing in common. She is uneducated, homeless, lost her children, unemployed and has a drug problem. What part of that, exactly, is like me?" The brisk pace was making her breathless, but Joshua strode along beside her as if they were strolling casually through the park.

"I'm not talking about all those superficial things," he said.

"Well those are the only things I saw," she said. "I'll thank you not to introduce me to any more of your friends, special or otherwise."

"She could really use your help," he said.

"She doesn't seem interested in my help or anyone else's."

"But she needs it."

"Joshua, you can't help people who don't want to be helped."

"How do you know?"

"You know because they make it clear they don't want it or appreciate it."

"No, how do you know you can't help them?"

Beata was confused. "You mean how do I know you can't help people who don't want to be helped?"

"Right."

"Well…everybody knows that. Some people aren't open to help. You can try and try, and it's a waste of effort."

They were in sight of her house by now. She would have picked up the pace but she couldn't do it without breaking into a run. Joshua was still breathing quietly, and she had a feeling he could have kept up with her if she were going twice as fast.

"I can personally assure you that is not the case," he said.

"So you know better than all the psychologists that have ever lived?" She exaggerated wildly.

"Right."

"I have no idea why I should take your word for that." With these words, she reached the back gate, which she yanked open, and turned to face him. "Please don't come in. And please tell your special friend not to come knocking on my door when the weather gets cold. And please don't get me involved in any more harebrained schemes to help people who don't want to be helped."

She slammed the gate and stalked up the back stairs. He'd hustled her out of the house so fast she had forgotten to lock it, and this fact made her even angrier as she ripped it open and stomped inside. She'd also left without taking the key. If she *had* locked the door, her grand exit would have been spoiled by having to stand helplessly on the back porch until she could pry the window open and climb in, but she was in no mood to be grateful for small blessings.

She ripped off her jacket and tossed it on the couch in the living room. The back was covered with flecks of lichen, tiny bits of fir needle and a film of dust, some of which settled onto the upholstery, irritating Beata further.

"Great. Ruin my couch, too," she muttered, unfairly blaming Joshua for the wholesale destruction of her wardrobe and home.

She stalked back to the spare bedroom which she used as a den, threw herself down on the sofa and turned on the TV. She surfed idly from channel to channel until she found a home improvement show, one of her favorites, and settled in to watch.

The next couple of hours passed quietly until a sound distracted her from the television. She hit the mute button and heard the hiss of strong wind in the trees and tap-tap of heavy raindrops against the window. Apparently it had turned into a wild night. She stretched out on the couch and turned the volume back up, but couldn't dislodge from her head a picture of Mary's flimsy tarp shredded by the wind and her grimy sleeping bag soaked through by the rain.

She arose from the sofa, wandered into the kitchen and put the teakettle on. The wind was rattling the windowpanes like castanets and the rain seemed to have lost all differentiation as individual drops and poured from the sky in one huge sheet. Beata could hear water hitting the ground as it cascaded from the roof. She turned off the kettle – she couldn't sit in her cozy den and sip hot tea in the midst of a maelstrom when Mary was out huddling under a piece of plastic. She walked to the front window and stared out. The shrubs in the front yard boiled in the gale and slapped against the window as if trying to climb inside out of the weather.

"What am I supposed to do?" Beata mumbled. "Go pick her up? There are shelters for people like that. Surely she can get to a shelter."

She marched to her bedroom, peeled off her clothes, put on her nightgown and climbed into bed. She lay on her side and clamped a pillow firmly over her exposed ear to block out the sound of the tempest. She couldn't take responsibility for the whole world. Mary wasn't the only homeless person out in the storm…what was she going to do, rescue all of them? She tossed and turned, yearning futilely for the sweet unconsciousness of sleep.

Before she could doze off, the phone interrupted her restless tossing. Beata sat up and groaned…who could be calling at this time of night? For a moment, she imagined it might be Joshua calling to order her to go get Mary from the park, but she hastily banished the thought from her mind -- surely it was impossible -- and reached for the phone.

"It's Dad," she said, startled at the caller ID display. "What's he calling at this hour for?"

"Hi, Dad. Is anything wrong?"

"Beata, your mother fell this evening and broke two ribs and her leg. We just got back from the hospital."

"Dad! That's terrible! How'd it happen?"

Beata's mom was over 80, and was having trouble adapting to the increasing frailty of her own body. She stubbornly continued the activities of her younger years and had an escalating succession of injuries to show for it.

"She climbed up on a chair to reach something down from the closet shelf and fell."

"Dad, she knows she shouldn't be climbing on chairs."

"I know, but she does it anyway. I didn't know what she was up to until I heard her fall."

"How is she feeling?"

"She's okay, but woozy from the pain medication."

"Oh Dad…"

"Honey, she needs you to come out."

"Dad, I can't just drop everything and fly out there every time Mom decides to climb on a chair."

"But we need you. Your mother can't use crutches; they make her too tired. She's in a wheelchair."

"Dad, you're going to have to handle this yourself."

"But honey, I can't. I can't lift your mom. What'll I do if she falls?"

Beata sighed. It was true enough; her dad could barely take care of himself, much less her now disabled mother. Her father suffered from a neuromuscular disease that made his legs and arms wasted and weak. He could barely walk with braces and crutches. Hefting a grown woman (with a heavy cast on) in and out of a wheelchair would be out of the question.

She got out of bed and made for the computer. "Dad, I'll book a flight as soon as I can, but there's no way I can be there before tomorrow night. It may even be the day after."

"The day *after*," her father whined, "we need you *now*."

Beata struggled for patience. "Dad, I'll come as fast as I can. You live on the other side of the country. There's only so much I can do. Not only do I have to find a flight, but I've got obligations here. I need to make arrangements."

"Well, I just don't know what we're going to do," her father complained.

"I'll be there as soon as I can," she promised, and hung up before he could say any more.

She searched the Internet for flights to Dulles, but most of them were already full. Near the end of the list, at full Coach fare, she found a two-stop flight leaving at 6:00 pm and arriving at 1:30 am with one middle seat left in the very back row.

"Great," she thought. "The most uncomfortable seat in existence and I get to occupy it for eight miserable hours."

Now what to do about Irene's dogs? No way could Gladys come over twice or three times a day, and there was no point in talking to Daphne about it…Daphne would grope for excuses and wind up resentful at even being asked. She grabbed the phone book and rifled through the yellow pages.

Under Pet Sitting, she found this sole entry: 'Home Away from Home Reliable House Sitting Services. All sitters bonded and back-ground checked. We do it all: Pets – Plants – Mail'.

By the time she'd finished booking the flight and finding the house-sitting service, it was well past midnight and the storm had calmed. Thank goodness she hadn't lost power or she'd never have gotten a flight. She tumbled back into bed and fell asleep.

The next morning dawned overcast, damp and cold. She shivered in her sweat clothes as she fished Irene's key out of the mailbox and went over to her house to let out Grover and Cleveland. They attacked her as if they'd been alone for a month, yapping and scratching her shins with their little nails.

"Hi, boys," she said, patting Cleveland's foxy head. She couldn't reach Grover, who had abandoned her shins and was tearing around in circles in the foyer. She opened the door and the two of them exploded into Irene's yard. Beata thought briefly about taking them to the dog park, but feared she would see Mary.

"I'll just take you guys over to my house," she told them, locking the door and heading for the gate.

Too late, she remembered their leashes. The instant she opened the gate, they dashed outside and, overjoyed at their unaccustomed liberty, tore straight up the middle of the street toward the end of the block.

"Grover! Cleveland!" she hollered fruitlessly, jogging after them. "Come here right now!"

As they reached the intersection of her street and the busier main road, Beata put on speed and started running in earnest. Fortunately, this intrigued the dogs…they assumed she was playing chase and frolicked back to signal their willingness to participate. At this, Beata craftily turned around and began running the other way down the street, and the dogs followed, nipping at her heels and yapping joyfully. She ran around to the back of her house and, without slowing, up the back steps. The three of them burst into the house in a tangle of legs and fuzzy bodies.

"You are a pain," she informed them as she dropped onto the couch, exhausted. They'd had few mornings so delightful, their bright eyes seemed to say, and it was a pleasure to be baby-sat by someone so obliging.

As soon as 9:00 rolled around, she called the house-sitting service. Could they look after her neighbor's dogs while she was out of town?

"Oh no, we can't do that," the woman said. "It's a liability issue. Your neighbor would have to call us about that."

"But my neighbor asked me to do it, and I have to leave town," Beata pleaded.

"Can't you ask your neighbor to call us from wherever she is and authorize this?"

"She's on the road," Beata said, "and I don't have her cell phone number. But she'll call me in a day or two from California. Can't you just do it for a couple of days and then I can have her call you when I hear?" No, they could not. Rules were rules. Sorry as they were about Beata's situation (Beata had the feeling they were not sorry at all), their hands were tied. Beata slammed down the phone. What was she going to do? Desperately, she dialed the number back.

"Hi," she said, lowering her voice to disguise her identity. "I have just been called out of town on a family emergency, and I need someone to look after my two dogs."

"Ma'am, didn't I just talk to you?"

"Why, no," Beata said. "What are you talking about?"

"Ma'am, I know I just talked to you. My caller ID has your number on it. You just called and I told you we can't take care of your neighbor's dogs without their authorization."

"But these are *my* dogs," Beata lied, trying to sound outraged.

"Ma'am, we can't help you," the woman said, and hung up the phone.

"*Now* what do I do?" Beata wondered aloud. Grover and Cleveland were in the kitchen, sniffing at the cabinet under the sink where she kept the kitchen trash. They seemed to think they could take care of themselves. Beata couldn't decide whether to cancel her flight or pack for it.

The doorbell rang, and the dogs went crazy. By now, Beata knew how to deal with this situation, and she ignored the bell long enough to shut them in the bedroom before answering.

"Hi." Joshua said.

"Joshua, I don't have any time to chat right now." Beata said, starting to close the door in his face.

"You have the dogs again," he observed, thwarting her efforts by moving into the doorway. The dogs' barking had risen to a feverish pitch, and it sounded like one of them was trying to dig through the bedroom door.

"Yes, I'm taking care of them for Irene while she and her husband are in California," she said. "You'll have to excuse me. I'm packing for a trip. My mother is sick and I have to fly to Virginia."

"With the dogs?" he asked.

"Of course not," she snapped. "I can't take two dogs to my parents' house. I'm finding someone to watch them."

"Who?"

He had her there. The question brought all her desperation avalanching back and she slumped back from the door. "That's the problem," she said. "I don't have anyone."

"I can do it," he offered.

"You?"

"Sure. I like dogs."

"But I hardly know you."

"True. Anyone else in mind?"

"Well…no."

"Okay, then," he said, as if that was the final word. Which it pretty much was, she guessed.

"I'm only doing this because I'm desperate," she informed him. "And you better not mess up my house or steal anything because I'll report you to the police in a heartbeat."

"Okay," he said.

"Come back in a couple hours. I have to go get all their stuff from Irene's and then I'll show you where it all is."

"Okay."

He wandered off the porch and out the gate. Beata wondered where he lived and why he always seemed to be around her neighborhood, but she didn't have any time to puzzle over it. She raced over to Irene's and loaded all the dog food cans into a box, threw the leashes and dishes on top and lugged it back to her place. By this time, Grover and Cleveland were almost hysterical, and the bedroom door was creaking under their combined assault as they hurled themselves against it like battering rams. She left the box on the kitchen floor and opened it. There were splinters of wood all over the carpet where they'd scratched a gash in the door.

"Thanks, guys," she told them. They sniffed the front door suspiciously and, finding no one, turned resentful gazes on Beata.

"We're only trying to protect the house," they seemed to be saying. "Why can't you let us do our job?"

Beata ignored them and returned to the bedroom to pack her suitcase. If Joshua was going to be coming in, she'd better bring along her laptop and camera...it wouldn't do to leave valuable items sitting around the house. Not that Beata owned anything really valuable. There was a lot of stuff she didn't want to lose, but she couldn't very well lug it all to Virginia with her. She'd have to hope for the best. Irene's key, though, was coming with her. She dropped it into her purse.

She took the bus to the airport to save on parking. The flight was as long and miserable as she'd feared. She arrived at Dulles late, and was delayed by the shuttle to the main terminal and again by the car rental company. It was well after 2:00 a.m. by the time she made her way out of the airport. Thank goodness she had GPS on her phone; she hated driving in a strange town late at night and had no idea how to get to her parents' house. It was close to 3:00 when she arrived. The lights were out and the doors locked. She rang and knocked...no answer.

"Dad! Mom! It's me!" she hollered, banging on the door and buzzing repeatedly. She saw the neighbors' upstairs light go on, but her parents' house remained dark and silent.

"Dad! Wake up!" she shouted, pounding more desperately on the door.

She retreated to the car and got her cell phone out of her purse. She dialed their number, but the phone rang and rang, then the answering machine picked it up.

"Dad, it's Beata. I'm outside in your driveway. Come to the door," she said. She hung up and dialed back. No answer. She dialed a third time and left another message, and another. Finally, giving up, she sat in the passenger seat of her rental car and, reclining the seat completely back, tried to fall asleep.

***

She was awakened by her father pounding on the window of the car. She sat bolt upright. It was broad daylight. The car clock said 9:00.

"Beata, what are you doing sleeping in the car?" her father said, now knocking more quietly on the window. Beata opened the door and climbed groggily out. She felt awful.

127

"You didn't hear the door," she said. "I got here at 3:00 and I couldn't wake you."

Her father sounded frustrated. "Why didn't you use the key?"

"What key, Dad?"

"The key sitting under the flowerpot," he replied, frowning as if to say 'did I raise an idiot?'

"Dad, how am I supposed to know where you keep your spare key? And besides, you shouldn't have a key out here. It's dangerous."

"I put it out for *you*," he said, sounding aggrieved. "And you spent the night in your car."

Beata shook her head and extracted her luggage from the car. There was no sense arguing with her father about the key, or about his assumption that she would magically sense its existence and whereabouts. She hoped that she'd be allowed a few more hours' sleep, but this didn't appear probable. Her father hobbled into the house and, before she had even figured out where to put her luggage down, said, "It's an hour past breakfast time."

Beata compressed her lips, but said nothing. Her parents, old and sickly, had started thinking of less and less except their own needs as the deterioration of their bodies gnawed away at their strength and self-sufficiency. It was unfortunate, she thought, that they lived so far away. It was expensive and exhausting to come all the way out here when they needed help. The day was not far off when she would have to insist that they move to Seattle where she could look after them without taking days off work.

She blinked back her sleepiness and went to say hello to her mother, who was perched on the edge of the bed, struggling to get into the wheelchair that was parked beside her without the brakes engaged. Beata rushed to her side.

"Mom, you're going to break another rib if you try to get into that wheelchair without locking the wheels," she scolded, applying the brakes and lifting her mom into the chair.

"Hello, dear," her mom said, kissing her cheek.

"I was just going to fix your father and me some breakfast."

"How can you do that in a wheelchair?" Beata asked.

"Oh, I've just been making frozen waffles," her mother said. "We've been eating them without syrup because we ran out of that, and your father is complaining about it, but now that you're here we can do some grocery shopping."

"Okay, Mom, I'll do that this afternoon," Beata promised, kissing her back. "Make a list."

"How was your flight, dear?"

"Awful. I got here at 3:00 this morning and I had to sleep on the driveway because you and Dad couldn't hear the bell."

"Oh, I'm sorry, dear. Your dad lost one of his hearing aids, and I sleep so soundly on this pain medication that I guess I just didn't wake up."

"It's okay, Mom. I'm going to need a little nap this afternoon, but I'll be fine."

"I'm glad you arrived today, dear. I didn't know how your father and I were going to get to church tomorrow."

Beata groaned inwardly. She hadn't been to church for over 30 years, but as a girl her parents had forced her to attend every Sunday until she'd left the house at age 18. Of course they couldn't miss church for such minor glitches as a broken leg and a few cracked ribs. The fact that, in these later years, both of them dozed through the whole service was immaterial. They went to church on Sunday, and that was the end of it.

"It might be a little difficult to get you in there in the wheelchair," she said.

Her mother dissented vigorously. "Oh, no. I'm sure we can get in just fine."

"Aren't there stairs? I thought Dad had trouble getting up the stairs."

"Well, he does, but some of the young men can help us."

Mom Has Spoken, Beata realized. To church they would go, and it was futile to discuss it any further. She wheeled her mom into the living room, and went to the kitchen to fix breakfast. As she cracked eggs into the frying pan, her mother's wheelchair appeared in the doorway.

"We have *fried* eggs on Saturday," she said, as Beata stirred the eggs in the pan into yellow homogeneity.

"This Saturday we are having scrambled," she said.

"Sunday is our day for scrambled," her mother persisted.

"Mom, you've been eating frozen waffles for two days. Wouldn't you like some eggs today?"

"I guess we can have fried tomorrow," her mother conceded.

"Scrambled?" her father asked, appalled, as she brought the eggs to the table. "We have *fried* eggs on Saturday."

"Today we are having scrambled," Beata repeated firmly.

"We'll have fried tomorrow," her mother promised.

"Where's the peach jam?" her father said.

"We're out," her mother said. "Beata and I are going shopping this afternoon and we'll get some more."

"Raspberry gives me diarrhea," her father complained, spooning a generous mound of jam onto his toast.

"Then don't eat any," Beata suggested.

"This is all we have," her father sighed. "Your mother doesn't think it's important to keep jam I can eat in the house."

"You could eat your toast with butter."

"Yes," her mother said, "just eat it with butter and stop complaining. We're going shopping later this afternoon."

"I can't tolerate dairy."

130

"Mom," Beata said to divert the conversation, "*we* are not going shopping. *I* am going shopping. You are going to stay at home and rest."

The truth was, Beata wanted to get out of the house alone. Her parents, with their rigid ways (*fried* on Saturday, *scrambled* on Sunday, breakfast at 8:00 and not 9:00) were frustrating to be around. She fretted under the burden of maintaining a seemingly infinite procession of meaningless habits and schedules. A solitary trip to the grocery store, armed with her mother's multi-page shopping list, gave her a chance to call Gladys.

"Gladys, talk me down."

"Hi! Where are you? I called earlier and your machine picked up."

"I'm in Virginia."

"Virginia? Is everything okay with your folks?"

"No, my mom fell off a chair and broke two ribs and a leg. She's in a cast and a wheelchair, and I had to make an emergency trip out here last night."

"Oh, Beata, that's terrible. How is she feeling?"

"Well enough to remember that they eat fried eggs for breakfast on Saturday, not scrambled, and to write out a three-page grocery list. I'm at the store right now."

"Oh good. I'm glad she's going to be okay. So tell me...you fixed them the wrong eggs this morning?"

"Yes, silly me."

Gladys had heard Beata's complaints for 12 years. She knew Beata's mother as well as Beata did. "A *good* daughter would know her parents' breakfast schedule," she said.

"Right...that's the difference between me and a *good* daughter."

"You better watch out," Gladys warned. "If you upset your father's digestive system, you'll be hearing about his diarrhea for the next two weeks."

"No problem. I'll just call you up and pass along all the details."

"That's my girl."

"Gladdie, can you do me a favor? I need you to drive by my house a couple times while I'm out of town. Yesterday, before all this happened with my mom, I told my neighbor I'd look after her dogs for a while. So when my dad called, I was in quite a pickle. I got someone to watch the dogs, but I don't know him very well. I'd sure appreciate it if you'd check up on him to make sure he hasn't burned down the house."

"Omygosh. You left a stranger in your house?"

"I left him the key so he could take care of Irene's dogs. I didn't have a choice. I had to find someone to do it. It's that Joshua guy who rescued me in the park."

"Oh, the stalker guy. Sure I can drop by. I'll keep an eye on the place."

"Thanks, Gladdie. I've gotta go now. I want to get this shopping done in time to take a nap before I have to fix dinner."

Beata finished the grocery shopping and loaded the groceries into the cupboard under her mother's stern eye. Putting away groceries took quite some time. There was no hasty stuffing of cans in front of cans or stacking the spaghetti on top of the cereal boxes. Beata's mother examined each item (tsk tsking over the fact that Beata had purchased the wrong brands) and directed its proper placement in the cupboard: recent items on the bottom and in the back; older items on top and in the front. Even the freezer was alphabetized, and they had a brief skirmish over the where the ground beef should go. Beata put it under 'h' for hamburger, but her mother wanted it under 'b' for beef, ground.

"It'll get mixed up with all the other beef," Beata said. "You've got beef comma steak and beef comma roast and beef comma ribs in here."

"Those go under 's' and 'r'," her mother said. "Your father doesn't eat fish or pork, so everything in here is beef."

The next morning they arose very early (in Beata's jet-lagged perception) to trek off to church.

132

"Don't you have anything nicer than that?" her mother asked, looking at her faded dress with disapproval.

"No, Mom. I packed in a hurry. This is all I brought."

"Well, you really should take more care with your appearance, dear. I realize there's nothing you can do about your hair. You always had bad hair. But at least you could wear decent clothes."

"Have you and Daphne been talking behind my back?"

"Daphne? No...why do you ask?"

"She doesn't approve of my clothes, either."

"Daphne is such a good girl," her mother said.

They arrived just as Sunday School was starting, and Beata had difficulty rounding up enough help to muscle her parents up the steps. She felt she'd stepped far enough out of her comfort zone in agreeing to attend the service; she wasn't going to pile Sunday School on top of it. So, while her parents sat through the Sunday School lesson, Beata explored the church.

It was an ancient, imposing structure. Beata shivered as she ambled through its gloomy hallways. The floorboards creaked dangerously, and it breathed an ambience of dusty quietude that felt at once stifling and yet cold. Beata loathed the formality of it. It reminded her of the church she'd attended as a child.

She'd had recurring nightmares about that church. In one, she was walking down a long hallway toward the pastor's office. She could see a narrow wedge of sunlight under the door, but the hallway was completely dark. Before she reached the door, the walls started closing in. She couldn't hear or see anything moving, but she could feel them getting closer and closer, until they were touching her sides, hemming her in. She couldn't move backward or forward; she was trapped there, staring at the bright wedge of sunlight under the door but unable to reach it as the walls smashed in on her tighter and tighter.

She'd had the dream so many times that the crushing walls stopped surprising her. As soon as the dream started, she'd see the long, dark hallway and the door with its glow of sunlight at the end, and her heart would start pounding. In the dream, she'd tell herself "The walls will not close in. They won't." And she'd start hurrying down the hall as fast as she could. But although she was running, her feet would move with maddening slowness, as if she were under water, and the door would drift away further, and the walls would start closing in long before she got there.

She always woke up before she got crushed, of course. She wasn't even afraid of being crushed. It was being trapped she dreaded, trapped in sight of a bright place of refuge, but always stuck on the wrong side of the door. She never told her parents about the nightmares, but every night when they sent her to bed, she'd lie awake as long as she could and whisper an incantation over and over: "I won't have bad dreams. I'll have good dreams, only the best."

Religion, Beata had concluded, was just like that – it promised safety, security and happiness and then held them just out of reach. She was forever trapped in the dark on the wrong side of the door. Beata wasn't the type of gal who took comfort in rituals. She wanted truth. She wanted freedom. She wanted, she sighed, to be happy. Why did that simple goal seem so far out of reach?

When Sunday School ended, Beata rejoined her parents for Fellowship Hour. She sipped watery coffee and noshed on store-bought cookies while her parents introduced her to two dozen people she couldn't tell apart.

"This is Guy," her mother said. "He's Sally's husband, and they're Darla's aunt and uncle. Remember the Champtons?" she asked, mentioning a family whose name Beata remembered from their phone conversations but about whom she could summon not a single detail. "Guy is their son-in-law. He married their daughter Candy. You remember Candy, dear." Beata did not remember Candy, but she smiled at Guy and shook his hand. "Look," her mother said. "There's Julie Brownwell. You'll want to say hello to her. Roll me over there, dear."

Beata rolled her over and dutifully said 'hello' to Julie Brownwell, another forgotten acquaintance of her parents' from 20 years ago. She forgot Guy's name even before she got as far as Julie, and then forgot Julie's name before her mom dragged her on to the next introduction. She hoped she could escape from the fellowship hall before Guy or Julie or any of the others her mother had introduced came over and wanted to chat.

In comparison with the social agony of Fellowship Hour, Beata welcomed the formal monotony of the church service, which was long on responsive readings and dirge-like hymns. The brief sermon came from Matthew 7:16: "You will know them by their fruits." It was a theologically uninspiring homily that seemed to boil down to "Be a good person". Beata's parents sat contentedly in a middle pew and nodded off while Beata tried to fix her drifting attention on the reedy voice and earnest, watery eyes of the preacher, whose rhetorical talents fell woefully short of his sincere desire to motivate his flock.

Mercifully, the service was over promptly at noon. Her parents seemed to want to stay and mingle, but Beata strode resolutely through the cluster of people by the sanctuary door, determined to evade further socializing. She could not, however, avoid the preacher standing in the vestibule to intercept everyone who approached the front door. He clasped her hand in his spongy grasp and pumped it weakly up and down in his version of a hearty welcome while her mother beamed at the middle of her back and introduced her to Chad Somebody, Associate Pastor of First Presbyterian.

"Mom," she hissed out of the side of her mouth, "we have to go."

"So good to have you here helping your parents," Chad said as Beata surreptitiously wiped her clammy hand on her skirt. "They are such fine, Christian people."

Beata nodded and smiled. "They certainly are," she agreed.

Chad and Beata walked the wheelchair down the stairs while her father tossed his crutches on the sidewalk and inched down, clutching the railing. It was hot and sticky, and poor Chad was as gooey as an overheated marshmallow by the time they wrestled her mom into the car.

"Thanks, Chad," she said, as she gratefully fired up the air conditioner.

"No problem," he wheezed, mopping his doughy brow with the back of one arm. "I'm looking forward to seeing you next week."

"Um, me, too," Beata lied.

"Isn't he the nicest man?" her mother beamed as they drove away.

"Hmph," her father said. "He's an Arminian. He's got no business preaching in the Presbyterian church."

Beata's father was an enthusiastic student of theology. He was also an ardent Calvinist, quoting frequently from Calvin's Institutes of the Christian Religion, and had a proprietary love for the Presbyterian church that demanded rigid adherence to its Calvinist roots. He was always debating people on obscure doctrinal points that had faded from relevance generations before he was born. No doubt there were others who maintained an interest in such matters as irresistible vs. prevenient grace, but aside from her father, Beata didn't know any of them.

"Dad, I don't understand how an Arminian could get ordained in the Presbyterian church. In fact, I don't understand why an Arminian would *want* to be ordained in the Presbyterian church. Furthermore, I didn't notice any radical anti-Calvinist leanings in the sermon today. I'm wondering how you know he's an Arminian, or if it's just a blanket pejorative for anyone who disagrees with you."

This was all the opening Beata's father needed. He zestfully began dissecting a sermon which bore no obvious resemblance to the sermon Beata had heard, pointing out the error in several arcane points that only he had noticed. Beata didn't really care whether Chad was an Arminian. She knew her father enjoyed this sort of thing, and figured it was a good way to keep him occupied for the next hour or so. She let the words flow over her without really listening.

When they reached her parents' house, her dad had just reached critical mass, and was beginning to quote Romans 3:23 for the seventh time. He seemed to want to stay in the car and finish up, but Beata turned off the air conditioner and hopped out. He hobbled along after her on his crutches, still talking as she unlocked the front door and disarmed the alarm. She helped him into the living room and deposited him on the couch before leaving him, still talking, so she could get her mom's wheelchair over the threshold.

By the time she wrangled her mother into the house, her father had abandoned his diatribe in favor of a higher call: the hollow rumbling of his empty stomach. "When is lunch?" he inquired.

"Just give me a minute, here, Dad," she said.

Meanwhile, her father had remembered the Sunday newspaper and was searching fruitlessly for the World News section.

"Where's the news?" he said.

"It's right here, dear," her mother said, handing him the front page.

"I don't want *that*," he said. "I want the *news*."

"Dad, that *is* the news."

Her father cast the front page aside. "Your mother knows I always read the news," he said, his voice rising to a whine that scraped on Beata's nerves. "Why does she always hide the news section?"

She willed herself to speak patiently. "Dad, which section are you looking for? This is the front page. It has news."

"The *news*. The *news*," he insisted, looking angrily at Beata.

"He means the World News," her mother explained.

"Well why don't you just say so?" she said. She sorted through the paper, but found no World News.

"Maybe it's on the dining room table," her mother said.

Beata found it on the table and brought it to her father. He snatched it without thanking her. "Why are people are always carrying off the newspaper?" he grumbled. Then, changing tactics, he began abusing himself. "Never mind," he said. "I know I'm too much trouble. I should just die and stop being such a trial to everyone."

Beata ignored him and went to the kitchen. Her father was always saying he should die. She was tired of reassuring him that they loved him and didn't want him to die, and equally tired of suggesting that, since he didn't seem likely to die anytime soon, maybe he should stop talking about it.

"Sweetheart," her mother said as Beata started making sandwiches, "you should know better than to use that mayonnaise. You know your father can't eat it. It gives him diarrhea."

* * *

Beata stayed with her parents for three weeks. Day merged into day, an endless succession of meal preparation, studded with periodic toilet and bathtub assistance. She worked when she could, which was not often. Her parents demanded frequent attention that broke her concentration and resulted in short, unproductive sessions at the computer.

The longer she stayed, the more inept she felt. Her parents didn't accept her help gracefully, but demanded that everything be done in particular ways that Beata either had forgotten or never mastered.

"I told you yesterday," her father would complain, "I like my bread with the crusts cut off."

"Yes, dear, you remember," her mother would chime in. "I told you that. The crusts upset your father's digestion."

"But Dad, I tried to cut them off and you said the bread was too small," she'd say.

"Oh, never mind," he'd sigh. "I'm too much trouble. I should just die and get out of everyone's way."

"Dad, please stop saying that. You have no idea how bad that makes us feel. We love you. We don't want you to die."

"Yes, that's right," her mother would say. "Just shut up about dying already."

Beata would put her hands over her ears and flee to the bedroom. She called Gladys almost every day, not only to hear a sane voice that wanted to talk about something besides food, bowel health and John Calvin, but also because she was nervous about leaving her house and Irene's dogs in Joshua's hands. Gladys had driven by the house several times and reassured Beata that everything seemed to be in order. A couple of times she'd gone to the door to talk to Joshua and check on the interior of the house as well.

"He seems really nice," she reported. "I don't think you have anything to worry about. He even mowed the lawn."

"Wow, that's great," Beata said. "I'm not sure it's such a good idea to raise the neighbors' expectations, though."

One day, near the end of the three weeks, Gladys had more disturbing news to report. "I went by your house again today," she told Beata. "Some woman came to the door. She was pretty hostile. I said 'Who *are* you?' and she said 'Who are *YOU*?' So I said 'I'm Beata's best friend and she asked me to drop by and check on the house. Did she give you permission to stay here?' She said 'If you're such a good friend, then why aren't you staying here to look after these dogs?' Well, that made me mad, so I was getting ready to let her have it when Joshua came in and said 'Hi, Gladys, how're you doing?' and I said…"

"Wait a minute, wait a minute," Beata interrupted. "There was a woman staying at my house? A *hostile* woman?"

"That's what I'm telling you," Gladys said. "And then Joshua came in and started a conversation like there was nothing in the world going on. And I have to say, he sure can make those dogs behave. They were as sweet as pie, didn't even yap once."

"Gladdie, try to focus," Beata said, feeling a knot in the pit of her stomach. "What was Mary doing in my house?"

"We never got that far," Gladys said. "Joshua came in, and we started talking about this and that. Like I said before, he's very nice. You ought to date *him* instead of that Frank guy."

"Gladys," Beata said, "Joshua is too young for me, and plus, he doesn't seem like the dating type. He likes everybody the same. At least, that's how it looks to me. Besides, I seem to recall you thinking dating 'that Frank guy' was a great idea."

"I thought it was a great idea for you to date *someone*," Gladys said. "It most certainly doesn't have to be Frank."

"Anyway, let's not get sidetracked. What is going on in my house?"

"It seems to be okay, Bea. I know it sounds weird, but everything looked fine. Except for a pile of junk in the corner of the living room – plastic and a sleeping bag and some other bags – everything looked normal. Clean, neat, nothing missing."

"Did you go back to my bedroom and the spare room? Did everything look okay there?"

"Yeah, you know me. I looked everywhere, even the bathroom. I didn't see anything missing, nothing was moved and everything was where it should be. Really, it looked as good as it does when you're there, maybe even better."

"So what did Joshua say about Mary?"

"He didn't say anything. We got to talking about my divorce, and I sort of forgot about everything else."

"You talked to Joshua about your divorce?"

"Sure, why not? He asked me about my family, and when I said I had kids he asked about my husband...one thing led to another. He's so easy to talk to Beata, I just spilled my guts to him. He's warm and sympathetic. I like him."

"Gladys, I'm really nervous about Mary being in the house. She's a drug addict."

"Well, I didn't see any evidence she'd been using drugs in your house. There weren't any needles or bags or anything strange sitting around. Besides, I can't believe Joshua would let her use drugs in your house."

"I guess not," Beata conceded. "I don't guess he would. He's nice and everything, but he doesn't seem like the pushover type."

"No, he doesn't," Gladys agreed. "So stop worrying. Everything's fine over there. How are your parents?"

"They're pretty much the same as usual. My mom is starting to heal; her ribs don't hurt as badly, and her leg is better also. The doctor gave her a walking cast because he says she should start bearing some weight on it to strengthen the bones. I think I'll be able to come home in a few days."

Although she'd told Gladys she was sure Joshua wouldn't let Mary run wild in the house, she was still nervous, and she decided she'd call him to check up herself. Not that she could do much checking from 2,500 miles away, but talking to him might make her feel better. She hung up on Gladys and dialed her own number. The phone rang several times and forwarded to the machine.

"Joshua!" she said. "Pick up! It's Beata!"

Suddenly, the answering machine clicked off.

"Hi," said Joshua. "How's your mom?"

"She's a lot better," Beata said. "Thanks. Say, how's everything going there?"

"Everything's fine," he said. We're doing just great here."

"We?"

"Me and Mary and the dogs. I heard from Irene, and she'll be back in town tomorrow, so the dogs won't be with us much longer."

"Irene called? Is she mad?"

"No. She was a little perturbed to hear you'd left town, but when I explained what happened with your mom she was okay with it. Plus, I put Grover and Cleveland on the phone so they could tell her how they were doing."

"She talked to Grover and Cleveland on the phone?"

"Right. She said she could tell they were happy and had been eating well."

"But....they didn't actually *say* anything, did they?"

He chuckled. "Not a whole lot, but it was enough for her."

"So I understand from Gladys that Mary is staying there."

"Yes, that's right."

"Joshua, I'm a little concerned about that. Mary is... well, she doesn't seem terribly stable."

"Not stable? Oh, you mean because of her drug problem?"

"Yes. Her drug problem. I really don't want people using drugs in my house. Or buying drugs and bringing them to my house."

"Don't worry about that," Joshua reassured her. "That's not going to happen. There've been no drugs in your house, and Mary's not using. She has a place lined up; she just needed somewhere to stay for a few days until that came through. It's been pretty rainy and cold here. It wasn't good for her to stay outside. Plus, she gets along really well with the dogs; they love her. She walks them twice a day and fusses over them just like Irene. Believe me, they've been good for each other."

"I'm glad to hear that, but I wish you had asked me."

"I knew you'd want to do the right thing," Joshua said.

At that, Beata felt hamstrung. Was she going to say no, she did *not* want to do the right thing? Or that sheltering a homeless woman was not the right thing to do even though she had apparently suffered no ill consequences from it? That she didn't want to help not because Mary had done something wrong but because Beata was nervous that she *might* have? That her own fear was more important than Mary's safety and well-being?

"You should have asked first," she insisted stubbornly. This was tantamount to saying 'it's not what you did that I'm upset about; it's the way you did it', which was a flat-out lie. She *was* upset about what he had done. She didn't like Mary. She didn't want Mary in her house.

Joshua was silent for several moments. She had the uncomfortable feeling he was digesting her statement and perceiving the falsity at its heart. Finally, he said firmly, "She needed your help." His tone was uncompromising. She was obligated to help a person in need. Her feelings about it were irrelevant.

"I'm coming home in a few days," she said. "I would like her out of the house before I get back."

"That shouldn't be a problem," Joshua said.

* * *

Beata flew back to Seattle a few days later. She arrived late and drove home, unsure what to expect when she arrived. The house was dark, but the back porch light was on as if to welcome her home. She intended to sneak in

143

quietly, but smacked her huge suitcase into the door frame with a resounding thump as she tried to jockey both it and herself through the door. A few seconds later, Joshua came out of the spare room, which also served as an office, looking rumpled as if he'd just emerged from bed.

"Um, hi," Beata said. "I didn't intend to wake you up."

"Welcome back," he said.

Beata peered cautiously at the dark hallway. "Mary's not still here, is she?"

"No," Joshua said. "She left a couple days ago."

"How's she doing in her new place?"

"Very well."

"I'm beat," she yawned. "I'm going straight to bed. I'll talk to you tomorrow morning."

The next day, she awoke early, being jet-lagged, and instantly smelled fresh coffee brewing. She stumbled into the kitchen and found Joshua competently manning the espresso machine.

"Latte?" he asked, handing her a steaming cup and turning to clean the steaming wand.

"Thanks," she said. "What's for breakfast?"

"Eggs and toast," he replied, bustling over to the stove.

"I was joking," she protested. But he'd apparently started cooking shortly before she awoke, because the eggs were just reaching perfection, and a plate of generously buttered toast sat on the counter. "Wow! Good service."

"I'm glad you're happy," he said. He carried two plates to the table, and they shared a quiet breakfast together.

"What are your plans for today?" he asked as he gathered up the plates and started the hot water running in the sink.

"Besides work, you mean? I have to check in with Irene and Gladys. What are you doing?"

"I have a number of friends to look in on," he said.

Beata felt she should make an appearance at the office, so she caught the bus downtown. From there, she called Irene and Gladys. Irene sounded surprisingly mellow, having nothing to say about Beata's desertion of her beloved animals, and even asking after her parents with seemingly genuine concern. Gladys, also, seemed relaxed and happy, and was bubbling over with big news.

"Beata, you aren't going to believe this," she breathed ecstatically into the phone. "I think I've met someone."

"You *think* you've met someone?" Beata asked. "How can you not know if you've met someone or not?"

"I know I've met someone," Gladys amended. "But I *think* he's someone special. Beata, it's just like those readers at the psychic fair predicted. They said I was going to meet someone, and I did."

"Oh Gladdie…really?" Beata felt a chasm opening in the pit of her stomach. She hadn't realized how much she relied on Gladys, how implicitly she'd assumed Gladys would always be there just the same way she'd been for the last 12 years. She wasn't sure she wanted to share Gladys with anyone else.

"Yes! Isn't that fantastic?"

Beata summoned up her game face and responded brightly, "Yes, wonderful! Tell me about him."

"I can't right now; I'm getting ready to go to lunch with him. His name is Stan."

"Stan." Beata said. "Well, I'm looking forward to hearing all about it. When can we get together?"

"I'll get back to you," Gladys promised, and she was gone.

Beata returned to work, but all the joy had been sucked out of the day. She had trouble concentrating. Who was this Stan character, she wondered. Who was she going to talk to if Gladys was always running off to be with Stan? She knew she was being selfish. Gladys had been longing for a relationship ever since her husband had summarily dumped her. Was she supposed to be contented with a platonic female friend just because it suited Beata's convenience?

"Not everyone is like you, you know," scolded herself, feeling forlorn and also somewhat victimized. This unanticipated shift in her life's infrastructure unsettled her, and as the day went on, she began, unreasonably, to resent it. When she returned home to find Joshua in the kitchen (almost as if he owned the place, she grumbled to herself), her sense of ill-usage increased.

"Still here?" she inquired. Contrary to her hope, he didn't look the slightest bit uncomfortable.

"Bad day?" he responded, stirring away at a bubbling pot emitting warm aromas of meat and spices.

"You might say that," she said, dumping her bag in the spotlessly neat dining room (had he polished the floor? It glowed like a loaf of new bread coated with egg wash).

"What happened?"

She hadn't planned to confide her problems to him. She preferred to keep her less admirable feelings to herself. But as he stood there, penetrating her self-pity with a kindly inquiring gaze, words began flooding from her mouth. She told him about her resentment that an interloper had pushed her off the top spot on Gladys' priority list. Then she admitted her fear that, without Gladys, she'd die lonely and bereft, that no one cared for her except Gladys and now Gladys didn't care, either. She was ashamed of her own feelings, she whined, of her inability to be happy for her friend. Finally, she put the finishing touch on her humiliation by bursting into tears. She ran into the bathroom, expecting him to follow. He didn't. He simply returned to stirring the pot.

A few minutes later, he called that dinner was ready. Beata emerged from the bathroom red-eyed and drippy-nosed. Her shame had morphed into anger, and she silently dared him to presume to say anything further about Gladys, but he didn't do that, either. He dished out some stew for each of them and sat silently at the table while they ate. His calm good humor seemed to suck all her hysteria into a bottomless void of peace. The longer they sat without talking, the better she felt. Her mind seemed to have stopped functioning; she tried to grapple with her feelings but couldn't summon the energy, so she let them drop and concentrated on the flavor of the stew.

"This is good," she finally managed to say. "Thanks."

"My pleasure," he responded. "By the way, I think you have some phone messages."

When dinner was over, she checked the machine. Indeed, she did have some phone messages: 8 of them, all from Frank.

"Oh *NO!*" she wailed. "I left without telling him I was going! I was supposed to meet him downtown the Saturday after I left, and I didn't show up! He must think I stood him up!" Quickly, she dialed his number. Apparently her name had come up on his Caller ID because his voice was as frosty as the North Pole when he picked up the phone.

"Yeah," he said.

"Hi! Frank! It's me, Beata. Listen, I'm so sorry I left you hanging on Saturday. I actually flew out of town the night we talked on a family emergency and I just got back yesterday. I was so caught up with making travel arrangements and all that I completely forgot about our date."

"Uh huh," he said.

"See, I had Irene's dogs, and I couldn't get anyone to watch them," she babbled. "I had to leave right away. My mom broke her leg. My folks called right after we made our date. Irene had already left the dogs with me and the service didn't want to watch them without talking to her, and plus I had to book plane tickets for the next morning…I was so frantic that I simply forgot we had planned to meet. Look, I'm really sorry. I should have called but it slipped my mind." This was getting repetitive, she realized, and it wasn't working. Frank wasn't thawing out.

"So what d'you say? Can we get together and at least talk about it?" What was she doing? Before she'd left for Virginia, she'd been wracking her brain for a way to get rid of Frank, and now she was falling all over herself to erase the bad impression she'd left on him. She'd given in to panic.

Frank seemed to be turning her proposal over in his mind. Finally, after an eternal pause, he agreed. "Okay," he said. "I'll come by tomorrow night." Beata heaved a sigh of relief as she hung up the phone -- great. She'd won. And her prize was…a date with a man she didn't want to see.

The next evening, when Frank pulled up in front of the house, Beata was in her room fishing under the bed for her flip-flops, which had migrated to the darkest, most remote corner of the room. She was lying on her belly wriggling like a caterpillar, trying to wedge herself into the space under the bed, a more demanding task than it would have been several years ago when she was 10 pounds skinnier. She didn't hear him knock, but as she emerged from under the bed, clutching the flip-flops and picking a dust bunny out of her hair, she heard the door creak open and Joshua say "Yes? Can I help you?"

She hurried out into the hallway and saw Frank standing on the porch, glaring at Joshua.

"Hi, Frank," she called, waving the flip-flops. "Come on in. I was just fetching my shoes from under the bed. This is my friend Joshua. He stayed here to look after Irene's dogs while I was away."

"Come in," echoed Joshua, opening the door wider.

Frank stood rocking back and forth on his feet as if nailed to the porch. He looked from Joshua to Beata and back to Joshua. His face reddened. Then, without saying a word, he turned and stomped back down the walk toward the street. He paused to rip open the gate, then slammed it behind himself as he stalked to his truck.

"Frank!" Beata called, coming over to the door to stand behind Joshua. "Wait! Stop! You don't understand!" But Frank ignored her, climbed into his truck and roared off into the night.

"I think he's mad," Beata said.

"It looks that way."

"Thanks to you," she said.

"Oh, are you upset about it?"

Beata was about to say that of course she was upset about it, and who did Joshua think he was to take up residence in her house and run off her friends as if he owned the place, when he turned and fixed her with a look that froze the lies on her lips. Somehow, there was no room for game-playing around Joshua.

"Not really," she said. "To be honest, I couldn't figure out how to get rid of him."

"Get rid of him?" he echoed, and Beata suddenly felt ashamed. She had no more consideration for Frank, she realized, than a worn-out pair of shoes…he was an inconvenience to be 'gotten rid of' like yesterday's leftovers.

"I guess that sounds mean," she said, turning and walking away from the door. "For whatever reason, I can't seem to value him like I should."

"Maybe that's because you don't respect him," Joshua said.

"I do too," she argued, "I respect him. He's a decent guy. He works hard. He's capable. He can build things. Just because I don't want to date him doesn't mean I don't respect him."

She kept on going, through the living room, and shut herself into the bedroom. She didn't want to hear any more uncomfortable truths from Joshua about Frank. Unfortunately, she realized, he was right; she *didn't* respect Frank. She tried to sugar-coat it by calling him a 'nice man' and a 'decent guy' and pretending she wanted to like him but inexplicably couldn't. But the fact was, she didn't particularly care about Frank. She didn't care what he thought about at night, alone in the dark. She didn't care how his mind worked. She didn't care about his private pain, or angst, or his private happiness, for that matter. She was perfectly willing to write him off without a second thought, as long as she could do it without looking like the bad guy.

"How did I get to be such a jerk?" she asked herself. She mentally added this flaw to a long list of character defects that she told over in her mind like toxic Rosary beads whenever she decided to focus on self-improvement. Enumerating all the faults she would fix if she were a decent human being was a common pastime of Beata's, and she hoped that one day her self-flagellation would pay off in substantive change.

She threw herself down on the bed, morosely contemplating her manifold evils. Then, she flipped over to retrieve the phone and dialed Gladys' number. The phone rang six times before Gladys picked up.

"Hello?"

"Gladdie, it's me."

"Hi Bea. What's up?"

"Can you talk?" Beata heard scuffling sounds, then Gladys giggled.

"Stop it!" she squealed.

"Stop what?" said Beata.

"Not you, Stan. Cut it out!" There was more scuffling and more giggling. Gladys dropped the phone and now Beata could hear thumping and laughing. Finally, Gladys came back on. "Sorry. What did you want to talk about?"

"I wanted to talk about Frank. Can you give me a few minutes?"

"Sure." Gladys muffled the phone against her chest and hollered instructions to Stan on how to find something in the kitchen. "Sorry, we're making dinner here."

"Gladys, I really need to talk to you," Beata said, feeling at once resentful and forlorn. Where was her best friend?

"Okay, okay, sorry," Gladys said. "Let me go into the bathroom." Beata heard a door close. "Now what is it?"

"Frank just came over and found Joshua here. He ran off in a snit and I think he's dumping me."

"Is that a bad thing?" Gladys asked. "I thought you wanted him to dump you."

"I did, but now I'm worried it was a bad idea."

"You're over-thinking this," Gladys said. "The whole time you were seeing him you wanted him to go away, and now, he's gone away."

"I guess," Beata said. At that moment, she heard someone knocking on Gladys' bathroom door. A male voice said "Help! The potatoes are burning!"

"I gotta go," Gladys said. "I'll talk to you about this later."

"Like when?" Beata asked.

"I was thinking of having you over to meet Stan this weekend."

Beata tried to muster some enthusiasm for this idea. "Oh....great. Okay. When?"

"Saturday, sixish? We can have a glass of wine and a chat."

A glass of wine and a chat? Beata and Gladys never had a glass of wine and a chat. They went out for tacos and slugged down beer. They didn't chat; they discussed, dissected, debated and hammered out. Beata felt she'd lost her moorings. Gladys was becoming a new person, part of a crowd that chatted and sipped and acted refined, and Beata was still an old cow in a holey tent dress.

* * *

She was slightly comforted, upon arriving at Gladys' house, to see that Gladys had not completely gone over to the lite side. She was swathed from head to toe in a shiny pink pantsuit, and her hair stood up from her head like a snowy paintbrush dipped in pink ink. She looked like a troll doll. Stan stood behind her with one hand clamped fondly on either side of her ample waist. He had coarse salt-and-pepper hair cut raggedly short, and wore wire-rim glasses. Behind the glasses, his dark eyes looked mischievous.

As Beata jumped out of the car, Gladys started waving madly. "Bea! Bea! Hi!" she hollered. "Come on in!"

Beata came on in, accidentally jostling the two lovers at the door because they could not detach themselves from each other to make room for her to enter. As a unit, Stan and Gladys migrated into the kitchen, where Gladys fetched three wineglasses and a bottle. She brought these into the living room. Stan, still glued to her waist, followed along behind her like a trailer. Beata wondered if he expected Gladys to sit on him, but when they reached the sofa, he detached one hand from her waist and slid to the side, still connected by one arm.

"So," he said heartily, "this is the famous Beata."

"Or the infamous Beata," Beata said. "Ha ha."

"Heh heh," Stan chuckled. "Good one."

Gladys busied herself pouring a generous glass of wine for each of them, then put down the bottle and popped up off the couch. "I'll formally introduce you two," she announced. "Stan, this is Beata, my best friend. Beata, this is Stan, the love of my life." She plopped back down into Stan's embrace and they rubbed noses and giggled at each other.

"Gah!" Beata thought. "This is a nightmare." She plastered a smile on her face and watched them play kissy games until one of them, Beata thought it was Stan, remembered that she existed and broke their eye-lock long enough to say "Now honey, let's not be rude," and wink at Beata.

Beata exposed her teeth in what she hoped was a reasonable facsimile of an indulgent smile. "Oh, don't mind me," she said. It was clear they wouldn't, so Beata finally launched into a conversational topic that she hoped would keep them from dissolving into puddles of hormone-rich goo.

"So, tell me how you met," she demanded.

"It was at the self-service car wash," Gladys said while gazing soulfully into Stan's eyes. "I was trying to make the wash wand work and I couldn't get any soap to come out. I kept putting in money and it kept coming out plain water. So Stan was in the bay right next to mine, and he came to my rescue."

"Really?" Beata said. "How did he fix it?"

"He didn't," Gladys said. "He took my car over to his bay and washed it with a different wand."

"Oh, that's....that was really sweet," Beata said

At this, Gladys actually looked Beata in the face, joy radiating from every pore. "Wasn't it?" She turned back to Stan again. "You are just sooooo sweet," she cooed.

"I *am* sweet," he agreed smugly.

Beata rolled her eyes. "We're all sweet," she said.

"Let's have some more wine," Gladys suggested.

"We aren't done with the wine we have," Beata pointed out, but Gladys sloshed more into each glass.

"What happened after the car wash?" she asked.

Stan now took up the narrative. "She looked so helpless," he explained. "I could tell she needed someone to look after her. I'm widowed for seven years, so I know what it's like. There was just some chemistry between the two of us. She bowled me right over. I knew right then and there she was the woman for me..." he squeezed her waist again. "So I asked her out for dinner. And the rest is history."

"You're widowed? And you've been single for seven years?"

"Not exactly single," he said. "I'm a sociable guy, I've had girlfriends here and there. But nothing serious. Not like this."

For an hour or so, Beata bided her time while Stan and Gladys cuddled and complimented each other and waxed sentimental about their newfound love. At last, she got the break she was waiting for: Gladys had to go to the bathroom. Despite Beata's fear that Stan would follow her even in there, the event did produce a temporary separation of the StanGladys unit, which Beata immediately took advantage of to yank Stan into the kitchen by one arm.

"What's the deal with the girlfriends," she hissed. "You better be on the level, buddy."

"What?" he protested. "Are you suggesting I'm not serious about your friend?"

"I'm not suggesting; I'm asking. Are you serious about my friend?"

"Serious as a heart attack," he promised solemnly, placing one hand upon his chest.

"Well you'd better be," Beata said pugnaciously. "Because if you screw her over, I will gouge your eyeballs out with a rusty spoon handle and mail them to the organ bank."

"Ugh," he said, pulling away from her in distaste. "That's sickening. What's wrong with you?"

"Nothing," she said. "I am a perfectly normal psychopath. So don't mess with me, and don't mess with my friend."

"I don't get how a sweet little woman like Gladys could be friends with *you*," he said. "What are you, a lesbian?"

"Oh wow…that's enlightened," Beata said. "You're being mean to me, you must be a lesbian? Is that the only possible explanation for not liking people who mistreat my best friend?"

"Hey, what's going on in there?" Gladys called, emerging from the bathroom. "What are you guys doing in the kitchen?"

"Sipping wine and having a friendly chat," Beata said. "We're discussing Stan's ocular health."

Stan hurried back to Gladys' tender embrace. "She was threatening me, honey," he said, dropping a kiss on her upturned lips. "I think your friend here is a little butch."

Gladys looked at him blankly for a second or two, then burst out laughing. "Butch? Beata? Don't be ridiculous. Beata is philosophically opposed to *all* sexual relationships regardless of gender."

Beata could've kissed Gladys herself, if she could've gotten around Stan. For a fleeting second, her old friend was back. Stan looked a little huffy, and Gladys was quick to soothe him. "Don't you worry about Beata, honey," she cooed. "That's just her way. She doesn't mean anything by it, do you Bea?"

"No," Beata sighed, "I don't mean anything by it."

"See," Gladys said, "I told you she didn't. Now I want you two to like each other because I love both of you."

Stan's responding glare said that he had no intention of liking Beata either now or when hell froze over. Beata regretted taking him on; she knew it was futile. Gladys loved him, and that gave him the upper hand. She would only cut herself off from Gladys by antagonizing him. Unfortunately, it didn't look like she would be able to insinuate herself back into his good graces. She considered throwing herself on his mercy, playing the weepy female card, sucking up and pretending she had been overcome with jealousy (or was it pretending?). She blinked a couple of times trying to summon up some tears.

"Stan," she began in a chastened voice, "I don't know what came over me. I truly, truly apologize for my outrageous behavior." Stan's glance was frigid. She was going to have to try harder. "Honest, Stan," she wheedled. "It was just such a shock to me to see you two so happy, so perfect for each other. Gladdie and I have been best friends for 12 years and I got used to having her all to myself. You know how wonderful she is. And I never thought she would meet anyone as fantastic as you. I thought things between me and her would just go on the same way forever. So when I saw you and I saw how happy you guys are together, I got jealous. I got scared. I know it was wrong. Please forgive me?"

Stan looked uncertain. These changes were going a little too fast for him. Beata managed to squeeze out a tear, and he started to thaw. Maybe she was a normal woman after all. He offered his hand. "Okay," he said gruffly, "We can start again."

"Thanks, Stan. You're a prince."

"No," said Gladys, "he's my knight in shining armor."

"Knight in shining Armor-All" thought Beata, and then mentally kicked herself.

***

156

When she got back to the house, Joshua was out. She'd gotten so used to him fixing dinner every night that she was a little put out that he was gone. She'd just have to do it herself. Although she was feeling a little woozy from the wine she'd consumed at Gladys' house, she figured she might as well have a little more…in for a penny, in for a pound, and opened up a bottle. By the time Joshua returned, she was two glasses into it. Her tolerance for alcohol wasn't high, and she was feeling pretty drunk.

He appeared at the front door (funny how he always used the front door while Beata always used the back) as she was weaving through the dining room setting out plates and napkins.

"Hello," he said from the living room. "I brought company."

"Company?"

Beata steadied herself against the table and tried to focus on the individual standing in the shadows behind Joshua.

"Yes, this is a special friend of mine. His name is Clayton." Joshua stepped back and dragged Clayton forward by the arm.

"Why are all your friends bums and drug addicts?" Beata asked. Her nerves had been frayed by the confrontation with Stan, and that, in combination with the wine, had stripped away any veneer of social grace that might otherwise have moderated her tongue.

Indeed, Clayton appeared to be a bum. His eyes were bleary and his flesh sagged from his bones like melting wax. He was gray and unhealthy looking, not thin, but scrawny and edematous as if he got plenty to eat but none of it was any good. His teeth were rotted and his shoes cracked and pocked with holes. He shuffled these uncomfortably against the polished floor as he stared around the room, everywhere but at Beata, and worked his mouth soundlessly.

"Oh good, you've got dinner on," Joshua continued, ignoring Beata's question. "Set a place for Clayton."

"We're having pork chops," Beata announced. "There isn't enough to go around." This was a lie. There were six pork chops under the broiler; Beata had fixed the whole package without even knowing why.

"Really," Joshua said mildly. His raised eyebrows told Beata that he knew perfectly well there was no shortage of food. "He can have my share."

Beata stomped back into the kitchen, but her histrionic portrayal of an outraged victim was ruined when she reeled drunkenly into the door frame and bounced off with a skull-cracking thud. It was difficult to act holier-than-thou when you were too inebriated to walk straight. She propped herself up on the counter and tried to clear the stars from her eyes. She realized she ought to pull herself together and act civilized; there was nothing to be gained by being rude. Clayton looked like he'd been the brunt of enough rudeness so that a little bit more from her was unlikely to dissuade him from taking advantage of a free meal.

Sure enough, when she brought the food to the table, he began shoveling it in like a starving animal, taking seconds and thirds. They'd run out of pork chops by then, but he vacuumed up the remaining mashed potatoes and string beans, and probably would have devoured the plates and silverware if Beata hadn't snatched them off the table. The bottle of wine she left in the kitchen, sneaking a swig every now and then when she had to retrieve the salt or butter or Worcestershire sauce, which Clayton poured on everything in a vinegary flood. Joshua and Beata said little, and Clayton even less. By the end of dinner, all she knew about him was that he had a good appetite, and that even without some of his teeth he could sure get through a pork chop.

"I'm glad you could come, Clayton," Joshua said while Beata was rescuing the dinnerware. "I get worried about you out on the street."

"Yeah, well...there's not too many places to get a good meal." He turned to Beata. "I don't s'pose ya got any booze?" he said.

"No," Beata lied firmly.

He seemed resigned. "Kay," he said, and rose from the table. "Thanks for the food."

He made his way to the door and banged out if it without further comment. Joshua sat serenely at the table, looking as delighted as if he'd just finished presiding over an intimate dinner party between bosom friends. Beata turned on him furiously.

"Who was that?" she demanded. "Where do you get off inviting drunks over for dinner at MY house?"

"*You're* drunk," he pointed out.

"But I'm not a wino. I'm a responsible working person. *I* pay the rent here. It's my house and I say who comes over for dinner. Oh, and by the way, it's my food, too."

"Oh, is it really?" he said. His tone was completely devoid sarcasm or blame; he spoke like he was stating an obvious fact. He observed her calmly, inviting her to see his perspective. What was he thinking, Beata wondered. How could he not see that he was acting outrageously? How many people would consent to have a stranger move into their house and bring seedy friends to eat there and even stay there without permission? But he did *not* see it. He seemed to be operating under a foreign paradigm where he was in charge of everything and everyone.

"I want you out of here," she said.

"You do?"

She wanted to reply with firm assurance, to say "of course, instantly", but the words stuck in her mouth. Did she want him out? She actually liked having him around, and she wasn't sure why. His peaceful demeanor seemed to be contagious. He made big, dramatic things seem like they were no big deal. He was comforting to be around, she realized, despite his odd ways. She wanted him to stay, but on *her* terms, the comfort and peace without any weird friends or high-handed behavior.

She tried to salvage a partial victory. "Can't you at least let me know before you bring people over?"

Joshua considered this. "No," he said finally. "That may not be possible."

"Why not? You said Clayton was a special friend of yours. Didn't you know you were going to bring him home?"

"Not exactly," he said. "I went looking for him, but I wasn't sure I'd find him. I wasn't sure he'd come, either. You know how it is. Sometimes it's hard to get people to let you love them."

Love? Love? What was all this about love? She took his words personally, as she took everything personally. But hadn't he intended her to take them personally? She opened her mouth to demand what he meant, but couldn't force the words out.

It appeared she was going to have to take Joshua as he was or not at all. She turned away wordlessly and walked toward her room. She wasn't going to say 'okay, I give up; you can stay. Bring over whoever you want.' If he thought she was still kicking him out, well, she would live with it. She wasn't going to completely cave; she had her pride.

"How did you like Stan?" Joshua called after her.

"He's a jerk," she said. "I can't imagine what Gladys sees in him." And she shut the door.

160

Stan didn't grow on her as the weeks went by, and neither did Beata grow on him. They maintained a watchful truce that threatened to burst into full, martial flower at any moment. Gladys sat in the middle, blissfully (and, Beata thought, willfully) oblivious to their veiled hostility. Perhaps she enjoyed their covert competition. Stan was over at her house almost every night, while Beata only appeared a couple of times a week. She felt herself constantly losing ground, missing the inside jokes, being condescended to like a half-witted relative at the reunion of a close-knit family of geniuses. Stan took obvious satisfaction from this situation and made no effort to include her. Beata had more and more trouble getting a lunch alone with her. Each time she called Gladys had 'previous plans' with Stan. The invitations began to subside, and finally trickled down to once every week and a half or so…no more often than she saw Daphne.

Daphne kept the usual contact, but it wasn't the same as seeing Gladys. Daphne eyed her askance, as if she expected her to rip off all her clothes and do handsprings around the town square. Beata felt that she *would* rip off all her clothes and do nude handsprings, but she was too embarrassed by her fifty-plus-year-old flab. Still, the idea held appeal for her. It nicely expressed her inner recklessness, along with an in-your-face, dare-you-to-object assertiveness that Beata wished, rather than believed, she possessed.

Daphne did not understand Beata's desire to compete with Stan over Gladys. As far as Daphne was concerned, Gladys was doing the natural, expected thing, and Beata, instead of whining about it, ought to go find herself a man, too.

Furthermore, she didn't approve of Joshua's peculiar status in Beata's life. What was he doing in her house, she wondered, if he wasn't working and pulling his weight? And what were they doing living together if they weren't "living together"? Joshua represented the thing most intolerable to Daphne, a piece that didn't fit into the puzzle. She'd met Joshua. Beata didn't hide him, and no one who came to her house could avoid him because he always stood at the center of anyplace he was, a natural focal point.

"I don't get that guy," Daphne complained to Beata. "He gives me the creeps."

"Why?" Beata asked. "He's not creepy at all."

"I know," Daphne replied. "He *isn't* creepy. But he doesn't make any sense. What does he do all day? Where did he come from? How can you feel safe around him when you don't know anything about him except that he has creepy friends?"

Beata, who had asked herself these questions numerous times, perversely rushed to his defense. "How do I know I'm safe with Sean, or Stan, or even Gladys for that matter? You could say that about anyone. I know Joshua. I've lived with him for weeks now."

"Well," said Daphne, "just don't complain to me when you come home to find he and his sleazy friends have robbed you of everything you own and taken off into the night to prey on some other gullible old woman."

Great, thought Beata. That's how my daughter sees me: old and gullible. She and Joshua didn't hang around with each other. They co-habited the same space, which meant that most days Beata sat at home working while Joshua wandered around town doing whatever it was he did all day, coming home in time to cook and clean up dinner and hear about Beata's day.

Beata never asked where he'd been and he volunteered nothing. She was content to lean on him while pretending he was expendable. She supposed people assumed they were romantically involved. Certainly Irene, who had started coming over looking for him every few days, spoke of him as if he were a semi-permanent fixture in her life. She acceded to this while privately maintaining distance between them, not wanting any entanglements.

162

Joshua never offered her money. He didn't help with the rent and he didn't buy any groceries, yet her food bill wasn't any higher, either. He seemed to stretch the money that had once fed her, alone, to cover them both without changing what they ate. He continued to bring people home for meals, too, always introducing them as "a special friend," but rarely bringing the same person twice. All of them looked grim and battered like life had chewed them up and spit them back out. Most of them didn't seem to know him at all; it was as if he banged into them on the street and immediately invited them over for dinner.

It was odd, therefore, when one Saturday morning he announced that he was going out, and asked Beata to come along.

"Where are you going?" she asked. "I was planning to do some housework." Beata was always planning to do housework but never following through, so she couldn't blame him for the skeptical look he gave her in response. Beata looked yearningly at the book she'd left open on the couch the preceding night.

"We're helping Mary move," he said. "We need the car."

That sounded about as fun as impaling herself on a rusty spike, but as usual, when Joshua said something had to be done, she complied. She drove him across the freeway to a seedy neighborhood south of Capitol Hill where decrepit tenements were planted cheek-by-jowl with liquor stores and all-night groceries with bars on the windows. They stopped in front of a three-story brick apartment building with several windows broken and patched with plywood.

The building's stairway was dark and smelled of urine. Beata was relieved not to see any active puddles on the black-painted wooden treads. They climbed two flights and then navigated a narrow, grungy hallway. They stopped before a door in the middle of the hall. Beata wondered how Joshua knew it was Mary's, for the numbers were off of it and most of the other doors, too. He knocked. The echoes thundered in the bare hall. They waited. He knocked again. They waited some more.

"I know you're in there, so open up," Joshua demanded, this time pounding on the door so hard it rattled in its frame. "We're not going away until you open the door." He pounded again, and this time kept pounding. A couple of doors up and down the hall cracked open to see who was causing all the ruckus. Beata wondered how long the door could withstand his assault, and feared the police would swoop in any moment and arrest them for disturbing the peace. Just as she was concluding that no one was home and getting ready to make a run for the car, the door opened a fraction of an inch. A noisome odor of mildew, solvent and stale food emerged.

"Who is it?" demanded a male voice. "Shut up. We don't want to be bothered."

"It's Joshua," said Joshua. "We're here to help Mary move."

"Move?" the voice said suspiciously, "Who said she was moving?"

"She did," Joshua replied, "so we're going to help her."

"She doesn't want to move today." The man slammed the door, and Beata heard a bolt click shut. "That's the end of that," she thought. "I guess I'll be reading that book after all."

But she reckoned without Joshua's quiet persistence. He reached for the doorknob and turned it. Apparently the bolt was malfunctioning, because the door fell right open as if unlocked. The man who had shut it was still standing in the front room. He was shirtless, and his worn jeans hung precariously from thin hips. An elastic underwear band and an inch of gray briefs showed above them. At the sound of the opening door, he whirled around.

"What the hell..." he said. "I locked that door."

"We're helping Mary move today," Joshua repeated. "Where is she?"

Beata looked around the room. She saw a few pieces of dilapidated furniture, the upholstered ones torn and the rest pocked with burn marks and scratches. A glass-topped coffee table stood in the center of the mess, and on it were some twisted bits of scorched foil, a handful of matchbooks, two ashtrays overflowing with cigarette butts, a jar one-third full of some clear liquid and a hypodermic needle. The floor nearby was littered with dirty dishes, empty food containers and assorted pieces of dirty fabric that might have been clothing, pillowcases or dishtowels, it was hard to say which.

The thin man shifted nervously. "Mary changed her mind," he said. "She's not moving. Besides, she's sleeping. You can't see her."

Joshua calmly surveyed the chaos. He moved to a closed door coming off the front room and applied his knuckles (which, Beata thought, must be made of iron) to it. "Mary, we're here," he called. "Get up. It's moving day." There was no response.

Joshua pushed the door open and stepped back. In the gloom created by windows half covered with tattered sheets pinned to the window frames Beata glimpsed a still form sprawled on its back across a mattress that sat directly on the floor. The thin man moved quickly to stand between the door and bed. He spread his arms slightly out from his sides, trying to block their view.

"She's sleeping," he insisted. His eyes darted toward the bed and then back to Joshua. Tiny beads of perspiration collected around his greasy hairline. Mary, if that was indeed who the form on the bed was, lay with unearthly stillness. One arm flopped half off the mattress. Her eyes might have been half open. Not a flicker of the eyelids nor the slightest rising of breath stirred beneath the dirty blankets which covered her.

"Go away," the man said. "She doesn't want to talk to you."

"She can tell me that herself," Joshua said. He moved further into the room. "Mary!" he called loudly. "It's Joshua!" The form on the bed didn't respond.

"You better leave or I'm calling the cops," the man said, advancing toward Joshua.

"Are you?" Joshua said, looking at the man. "Go ahead, then. Call them."

The man stopped, not seeming to know what to do next. He had now progressed from nervous to panicky. His eyes darted around the room as if searching desperately for an escape route. Joshua looked him up and down, then walked forward and grasped him by the shoulders.

"Look," he said gently. "There's no need to be afraid. Why don't you just sit down on the sofa and let me help Mary?" He turned, put his arm around the man's shoulder, guided him out of the room and deposited him on the couch.

Then he turned and, standing outside the bedroom, faced the open door and called, "Mary, come out."

So commanding was his voice that Beata's heart leaped in her chest as if it wanted to burst forth from her ribcage and run to Joshua. The figure on the bed sat bolt upright. Her head turned toward the door, eyes open wide.

"Joshua?" said Mary's voice, sounding sleepy and vulnerable, like a child just awakened from a deep sleep.

"Get up, Mary," Joshua said again. Obediently, she threw the blanket off and stood, swaying slightly. He rushed forward to steady her with a gentle arm around her waist.

"It's time to leave," he said. "Let's get your things."

"Where are we going?" she asked.

"Someplace safe," he said. "Let's gather up your things and get going. Look, Beata's here. She brought her car to help you move."

"Beata?" She echoed.

"Hi," Beata said.

Mary turned away without acknowledging her. She looked around the room. "My things? I -- I don't know where they are," she said helplessly.

Joshua dove into the closet and started rooting around. "I'll find them," he said. He pulled out a fleece jacket and a pair of tennis shoes, which he handed to Mary. Then he began to extract boxes and bags. She didn't have much. Within ten minutes, it was all piled in a heap on the bedroom floor. Meanwhile, she had put on the shoes and the jacket, and was beginning to look more like her normal, sullen self.

When she emerged from the bedroom, the man on the couch sat up with his eyes bulging. "Mary!" he gasped. "You're al...you're okay!"

"No thanks to you," she rasped, turning her back on him. He fell back on the couch as if hit by a taser gun, and stared wordlessly at the three of them as they divvied up Mary's few belongings and prepared to carry them down the stairs.

"You two go on ahead," Joshua directed Beata. "I'll be down in a few minutes."

The two women each carried a box down the stairs and stashed it in the trunk of Beata's car, then returned for a second load. They found Joshua sitting on the couch beside the thin man, talking so quietly that Beata couldn't make out his words. The man slumped away, eyes fixed on the floor, giving Joshua a view of the back three-quarters of his head, but nevertheless seemed to be listening intently. When they returned for the third and last load, the man's elbows were on his knees and his head was hanging low between his shoulders. He might have been crying. They loaded the last of the bags into the car and then climbed in and waited. It was a quarter of an hour before Joshua finally came out.

"Got everything?" he asked, climbing into the back seat.

Mary stared out the side window without responding, so Beata said, "I guess so. Where do we go now?"

Joshua guided them across town to a modest bungalow set in an older, working class neighborhood south of the main part of the city. He and Beata left Mary there with two other women who absorbed her into their clan with little fuss. Mary accepted their hospitality with uncharacteristic meekness. All three seemed, without any discussion, to recognize a shared experience that bound them together in fraternal companionship. They respectfully stowed her oddments of camping gear and bedraggled clothing as if cherishing bits of torn plastic, dented pots and cast-off menswear were the most natural thing in the world. When they found she had nothing with which to make a regular bed, they rolled her threadbare sleeping bag out on the mattress without any display of shock or pity and wrapped a throw pillow from the couch in an extra pillow case to place at its head. Joshua hugged her goodbye, and for good measure, hugged the other two women as well, both of whom he seemed to know by name. Then he and Beata drove home.

"Mom," Daphne's voice on the phone was urgent, "I have to talk to you."

"Of course, honey, go ahead. What's wrong?"

"I went to the doctor today," she said. Her voice sounded tense, and Beata's stomach lurched.

"What is it? What's wrong?"

"I have breast cancer, Mom."

Beata's heart froze in her chest. She looked around the room in wonderment. The walls stood; the ceiling was still in place. Outside the window, the sun was still shining and the grass still stood knee-high in the yard. How could everything look so normal when the entire world had just come unmade?

"Breast cancer," she said, forcing the word past the knot in her throat.

"Yes," Daphne said, beginning to cry. "I have to go in for surgery on Thursday. I – I didn't notice. I waited too long." Daphne rattled on and on about tests and stages, but Beata's brain had dissolved into a puddle of molasses. She didn't take it in until she heard Daphne say "50 to 60% survival rate."

Beata leapt immediately to the worst-case scenario. "50%? You have a 50% chance? What about chemo? Radiation? What are they going to do for you?"

"Surgery. I have to have surgery. Then they're going to do chemo and radiation treatments."

"Why didn't you tell me?" Beata shouted.

"Oh Mom…"

Now they were both crying. Beata scolded herself savagely; she had to pull herself together.

"I'm coming over," she said. "I'm coming right now."

"No, Mom, please don't come," Daphne sobbed. "I can't deal with it right now. I need some space."

"But Daphne," she pleaded, "I *have* to come. Please don't push me away. I want to help."

"Fine," said Daphne, "you can help. But don't come over right now."

Beata leaned against the wall and wept. What had she done to make her own daughter see her as a burden instead of a support, she wondered. Was she so weak, so useless, that Daphne would rather face this alone than have her mother hanging around her neck like a millstone? Whatever Daphne's reasons, she wouldn't compound them by pushing herself in where she wasn't wanted. She swallowed her pain and forced herself to speak matter-of-factly.

"Honey, I only want to do what you want me to do. How can I help?"

"Come to the hospital with me on Thursday. Sean has to work. He can't take me."

Beata bit back a caustic remark – how could Sean be busy working when his fiancée was fighting for her life? "I'll be there," Beata promised. "I'll pick you up."

"Good," Daphne said. "I'll see you at 6:30."

***

Beata was there at 6:00; too nervous to sleep. The last few days, she'd struggled unsuccessfully to focus on work. She measured the significance of each moment against the unthinkable thought: what will this mean if I lose my daughter?

Against this possibility, all her former problems faded to background noise. Her relationship with Glan/Stanys (Stan and Gladys had now morphed into some sort of unitary entity), formerly food for endless worry, had ceased to occupy her mind. She'd told Gladys about Daphne, of course, but flatly rejected her syrupy expressions of sympathy. How could she, adrift in a sea of euphoria over her blossoming romance, sympathize with Beata's ugly despair? Even the pretense, although well meant, was insulting.

She noticed it hadn't motivated Gladys to detach herself from Stan long enough to come over and

170

commiserate. Even within the space of a phone call, Gladys interrupted herself repeatedly to bring Stan into the loop, fetch his beverages, find his keys, and in other ways reach out to ground herself on him as if to discharge the static electricity that collected when she was unconnected. Beata'd lost all patience with her. If she wanted to float around in a pink fog, fine, but Beata had other things to deal with.

In the vacuum created by Gladys' defection, she'd turned to Joshua for comfort. He'd steadied her. He'd spent hours listening to her fears and self-recriminations. But she felt inconsolable. Daphne's prognosis broke over her like an evil flood that drowned the tiniest glimmers of hope.

"I can't lose my daughter," she sobbed. "I can't bear it."

"Have faith," he said.

"Faith?" she cried. "Faith? People die of cancer every day! Faith isn't going to stave off death."

"I know," he said. "Have it anyway."

"I can't. What's the use? What difference does it make?"

He just sat there, patting her hand or putting his arm around her shoulder, and listened to her rail against fate. Every time she did this, she fell deeper into the hole of her own despair.

She called Daphne every day, offering (or was she begging?) to come over, but Daphne always refused. At the hospital, Beata padded around after her as she went to the check-in desk, the lab, the pre-op waiting area. She hovered anxiously, hopping out of her chair every few seconds to fetch Daphne a magazine or a pen or a glass of water which she wasn't allowed to drink.

Daphne didn't speak much. Whether she was wrestling with her own internal demons or simply focusing on the business at hand, Beata couldn't tell. Even as a young child, Daphne's mind had been foreign territory to her. Neat, antiseptic, dry and orderly…she always had been the opposite of Beata's emotive turmoil. Now that Daphne

171

faced, for the first time, a situation that was beyond the reaches of her determined competence, Beata wondered whether she truly had been as stoic as she'd seemed, or if this had been Daphne's way of protecting herself from an intrusive presence she'd found unsettling.

Daphne brushed aside Beata's fussing as if it were a bothersome insect. "Sit down, Mom," she ordered. "I don't want you bringing me stuff. Just be still."

Beata dropped into her chair obediently and tried to read her magazine, but kept stealing glances at Daphne from the corner of her eye. Was she reading? Or was she pretending to read while secretly fretting? Daphne turned the pages of her magazine and tossed it on the table, then sat staring at the wall. When Beata leapt from her seat to find her another, she glared at her fiercely and commanded her to sit down again.

"Oh, honey, I'm just so nervous," Beata defended herself. "I just wish there was something I could do."

"Mom, this isn't about you," Daphne said coldly. "Don't make me sorry I brought you."

A nurse came to the door. "Daphne, we'll take you now."

And Daphne was gone.

***

Hours later, in Daphne's hospital room, Sean made his belated appearance. He seemed annoyed at finding Beata there and stood clutching a bedraggled bouquet of daisies and carnations, eyeing her with hostility.

"Hey," he said, looking at Beata. "How're you feeling?" Beata realized, after a moment of confusion, that he was talking to Daphne. He wandered over to the window and stared out at the tar and gravel roof of the lower hospital wing spread out below it. He didn't meet Daphne's eyes.

"I'm okay," Daphne replied, reaching out to touch the hem of his jacket. "How was work?"

172

"It was okay. We're pretty busy right now, so I can't take a lot of time off. Your office called, though, to ask how you were doing."

He shifted the bouquet from one hand to another, and, discovering nothing to put it in, deposited it in the sink. He pulled a chair up on the side of the bed opposite to Beata, and sat contemplating Daphne as if she were something he'd never seen before: a cadaver, perhaps, or an obscure piece of farm equipment, something intellectually interesting but not emotionally compelling. Daphne commandeered his hand, which he left lying in hers like a dead fish.

"The surgery went fine, thanks for asking," Beata said. "They think they got all the cancer."

"Mom," Daphne turned to her, "would you please give us a moment here?"

Beata headed for the hall. "And close the door, please, Mom," Daphne called. Beata paced up and down the hall, staring at the closed door each time she passed. After a time, Sean emerged and, without glancing at her, made his way toward the elevator. Beata hurried back into Daphne's room and found her lying rigidly in bed.

"What's up with Sean?" she demanded. "He seems to be acting very strange for a man whose fiancée has a life-threatening illness."

"It's none of your business, Mom," Daphne said. "Sean is having a hard time with my – with my deformity, that's all."

"Your *deformity*. What are you talking about? You lose a breast and you're deformed? What, does he want you to keep the breast and die? Aren't you anything more than a couple of breasts with legs?"

"Shut up, Mom. I don't want to talk about it. He's having a hard time but we're fine; everything's fine."

But everything was not fine. As the weeks passed and Daphne entered chemo, her health deteriorated. Her skin turned pale and friable and there were dark rings around her eyes. Her hair started coming out and she was frequently sick. She wasn't able to work. Meanwhile, Sean stayed away long hours each day, supposedly working, coming home late, reeking of cigarette smoke and alcohol.

"I stopped by for a drink after work," he'd say. "I only stayed for 20 minutes."

His lengthy absences drove Beata crazy. "Come stay with me for a while," she would beg Daphne. "I'll feed you. I'll take care of you. You shouldn't be alone all day."

"I'm fine, Mom," Daphne insisted. "I need to be at home."

"But honey, there's no one taking care of you at home."

Even this oblique criticism of Sean made Daphne angry. "You don't know what you're talking about," she said. "I'm getting along just fine. Stop interfering with my life."

"Honey, I don't interfere. You wouldn't let me interfere even if I wanted to. I'm worried about you. Let me bring you some dinner."

Daphne accepted the dinner, but reluctantly as if worn down by Beata's persistence and too weary to resist. For all Beata knew, Daphne waited until she was gone and threw it all down the garbage disposal. But it was the only thing Daphne would let her do. Sean, when he was around at all, was terse with Beata and kept his distance from Daphne as if he couldn't bear to touch her. Beata would mill around the apartment aimlessly, straightening things that weren't out of place and brushing invisible specks of dust off the furniture until Daphne all but threw her out of the house. Then Beata would return home for another few days until she did it all over again.

It was obvious that Daphne took no comfort in her visits, her dinners, her offers of assistance. But she didn't know what else to do. She slept little, worked less. She was haunted by visions of Daphne lying on her deathbed, Daphne's cold, white body in a coffin, Daphne buried in the ground, consumed by worms. She wept, paced, and made gallons of soup which Daphne and Sean steadfastly rejected. She was afraid to leave the house, afraid Daphne would call when she was out, afraid Daphne would not call but a strange doctor would, with the news of her death. The world collapsed into a tiny box the size of her living room, bedroom and kitchen.

"Where is Sean?" she raged at Daphne over the phone. "What's *he* doing for you?"

"He's at work," Daphne always replied.

"Funny how he has to work twice as much now that you need him than he did when you were well," Beata said. "How are you supposed to manage all day and half the night by yourself? You're sick! You need to rest!"

"Mom, I haven't been to work in weeks. I'm not making any money. Someone has to pay the bills."

"Is that what this's about?" Beata said, "Money? He's treating you like this because you have no money?"

"You're the one who's upsetting me, Mom, not Sean." Daphne broke down in tears and hung up on her.

The good days, Beata realized, were the days that were worst for Daphne, the days she spent retching at the very smell of food and couldn't get out of bed. Then she would call Beata and ask her to come over, and Beata would race to her side. She'd clean the bathroom and help Daphne change into a fresh nightgown, prop her against the pillows and tenderly sponge her exhausted, gray face with lavender-scented water. She felt needed on those days. They were infrequent, though, and usually came to a tense and abrupt end when Sean clattered into the house.

Sean had transformed from a mild young nobody into a pit-bull bristling with resentment over Beata's presence in his territory. When Daphne wept, in a weaker moment, that he had blamed her for the avalanche of medical bills, Beata wrote her a check. Later, Sean handed it back to her, frigidly recommending that she mind her own business and stop interfering in their affairs. Beata couldn't figure out what was wrong with him. Didn't he expect

175

Daphne's own mother to be at her daughter's side during a life-threatening illness?

She begged Gladys to help her understand.

"How old is Sean?" Gladys replied. "Twenty-five? Twenty-six? He's young. This is a huge responsibility for him. Don't be so hard on him." But Beata couldn't help it. He was keeping her from her daughter, who soon would be dead.

So convinced was she that Daphne would die that the news her cancer appeared, after a savage battery of chemo and radiation, to be in remission, came as a shock. She'd spent months preparing for the worst, reliving a thousand times, in her mind's eye, Daphne's last breath, her lifeless body being carried from the bower of death, hearing the weighty strains of Chopin's funeral march as she cast herself over the icy form lying in the casket. She'd kept up this macabre repetition of agony-in-advance as if believing it would somehow blunt the edge of the devastation when the worst actually happened. And now, it appeared it wasn't going to happen, at least not right away.

She should have been relieved. She should have been triumphant. She should have been singing Hallelujah and dancing in the street. Instead, she felt numb and dazed. She kept on replaying the imaginary funeral as if her mind was stuck in that dark groove and refused to accept the reality of a happier alternative. From staying awake multiple hours a night, she fell into twelve-hour marathons of nightly slumber, arising to gulp cold coffee and pretend to read her email before falling on the couch to doze over the most depressing book she could find in her collection. Daphne's remission, far more than her disease, made her feel useless and unwanted.

Daphne was recovering, but she'd had nothing to do with it. Aside from spending a few hours in the hospital and forcing a few home-cooked meals through the front door, she'd done nothing for this, the dearest person in her life. Never before had she so longed to be another person, someone Daphne could rely on. Heretofore, she'd assumed the wrong was on Daphne's side, that Daphne was unnaturally rigid, she needed to loosen up and be more like her mother. Now she wondered…was her fetid, roiling broth of self-contemplation, her endless deconstruction of her own feelings into ever-more-microscopic particles, really as mature and freeing as she'd cracked it up to be? Or was she mired in a pathological obsession with her own inner workings, as Daphne's subtle disapproval always seemed to imply?

She would reform herself, she decided. She would behave like a normal mother and mother-in-law. She would stop over-analyzing everything and start to consider how regular folks would do things. She would take Daphne out for a pedicure and talk about the weather. She would join a Bridge club and invite Irene over for tea. She would stop ranting and raving about Love being a four-letter word.

She felt better having made this decision. An action plan always gave her solid ground to stand on. Now, she could focus on moving forward. This tea thing, for instance – what kind of tea should she buy? Green tea? Black tea? Herb tea? What were the relative merits of loose tea vs. teabags? Maybe she should get a variety of teas.

Sternly, she halted herself. Regular folks did not agonize about tea; they simply bought what was there. She would go to the grocery store and buy the most normal tea on the shelf, and then she would come home and look through the Yellow Pages for a pedicure salon. But first, she called Gladys.

"Gladys, this is Beata. I'm wondering if you would be interested in learning to play Bridge."

"Bridge?"

"Yes," said Beata. "I think it would be a marvelous way to spend my free time."

"Don't you need four people to play Bridge?"

177

"Yes, but I can't play with three other people who already play unless I learn how. How does one go about learning to play Bridge?"

"I have no idea. I don't play Bridge. Buy a book, I guess."

"Well, how would you feel about learning with me?"

"I don't want to play Bridge. I didn't know *you* wanted to play Bridge. When did you get this burning desire to play Bridge?"

"Oh, I've been wanting to play for a long time," Beata lied. "It seems like an interesting game."

"I used to play Pinochle every now and then," said Gladys. "Do you want to learn that?"

"No, I don't think so," said Beata.

"Just as well," said Gladys, "because I don't remember how."

"So how do you feel about the Bridge thing?"

"Beata, I'm really busy these days," Gladys said. "My time is taken up with work and Stan. I don't have time to play Bridge. Sorry."

Okay, she could put off learning Bridge for the time being. Tea and pedicures would make a good start, and she'd work out the rest later. She was searching for her purse when Daphne called to give her the news that Sean had apparently survived the agony of her disfigurement and come to terms with the thought of being forever yoked with the half-woman she had now become.

"We're not going to put it off any longer," Daphne announced. "We're getting married."

Married? Beata thought blankly. Her daughter, who was not, apparently, going to die in the next little while, was getting married? She was having trouble keeping up with all these changes. However, she realized this was a golden opportunity to practice normal motherhood, and she seized it with both hands.

"Oh, Daphne, honey, I'm so happy for you," she said. "What kind of wedding do you want? I can't wait to start planning!"

This was a lie. The thought of feigning interest in the meaningless trivia of decorations and party dresses, which, it seemed to her, was most of what planning a wedding consisted of, was as appealing as consuming rotten flesh. But if Daphne and Sean were getting married, she *would* be involved. She would ooh and ah over a hundred identical white dresses; she would agonize over which flowers the guests would rather have sitting on the tables where they guzzled free liquor. She would offer no commentary on the momentous significance of childbirth or raising teenagers or succoring dying spouses when Daphne referred to her wedding as 'the most important day of my life'. She would behave as people expected, and so, redeem herself in her daughter's eyes.

But Daphne had other ideas. "We're going to have a small, private wedding," she continued. "We'll travel to Bali and get married on the beach."

"Bali? You're getting married in Bali? Honey, won't that be kind of expensive? How will everyone get there? Where will they stay? Do you have a hotel in mind?"

"It's going to be private, Mom. Sean's parents won't even be coming."

Alarm bells sounded in Beata's mind at the mention of Sean's parents. "Does – does that mean you aren't inviting me?" she said.

"Mom, it's not a matter of inviting you. We agreed to have it private; that's the way Sean wants it."

Perversely, Beata moved instantaneously from dreading the planning and the pomp to feeling wounded over being left out. "Private meaning no mothers? Honey, how can you do this? I can't tell you how hurtful it is to not be invited to my own daughter's wedding."

"Mom, it's our day. We have a right to get married the way we want. Sean isn't comfortable with a big wedding."

"Daphne, you don't have to have a big wedding in order to invite your mother. I'm not that big a person."

"Ha ha," Daphne said. "Look, Mom. I'm only just now recovering from radiation therapy. I'm tired and I'm ugly. I don't have any hair left. I don't want to have a big party. I just want to get married. Can you please, please not harass me about this?"

"Oh, honey, you know you look beautiful. You don't have to hide yourself away just because you've been sick."

"Mom, this isn't open to discussion. Sean and I've decided."

It was only natural that Daphne gave more weight to Sean's feelings than to hers, but inside Beata railed against being displaced as the most important person in her daughter's life. She couldn't help believing that Sean had thrown his own parents out of his wedding because he didn't want Beata there: problematic Beata, the oddball, the idiot child, the family embarrassment.

She deflected her distress by seizing upon a logistical problem. "Who's going to perform the ceremony all the way over in Bali?" she demanded.

"We have a friend who's an ordained minister. He's going fly out there with us."

"Ordained as what? He's a minister in a church?"

"No, he's a non-denominational minister; he's not associated with a particular religion. Anyway, what difference does it make? You don't go to church. We don't go to church. We don't care who marries us as long as it's legal."

There seemed nothing more to be said. Daphne clearly didn't want to discuss it any further. She had called to notify Beata, just one of many people that had to be informed, and now was ready to move down through the rest of her list. "I have to go," she said, "I have a bunch of people to call. Love you, Mom." And she hung up the phone.

With Daphne going to Bali, buying tea didn't seem such a high priority. "So much for normalcy," she told Joshua.

"*I* like tea," he said.

* * *

The day of the wedding came and went. Joshua suggested they celebrate by having a dinner party, so he gathered up twelve of his rag-tag 'special friends' and made them all a feast of roast chicken, mashed potatoes and gravy, baby lima beans, broccoli, salad and apple pie. He spent the entire day in the kitchen, humming and stirring, emerging occasionally with a dripping spoon in hand to demand that Beata taste the gravy or salad dressing. Beata was too numb to object and too sorry for herself to participate. She drowned her sorrow by drinking an entire bottle of wine before dinner, and got so tipsy that, on the way to the table, she almost fell into the lap of a particularly redolent bum. Joshua didn't let her bring her wine glass to the table, so she sat and picked at her dinner for half an hour before stumbling into the bathroom to throw it all up again.

The next day she had the king of all hangovers, which for Beata meant a full 12 hours of nausea and lightheadedness that rivaled the stomach flu and made her feel that death would be a mercy in comparison. At 9:00 p.m., Joshua brought her a plate of scrambled eggs and toast and a shaker of salt.

"Ugh," Beata moaned. "Get that away from me. I can't eat anything. I'm still sick."

"It'll make you feel better," he promised.

"How do you know?" she said. "Have you ever had a hangover?"

"No," he said, "but I know a lot of people who have. Eat the eggs. Eat the toast. The salt will help settle your stomach."

"You are a very comforting person," she said, sitting up in bed and forcing down the toast, which did, as promised, settle her stomach. "How did the party turn out?"

181

"It was good," he said. "Everyone ate a ton."

"I'm sorry I missed it," she said, and to her surprise, she *was* sorry. She'd been so caught up in her own troubles, longing for her old relationship with Gladys to be magically reestablished and worrying about Daphne's cancer, that she had barely noticed Joshua's existence for the last several months. She looked around her room as with new eyes. Everything was clean and neat. There wasn't a speck of dust on the furniture or a spot of dirt on the carpet. No dead flies on the windowsill, no cobwebs in the corners of the ceiling. All the clothes she habitually flung on the floor were laundered and hanging neatly in the closet. Although she hadn't paid any attention to it for many weeks, she realized it had been this way all along. She never saw him clean, and certainly never saw him enter her room, yet somehow he quietly kept the house spotless and cozy.

"Thank you, Joshua," she said. "Thanks for looking after me."

"No problem," he said, patting her hand. "I'm very fond of you."

* * *

Sean and Daphne returned from two weeks in Bali and invited Beata over for dinner. Beata'd spent the time pampering herself, getting a haircut, a massage, a chiropractic treatment and whatever else she could think of. She'd even managed to pry Gladys out of Stan's arms for a girl's day out, and they'd gone shopping. Gladys had purchased some pink satin lingerie, and helped Beata look for a wedding gift for Sean and Daphne.

"It's not like they need anything," she said. "They've been living together for two years anyway, and besides, Daphne likes to pick out her own things."

"So you don't think she'd like these?" Gladys suggested, indicating a set of cow-motif ceramic canisters.

"Mmm. Tempting." Beata said, studying the canisters. They were white with large black splotches and sported little cow-arm handles with hooves at the bottom. The lids were shaped like bovine heads (in graduated sizes) with ears and bulbous, pink noses. When Gladys opened one of them, it emitted a deep moan that, Beata imagined, was supposed to sound like a mooing cow.

"I'm afraid I'll have to pass on those," she told Gladys. "I don't think Daphne would see the humor. I'm trying to get back in her good graces by being as normal as possible."

"Get *back* in her good graces?" Gladys said. "When were you ever in her good graces to begin with?"

At that moment, she was diverted by a hand-held waffle iron that she was sure Stan would absolutely die for, and the discussion veered off in his direction.

"Just look at this!" She squealed, working the spring-loaded plastic handles to snap the waffle iron open and shut like a pair of crocodile jaws. "It's absolutely perfect for making single-serving waffles. Stan would adore this; he's a wonderful cook."

"Wouldn't it be better to have a waffle iron that made two waffles at once?" Beata suggested.

"No, because Stan doesn't like waffles," Gladys said. "This is for him to make *me* waffles. He's soooo sweet," she sighed. "He takes such good care of me."

Beata didn't want to participate in a coo-fest about Stan, so she grabbed the waffle iron from Gladys. "And when you're not using it to make waffles, you can hang it from your clothing for convenient storage," she helpfully demonstrated by locking the jaws shut on her sweatshirt so the waffle iron dangled from its hem. "Perhaps you can find clip-on cooking utensils and a can opener to match."

"Right, or I could use it to curl my hair," Gladys suggested, grabbing it back and clamping it onto her white fluff.

"Or protect yourself against unpleasant household odors," Beata offered, fastening it onto her nose.

"Okay, this is getting gross," Gladys said, whisking the waffle iron off Beata's nose and returning it to the shelf. "I don't guess the store will be happy about you wiping your nose on their waffle iron. Let's go look for something Daphne *would* like."

They finally settled on a tasteful but generic pair of crystal candlesticks of the sort people receive for Christmas from their great-aunt Mildred and then sell in a yard sale a month later.

"It's either these or the fake cross-stitched throw pillow saying 'Bless This Mess'" said Gladys. "Myself, I'd go for the pillow. It has more personality."

"Are you kidding?" said Beata. "If I get Daphne something with the word 'mess' on it, I'm a dead woman. She'd probably think I was making a snide comment about her housekeeping."

"It's supposed to be funny," Gladys said.

"Well, Daphne will not appreciate it; I guarantee. I'm going with the candlesticks. But feel free to get the pillow and give it to her yourself."

"No way," said Gladys. "Daphne *likes* me. I plan to keep it that way. Maybe I'll get her the waffle iron you wiped your nose on. By the way, how'd the wedding go?"

"I don't know," Beata said. "I haven't heard from them since they left except for Daphne leaving a message on my answering machine inviting me over for dinner next Saturday."

"So, did you call her back? You're going, aren't you?"

"Yeah, I called her back but she wasn't there, so I left her a voice mail saying I'd come."

"That's such a raw deal," Gladys said. "I can't believe they didn't invite you to their wedding. And now you're reduced to making appointments with your own daughter by exchanging voice mails."

Beata paid for the store to wrap the candlesticks in a white and silver box with silver tissue paper inside to keep them from chipping each other. They made an enormous bow to go on top with silver spangles and white fluff sticking out like a goose-down Mohawk.

"The box looks like it cost more than the candlesticks," Gladys said. "She'll know you had the store do it."

Beata customarily wrapped gifts in whatever paper she had lying around. Sometimes she wrapped wedding and birthday presents in Christmas paper bought right after the holidays at a 75% discount and stuffed into the hall closet to wrinkle and turn yellow until she unearthed it several months (or years) later. Other times, she used newspaper, a flattened paper grocery sack, or even green-and-white lined computer paper with the perforated edges torn off. If there were no recycled Christmas bows to be had, she made a bow from string, or drew one on with a magic marker. The white and silver box with its Mohawk bow would definitely scream 'store-bought', and in a *good* way, Beata decided. A *normal* way.

Beata arrived for dinner on the appointed evening, carrying the box ostentatiously in front of her like a peace offering. Daphne had been putting on weight, she noticed. Her cheeks were filling out and her skin was beginning to lose its papery look. She had a suntan, but it looked superimposed over her former unhealthy gray like a thin wash that might rub off if she scrubbed too hard.

"Congratulations, honey," she said, thrusting the box at Daphne and kissing her cheek. "You look wonderful."

"Hello, Mom," Daphne said, kissing the air beside Beata's face and accepting the box. "Thank you for the gift. It looks lovely. Look, honey," she waved the box at Sean, "isn't this a lovely gift?"

"Thanks, uh, Mom," Sean said awkwardly, placing the box on the coffee table and backing away as if it contained a live viper.

"So." Beata said, plopping herself down on the couch. That fake cross-stitched throw pillow might have come in handy, she thought as her back protested. Daphne's couch was padded but not soft, as if to encourage everyone to maintain good posture and not overstay their welcome. "Tell me about the wedding."

"We have pictures," Daphne said, indicating a photo album embellished with metallic lace. She perched tentatively on the edge of the sofa (no danger of any bad posture here, thought Beata) and looked over Beata's shoulder as she leafed through the album. The pictures showed Sean and Daphne in a variety of paradisiacal settings, always standing stiffly with their arms clasped around each others' waists, always smiling brightly at the camera as they squinted into the sun.

In the photos, Daphne looked fragile. Although she'd bought an expensive wig to conceal her baldness, the color was a tiny bit off and it was fashioned differently than her normal, somewhat severe style. It made her look young, as if the hair was a shade too big for her head. Beata realized, suddenly, how vulnerable she'd felt over Sean's threatened defection and how badly she needed to be reassured of his commitment.

"How is Gladys doing?" Daphne asked. "Have you seen her lately?"

"Stanys is fine," Beata said. "They are blissfully happy making waffles for each other."

"Waffles?" Daphne repeated blankly.

"We found them a personal waffle-maker when we went shopping for your wedding gift," Beata explained. "Gladys is doing great, but she isn't the same Gladys any more. She's half of Stanys now instead of being an independent person. Stan infiltrates everything she does like an infectious bacterium."

"That's how couples are supposed to work, Mom," Daphne said. She glanced at Sean, who was hovering over the couch. "That's not bacteria; it's love. Right, honey?"

"Right," said Sean firmly, putting his hands bracingly on her shoulders.

Another error, Beata realized. This quest toward normalcy was not going as smoothly as she'd hoped.

Daphne was happy with the candlestick holders, as far as Beata could tell. She seemed relieved at how impersonal they were, as if she dreaded Beata's personality and couldn't get too little of it. Their dinner party was cordial and brief. Beata found herself out on the sidewalk before 7:30, looking up at Daphne's lit windows and wondering what her daughter and her new husband were doing now…were they jointly thanking God she was finally gone? That the first meeting after the Great Divide had gone so smoothly, Mom hadn't broken down in hysterics in the middle of the living room or confronted them in the hallway, screaming abuse so loud the neighbors could hear? Or were they just doing the dishes?

Beata was happy for them, she told herself. Blissfully happy. Who wouldn't be happy that her daughter had found her soul mate? This dull feeling in the pit of her stomach was happiness. Absolutely.

It was mid-morning on a Wednesday. Beata was at her computer when the phone rang. "Can you come into the office?" her boss was asking. "Today? This morning? There's something I need to discuss with you."

"Um, sure," Beata said, glancing at the clock and mentally calculating the bus schedule. "I can be there in about an hour and a half."

"I need to see you before that," her boss uncharacteristically insisted. "Drive in if you have to. We need to meet in my office in half an hour."

That wouldn't give her time to suit up, she thought. She glanced down at her dress, which she'd been wearing for the last three days. There was a gap where the bodice had come unsewn at the waist and some ugly stains on the front.

"I'll do my best," she promised. She tore the dress over her head and put on the most serviceable sweater and pants she had, cursing her laziness for leaving her best clothes at the dry-cleaners for almost a week. She'd have to drive, all right, and pay to park. It would be an expensive day.

Forty minutes later she was standing in her boss's office, and he was staring over her shoulder, not meeting her eyes.

"Close the door," he said, and her stomach lurched. She dropped into one of the chairs across from his desk and wiped her sweaty palms on her knees.

He told her, awkwardly and with spurious sympathy, that the company was "readjusting priorities" and no longer felt they needed the specific skill-sets represented by her and her teammates in the Seattle area. They were planning to offer these functions from a lower-cost region using a service-bureau model. Beata had been working in corporate America for over twenty years; she had no difficulty interpreting the euphemisms. He was saying, in the most politically correct way possible, "we're laying you off and moving your job to a third-world country where we can pay someone a quarter of what you make to do the same thing."

"The least you can do is look me in the face while you are firing me," she told him. "The other least thing you could do is pay for my parking, since you forced me to drive down here to listen to this drivel. Couldn't you have let me ride the bus and fired me just as well an hour from now?"

"You're not being fired," her boss insisted, clearing his throat and shuffling papers around his desk, still not looking at her.

"Fired, laid off, whatever. The bottom line is, I don't have a job."

He floundered into a second speech (Beata suspected he'd prepared it in advance) about corporate realities, the demands of the competitive marketplace, leveraging business assets and the needs of the shareholders. Unctuous corporate platitudes flowed from his lips in a meaningless yet inexorable tide. She sat helplessly across the desk, waiting for the flood to abate and mentally assessing her bank balance to figure out how long she could make it without an income. Looking at his perspiring face, Beata decided he had probably determined to complete all his unpleasant interviews before lunch so he could go have a beer afterward, hence the need for her to drive down. She also saw that he was more relieved than sorry about the layoffs, probably grateful he hadn't been canned with the rest of them…yet.

At length, he ran out of words.

"I hope you're not thinking any of your corporate double-speak makes this okay with me," she said. "I'm furious, and I think our executives would sell their own mothers if they though they could make a dime off it."

Her boss launched into yet another speech, apparently wanting to enumerate the benefits of a healthy, free-market economy, but Beata had heard enough.

"No," she said, holding her hand up and getting out of her chair. "No more. I think our business here is done, no need to add insult to injury."

"Wait," her boss said. He'd gotten so distracted explaining why this seemingly callous betrayal of a long-time employee was actually a good thing for America and, by extension, for all Americans including Beata, that he had forgotten the rest of his HR-concocted spiel. He wanted to emphasize that all employees affected by the resource action were welcome to stay with the company in other capacities, although he was not aware of any positions available locally. However, he had a list of on-line resources to assist in placement, etc. etc.

She took the paperwork he was waving at her and glanced over the legalese outlining her rights (she had none) and her obligation, incurred at hire, to protect and return all company assets, including intellectual property a.k.a. information.

"I didn't bring my laptop," she said, "as I was in such a hurry to get here."

"Oh, you don't have to do that today," he assured her. "You still have 30 days to find another placement within the company."

As what? she wondered. What could she possibly do that someone in Bangladesh couldn't do cheaper? She hurried out of the office, avoiding the eyes of curious co-workers who'd been watching people troop in and out of the boss's office all morning. She felt embarrassed, superfluous, and didn't want to see the relief and pity mingled on their faces nor hear their hollow assurances that everything would be fine, that she would surely find something else.

She retrieved her car from the parking garage, wincing as she handed over her credit card. Was there any way, she wondered, that she could expense the $8.00 which she now could not spare? She bitterly regretted all the money she'd wasted on fancy coffee and meals out…that money could have swelled her savings account and given her another few days of rent and food.

She drove numbly out of the garage and through the downtown streets, choked with cars, trying to formulize an action plan. "Action plan." Even her personal thoughts, she realized disgustedly, were framed in corporate-speak phrases. What she needed was not an action plan but a rescuer, a friend...her best friend. She made her way through the downtown grid as fast as she could, to an affluent neighborhood just north of the business district, pulled over in front of someone's house and dialed Gladys' work number.

"Hi," said Gladys, sounding distracted.

"Am I bothering you?" Beata asked.

"No – well, I have to get these entries done, but I have a couple of minutes. What's up?"

"I've been fired," Beata announced tragically.

"Oh *no*," said Gladys, immediately sympathetic. "Fired? What for?"

"Not fired, exactly," Beata clarified. "But laid off. You know...resource action. The usual. Moving jobs to China, that sort of thing."

"Oh Beata, that's terrible," said Gladys, and Beata's heart lifted a little. She could count on Gladys. Gladys would always be there for her.

"So, I was wondering," she said, "whether I could, you know, rent a room from you, move in with you and cut my expenses. Just for a little while until I find something else."

There was a long pause, and Beata's stomach twisted. Maybe this wasn't going to work out as well as she'd hoped. "Well, actually," Gladys finally said, "Stan and I are moving in together. We're planning a house-warming party next Friday, and I was going to invite you. Stan owns a house," she continued happily, "and he suggested I move in with him. He's over at my house all the time, or I'm over at his place, and he says it doesn't make any sense to pay for two households. Isn't that wonderful?"

"Wonderful," Beata echoed dully.

"So can you come?"

"I guess. I mean, sure. I'd love to."

"That's great! It'll give you a chance to get out. It'll distract you, give you a break."

"Yeah."

"Say," said Gladys, "why don't you ask Daphne if you can stay with her?"

"Gladys, you know Daphne won't go for that. They only have one bedroom, and Sean would rather take in a carton of spiders than his mother-in-law."

"Oh, well, that's too bad." Gladys seemed not to recognize the tragedy of a son-in-law who preferred a carton of spiders to her best friend. She had, Beata realized, other things on her mind.

"And listen Beata," she said, "don't worry. Everything'll be fine. You'll land on your feet. You'll find another job."

"Sure," Beata said, and pushed the 'end' button. She rested her forehead on the steering wheel. So much for a rescuer. She felt like a swimmer in a vortex, clutching at a toothpick to keep from drowning. Well, she couldn't sit here and drown on someone's front lawn. She got out of her car and walked a couple of blocks until she found a coffee shop. Forgetting her self-recriminations of a few minutes ago on the topic of waste and fancy coffee, she went in and ordered an $11.00 coffee and sandwich, paid for by credit card, then sat by the front window and shuffled through one of the papers thoughtfully provided by the coffee shop. If Gladys couldn't offer her a room, she'd have to find a cheaper place on her own.

She spent the rest of the day driving around the city looking at studio apartments. She wanted a place that was cheap, which eliminated the complexes with covered parking, communal amenities such as spas and pools, and washer-dryer hookups. On the other hand, she couldn't live in a tenement. At her age, she felt like a target for Social Security check-stealing drug addicts and drive-by shooters.

She compromised by renting a place under the flight-path of the airport. It was a cottage-style complex with a sprawling but apparently inadequate parking lot, as residents' cars overflowed onto surrounding streets. The buildings sprawled as well, about 150 units, clustered around tiny courtyards mulched under the windows and around the porches with red bark and planted with azaleas and hydrangeas, and with a scrap of lawn at the center. Each unit's back faced the parking lot, and each fronted on one of these courtyards. It had a homey, peaceful look to it, interrupted every few minutes by the window-rattling thunder of a jet flying low overhead as it made for the runway.

Beata paid a year's rent in advance to ward off uncomfortable questions about employment. She was, she carefully explained, between jobs. The rental agent seemed unconcerned. A year's rent in hand was good enough for him. She could move in on the first of the month. He showed her the outside of her unit (currently occupied) and the inside of another unit. It included a smallish room that would have to serve as living room, dining room and bedroom, a bathroom and a tiny kitchen. Beata mentally tabulated her furniture…she could accommodate maybe an eighth of it. The rest would have to go into storage, yet another expense.

It was dark before she returned home, and Joshua was bustling around the kitchen, preparing dinner.

"Hi," she said, bursting in the back door and tripping over the throw-rug she'd placed there to wipe her feet on.

"Hi," Joshua said back.

"Listen, I have to talk to you."

Joshua handed her a cup of tea, and took one himself. He moved to the dining room table and sat down. "Sure," he said, sipping the tea and looking at her over the rim. "What's up?"

"Joshua, I got laid off today. I'm going to have to move to a cheaper place, a small place. I'm leaving in a week and a half, on the first."

"Need help?" he asked. His lack of concern about losing the only home he'd had for the last several months confused her.

"Help moving?" she asked.

"Right."

"Yeah, of course. I mean, I'd love some help. But... you realize, don't you, that the place is too small for two people. You're going to have to find someplace else. I'm sorry about the short notice, but I didn't see this coming. Do you have any idea where you could go?"

"I don't have much stuff to worry about," he said, and she realized he hadn't amassed any possessions other than what he'd brought with him: a bedroll and a small, shabby duffle bag full of clothes.

"But you've got to live somewhere, don't you?"

"Oh, I'm not worried about it. Something will turn up."

Beata wished she could be as confident. They spent the next few days packing and moving things to the storage locker, which she'd also paid a year's rent on. By the day of Gladys' housewarming party, her house was looking quite sparse. She'd kept only a few basic items of furniture. Most of it, and her kitchen stuff, too, had gone into storage.

"After all," she told Joshua, "how may pots and pans does one person need? There's one of me. Surely I can make do with a couple of plates. I'm not planning to throw dinner parties."

He nodded and kept wrapping cups in newspaper. She had a suspicion she could have taken more comfort from him, but she was too wound up in her own misery to pay him much attention. He seemed cheerful, humming as he washed the floors with Murphy's Oil Soap and bleached the

194

grout in the bathroom. He spent no time looking for a place to move, and she wondered what he'd do once the door was locked and the key turned over to the landlord.

"We'll miss you," Irene had said when Beata came over to tell her she was moving. "The doggies will miss you, won't you sugar pies?" She nudged Grover and Cleveland back with the side of her foot, as they were threatening to burst through the front door to get at Beata's ankles. "And we'll miss Joshua, too. Where are you two moving, anyway?"

"Oh, we aren't moving together," Beata said, and Irene looked shocked.

"What do you mean? Are you breaking up?"

"No, we're not breaking up. We were never together."

"I think that's a shame," she said. "Joshua's a good man. There aren't that many of them out there that are still single. At your age."

"It's not like that," Beata said. "Anyway, I came to let you know you'd probably be getting a new neighbor soon and to offer you these pans." She held out two Pyrex baking dishes and a ceramic casserole. "I can't use all this in my new place. It's really small. So I thought maybe you'd like to have them."

Irene glanced over at Beata's yard. She seemed to struggle with several conflicting emotions: relief that a more conscientious yard manager might be moving in, distress that Joshua was moving out, and distaste at being offered used kitchenware by a woman she strongly suspected did not keep her baking dishes in the same pristine condition Irene demanded of herself.

"Oh, no thanks," she said, backing away from the cookware as if it contained raw sewage that might spatter filth on her ivory sweater set. "I have everything I need already."

"Okay, well, it's been nice having you as a neighbor," Beata said, stooping to cup Grover's soft muzzle in her hand. His beady eyes gleamed at her and he gave a half-hearted yip, as if to emphasize that, old friend or not, she was on his turf and therefore had to be treated as a potential threat.

"Nothing personal," he seemed to say. "I have a job to do, here."

"You be good, boy," Beata said, scratching behind his ears. "Bye, Irene. Maybe I'll see you around."

"You take care, now," Irene said, and shut the door.

Instead of going directly back to her almost-empty house, Beata walked through the neighborhood wondering why she hadn't appreciated it more while she'd live here. The streets were pleasant, quiet, lined with trees. Occasionally, between two houses, one caught a distant glimpse of the Sound. She mulled over Irene's reaction, and Gladys', and Daphne's. All of them seemed, beneath the sympathy or neighborly regret, fearful that she'd land on their doorsteps like a foundling child, and drag them down into the sump of financial ruin with her. Each seemed relieved to discover she had somewhere to go that wouldn't inconvenience them.

Daphne – Beata's heart twisted when she thought about Daphne. She'd called her the same evening she'd lost her job to tell her of the impending move. Daphne'd tightened up like a guitar string and said, "I'm drowning in medical bills, Mom." As if she had called to ask for a handout. She'd also been relieved to hear Joshua was helping Beata move, as she and Sean were going to a trade show and would be tied up all day on the first.

"Sean and I need to spend time together," she'd explained, sounding a little ashamed. "I hope you understand, Mom. It isn't that we don't love you. But we have our own lives to live."

"How is Sean doing?" Beata obediently asked. "How is married life treating you?"

"Oh, just wonderful," Daphne said, and Beata hoped it was true. She desperately wanted Daphne to be happy, protected, secure. If Sean was the man who could give her that, Beata wanted it with all her heart. She quailed at the thought that Sean might leave Daphne the way Gladys' husband had left her, lonely and betrayed, her self-esteem in tatters. She had no idea what the internal strains and shifts in their relationship had been as Daphne fought her cancer, but she knew there'd been problems. She hoped they'd been resolved, for good, not plastered over and waiting to cause future disintegration. All attempts to discuss this with Daphne had been rebuffed, vigorously.

"Honey, that's great. Don't worry about me. I'll be fine. I've already found a little place south of town and paid a year's rent in advance."

"That's *great*, Mom," Daphne brightened. "We'd love to come see it."

They had come to see it, and been taken aback at its small size.

"Um, where are you going to sleep?" Daphne asked.

"On the floor, in the living room." Beata said airily, as if she'd been sleeping on the floor for the last 50 years and thought anyone would be a fool to sleep anywhere else.

"On the floor." Daphne said. She clearly didn't want to put any ideas into Beata's head, like "wouldn't it make more sense to live with your daughter and sleep in a bed," so she carefully refrained from criticizing, but she eyed the brown shag carpet with distaste. Sean scuffed at it, raising a small cloud of dust, which he hastily shifted as if to conceal, or to stop it from settling on his shiny loafers, Beata couldn't tell which.

"Yes, I thought I'd put the couch here, on the back wall, and tuck the bedding down behind it out of sight during the day."

"Oh, good idea," Daphne said. Sean stood with his hands in his pockets, determined to say nothing. One false move and he'd have Beata hanging around his own neck like an albatross; better to keep silent.

"I'm sure you'll be very comfortable here, Mom," Daphne persisted. "It's a cute little place." She walked over to the kitchen, separated from the main room by a half-wall. "THIS IS GREAT," she bellowed, ignoring the rumble of a plane flying overhead, which caused the whole apartment to vibrate as if in an earthquake.

"Yes," Beata said, "and the planes hardly ever fly over at night."

"I'm sure you'll get used to it," Daphne said.

In truth, Beata had already adjusted to the idea of moving. She didn't really care where she lived, as long as her life wasn't endangered whenever she stepped outside her front door, and she figured this place was as good as any. It was small, and that meant easy to keep clean. It was convenient to stores and buses. It was cheap.

"I'm sure I will," she agreed.

Gladys' housewarming party was scheduled for the evening before Beata's final move. Most of Beata's clothes were packed, so she wore the same dress she'd been packing and hauling boxes to the storage locker in all day, simply sponging the dust off the front and confining her untidy hair in a pony tail. She was greeted at the door by Stan, resplendent in a shiny polyester shirt with dragons embroidered on the front. His genial smile became somewhat strained when he saw who was standing on the stoop.

"Oh...it's you," he said, and then covered hastily. "Hi. Come on in."

"Gladys!" he hollered. "Your friend's here!"

He abandoned the door, leaving it hanging ajar, and left Beata to find her way in, throw her hoodie on the pile of jackets sitting on a table in the foyer, and make her way toward the kitchen to see what food and drink were available. She saw Gladys across the room, chatting gaily with three women, but Gladys couldn't seem to detach herself from the crowd to come and greet her. She merely waved Beata toward the kitchen.

There Beata found a couple of uncomfortable looking husbands milling around the counter, where a sizable collection of liquor bottles was displayed along with some picked-over plates of deviled eggs, crudités with ranch dip, and crackers squirted with cheese whiz and crowned with pimento-stuffed olives. She introduced herself to the gentlemen, offering each a firm, hearty handshake, which they limply returned and then jumped back from as if afraid she would take advantage of the physical contact to fasten vampire fangs on their necks and begin sucking their blood.

She turned away from the men and located a plastic cup and a few watery ice cubes, then spent several minutes contemplating the liquor. She wondered how much time she could possibly waste pretending to decide which variety of low-grade booze she could nurse for the next hour without throwing it back up again.

"There's beer in the fridge," one of the men offered before fleeing to the living room.

Beata finally splashed a generous dollop from a quart of gin into her plastic cup and returned to the main party. She made her way over to Gladys, who was glowing like a little pink dewdrop amid the trio of women who towered over her like stately, manicured conifers.

"Hi, Bea," she chirped. "Let me introduce you to my new neighbors. This's Trish, and this's Kitty, and this's Layla. Ladies, this is my friend Beata."

All three were fiftyish, with hair that appeared to have been carefully styled in helmets of curls and epoxied into place with a substance that reflected the light in a way that reminded Beata of trying to see through her windshield when driving into the sun. Trish's hair was pale lemon colored, Kitty's was a tasteful chestnut, and Layla sported salt-and-pepper tones that turned out, on closer examination, to be a frosted effect that reminded Beata of a zebra. Trish offered her hand, palm down. Beata stood for a moment before she took it, wondering if she was expected to kiss it.

"Nice to meet you, Beeta," Trish condescended, raking Beata up and down with an appalled gaze that took in her flip-flops, dusty dress and untidy hair and telegraphed her revulsion.

"BeAHta," said Beata, releasing the royal hand. "My name is Beata."

"BeAHta," the trio repeated mechanically. "Nice to meet you."

"We're so happy to have Gladys in the neighborhood," pronounced Trish, apparently the leader of the triad. "She's a breath of fresh air."

Gladys beamed. Her snowy gumdrop hairdo seemed out of place among these helmet-coiffed women, and her sparkly pink scarf and flowing caftan, adorned with giant roses, was flamboyant next to their rigidly creased pants, cashmere-blend sweaters, patent-leather belts and faux pearl necklaces. They seemed to view these aberrations tolerantly, though, as they were balanced by Gladys' warm disposition and eagerness to please.

"Yes," Kitty agreed, taking a delicate sip of beige liquid from her glass. "She is just too, too marvelous."

"So tell me, BeAHta," Trish continued, "what do you do?"

Beata considered regaling them with stories of ritual animal slaughter, or maybe a burgeoning career in child pornography, but these were Gladys' neighbors. She didn't want the police being summoned every time she crossed the borders of the neighborhood. "I'm between jobs," she explained.

"Ahhh," said Trish. That explained the flip-flops and the pony tail...Beata was a bum.

"And your husband," she persisted. "What does he do?"

"Gamble," Beata said without thinking. "And hang around seedy restaurants trying to seduce innocent young waitresses, maybe. I dunno." Catching sight of the slight frown crossing Gladys' face, she hastily amended, "We got divorced a long time ago. I don't really keep up with his activities."

"Divorced." Trish's glance became icy. She did not approve of divorce. She didn't approve of divorcees, either, who generally lurked around trying to steal other women's husbands. Still, this divorcee didn't look very threatening with her dirty clothes and disheveled hair. What self-respecting man would want her? She decided to extend the sisterly hand of compassion to the poor creature, maybe clean her up and introduce her to an elderly widower who wouldn't be too picky about personal grooming.

"You need to get involved in a nice church," she said. "Our women's circle meets every Tuesday evening. Why don't you come over sometime and get acquainted?"

"You go to church?" Beata asked. She couldn't imagine Trish feeding the hungry and clothing the naked. "What does your women's circle do? Make soup? Knit sweaters?"

"At the moment, we're discussing plans for our Country Club night. It will be a lovely dinner dance, one of our main fundraisers for the year. Our church is very large," she said smugly, as if this explained the spiritual significance of a dinner dance.

"And what are you raising funds for?"

"This year we're all going on a cruise," Trish said.

"Oh, I see," Beata said. "I thought you meant you were fundraising for charity."

"We do that, too," Trish said. "We tithe the proceeds from our functions for various charitable projects. This year, we're contributing to the new Senior Center."

"So 90% of it goes to the cruise and 10% to the Seniors?" Beata said. She was fascinated by this foreign concept of what constituted appropriate use of church funds. Her parents' church, although not given to spontaneous healings, TV evangelists or personal relationships with Jeeezus, seemed positively Fundamentalist in comparison with this one. Her parents couldn't have conceived of throwing a fundraiser to send themselves on vacation.

"Tithing is Biblical," Trish explained loftily. "We always remember our duty to the Lord."

"Very commendable, I'm sure," Beata said. "This fundraising dinner sounds awfully exclusive, though. How do you reconcile that with your Biblical principles?"

Trish took no offense at this question. She seemed to feel that exclusivity was praiseworthy if in service to the Gospel. "Yes, I guess it is exclusive in a way," she said. "The community is invited, of course. But we only have nice, Christian people there. Not just anyone can afford the tickets, you know. It is a *formal* occasion." She eyed Beata's attire as if to make it clear she'd have to polish up a bit if she expected to be welcome among nice, Christian people.

"Gosh," said Beata, recklessly deciding she couldn't care less whether she became a neighborhood pariah, "that sounds mighty tempting. But I'm just so busy I don't think I can fit it in. Between my Coven meetings, my Circle of Power spell-casting class, Sufi dancing and the Homewreckers Anonymous meetings I simply can't spare a minute to plan gala dinners for nice, Christian rich people." Defiantly, she threw the remaining contents of her glass into the back of her throat, swallowed, gave a tremendous belch, and smiled at them beatifically.

"Well!" exclaimed Trish, offended to speechlessness by this display of crudity.

"Beata," said Gladys, grabbing her by the arm, "Let me show you the house." Gladys swept her away from the Bakelite Matrons just before the three of them burst into outraged gobbling like a flock of irate turkeys.

She took her on an exhaustive tour of the house, including the dank half-bath in the basement and the storage area in the garage. If it had been daylight, Beata thought, she would have shown her the tool shed as well, but in the dark they couldn't venture beyond the floodlights illuminating the palatial deck in back. They made a lengthy stop to admire Stan's splendiferous chrome grill, which took up a quarter of the deck and, Gladys assured her, although currently abandoned, was, in the summertime, the focal point for many social wonderments such as block parties and family reunions that Gladys couldn't wait to hostess.

As she guided Beata, she also scolded her. "You can be so charming when you want to be, Beata. I just don't understand why you have to be so nasty to my new friends.

"Because they were treating me like a decaying rat corpse," she defended herself. "Didn't you see the way they were looking at me?"

"Okay," Gladys conceded, "maybe they were a little snobby. But you don't even *try* to fit in, Bea. You want to rub everyone's nose in what an oddball you are."

"Gladys," Beata said, stopping and turning Gladys to face her. "Do you *like* these people? Since when did you want to fit in with a bunch of mean-hearted Stepford Wife types whose idea of Christian charity is having a black-tie dinner that nobody but themselves can afford?"

"Oh they just seem that way when you first meet them," Gladys said. "They're wonderful, really. They've been so sweet to me, having me over for dinner and bringing me banana bread."

"I'm glad they're nice to you," Beata said. "Personally, I don't feel like being reformed by the acrylic automatons. If I'm going to change, which I grant you is not such a bad idea, I don't want to be changed into them."

"Beata, these are my friends."

"Really? How friendly would they be if you broke up with Stan? How friendly would they be if you lost your job? How friendly would they be if you called them up at 2:00 in the morning because you had a family crisis?"

"I know they aren't friends like *that*," Gladys said. "A person doesn't have very many of those friends. But they're my neighbors; they've been nice to me, and I want to get along with them. Please don't antagonize them."

She whirled away from Beata and went back inside, leaving her on the deck. Beata knew she was being unreasonable. Who was she to throw rocks at others just because of what they wore and what kind of entertainment they preferred? It was the very thing she accused them of doing to her. She peeked in through the sliding glass door. The Bakelite trio had broken up and were now hanging on the arms of their respective husbands. Gladys was circulating with a tray, soothing wounded feelings with alcohol and hors d'oeuvre. Beata slunk down the stairs of the deck, groped her way to the side gate and out of the yard. She couldn't face any of those people in there. She hadn't felt like this much of a social leper since she was a teenager.

The next morning, she called Gladys to apologize, but Gladys seemed to have forgotten it, and brushed off Beata's apology with barely a word. She was full of her own news. She and Stan were planning a trip to Hawaii, a place Gladys had always wanted to go but never could afford. The opinion of the neighbors paled in comparison with her dream vacation: two whole weeks in Hawaii. She had to run, she said, they were leaving in few days and she had a thousand things to do. She'd send Beata a postcard.

Gladys' postcard duly came, an idyllic picture of a
tropical beach with palm trees and turquoise water. Gladys
covered the back with a few words in a large scrawl: she had
gone snorkeling; it was amazing; she would call Beata when
she got back.

Beata, now moved into her apartment and living
alone for the first time in months, missed her terribly. She
missed Daphne, too. It seemed everyone in her life had been
whisked away by a happy force that swept them off on
exciting new adventures and left Beata stuck in the same old
place. She was so depressed she'd even contemplated
dropping in on Trish's Tuesday night women's circle, but she
figured by now the Country Club dinner was over and the
Bakelite People were probably off enjoying their tropical
cruise.

When Gladys had returned, she'd dropped in to see
Beata's new place and give her a report on her vacation.
She'd raved enthusiastically (between interludes of window-
rattling jet noise) about the tidy way Beata had folded
herself into the tiny space.

"Everything's so convenient," she said. "You've
always thought large spaces were wasteful, and now I see
why…the way you have this organized is very efficient."
She looked around the room, puzzled. "But where's your
bed?"

"Here," said Beata, pulling a wad of pillows and
blankets out from behind the couch. "I sleep on the floor."

"Don't they have any one-bedroom apartments
here?"

"I don't mind sleeping on the floor," Beata said. "It's
good for my back." She didn't care to admit that her savings
account wouldn't have covered a year's rent on the one-
bedroom unit. She tried to keep a bright face on everything.
She didn't want Gladys to think she was angling for a free

room at Stan's house, thus triggering a spate of embarrassed excuses. "So fill me in on what you guys did in Hawaii. Did you like it as much as you expected?"

Gladys had chirped happily on about Hawaii for the next 45 minutes, waving fistfuls of pictures and comparing her tanned arm to Beata's pale one. In every sentence, Stan's name was prominent except when he was subsumed into the pronoun 'we'. Gladys apparently did nothing on her own anymore. 'We' did everything, thought everything, said everything.

Beata realized this was customary for married couples, and Gladys was now married in all but name. She didn't mean to exclude Beata, and in fact, believed that she wasn't. She was here, wasn't she, taking time out of her busy schedule to visit? But Beata wasn't used to 'visiting' with Gladys. She'd come to rely on a deeper, almost familial bond.

Gladys had been the friend she could call at midnight if she heard weird thumping sounds in the basement. Gladys was the one that called her at 5:00 a.m. to report bizarre and, Gladys suspected, prescient dreams. Of course Gladys was still there, and she knew Gladys was too nice to hang up the phone if she received a midnight call, but Gladys had other concerns now. She would listen out of kindness, for the sake of what *had* been, not because she was as interested in the thumping noises as Beata was. And when she was done listening, she'd turn over in bed and tell a sleepy Stan: "That was Beata. She's freaking out about weird noises again." And Stan and Gladys would tsk tsk about poor, old Beata who was so lonely she called up her married friends in the middle of the night to complain about imaginary noises.

Beata was determined not to become an object of pity. She didn't want Gladys, or anyone else, tsk tsking about poor, old Beata. Wasn't she the Evangelist of Self-Sufficiency? Hadn't she insisted that self-reliance was the foundation of a secure, emotionally stable life? Well, now she was having to live it out, and she was determined to show that it could be done.

For the first few weeks, she maintained a rigid schedule. Up in the morning, peruse the Want Ads, mail off resumes, make phone calls. That took maybe an hour, on a lucky day two or three, if she had an interview. There were few of these. Then, she cleaned house. The house, all of 500 square feet, couldn't stand up to the daily assault of cleaning products. By the end of the first month, she was wearing holes in the kitchen floor, and the shower tiles were looking a bit faded from constant bleaching.

Next, she decided to embark on a campaign of serious reading. The library was over a mile away, and she trudged this mile three times a week, carrying a huge satchel full of books each way. She spent longer and longer each visit shuffling through the shelves, reading dust jackets, trying to find books she had even the remotest interest in that she hadn't already read. Then, giving up on finding interesting books, she decided to read the entire library from one end to the other. The shelf nearest the door contained a collection of large-print romance novels. She would start with those.

"Melanie's enormous eyes sparkled in her heart-shaped face as she watched Nigel stride across the ballroom floor," she read. "'Nigel!' she cried, and tried to leap from her chair, but sank unwillingly back as her fast-pounding heart caused her knees to buckle. Oh, would he see her? Would he notice her agitation? She wrung her lawn handkerchief in delicate, gloved hands, willing him to look in her direction."

Good grief, Beata thought. This poor woman sounds like a circus freak. Enormous eyes? Heart-shaped face? She must look a fright.

"Nigel seemed determined to ignore her. She watched as he smiled, bowed, greeted the gaily-clad ladies who fluttered their fans and glanced up at him with saucy smiles. His powerful shoulders and muscular thighs seemed inappropriately confined in the wasp-waisted coat and satin knee-breeches proper in a ballroom. Riding garb would better become him Melanie felt."

Oh, no. Here was Nigel practically bursting out of his clothes. Did he take steroids? Would they make him sterile? Maybe it would be better that way. Beata shuddered at the picture of Nigel and Melanie's children: muscle-bound bruisers with heart-shaped faces and enormous eyes. Nigel and Melanie seemed oblivious to the looming disaster of having deformed offspring. Their romance proceeded apace.

"Nigel clasped Melanie to his powerful chest…she was fainting…she couldn't stand…the world was spinning. His arm encircled her tiny waist like a band of iron. He fastened his sensuous lips on her soft ones, demanding yet gentle as his tongue explored her mouth."

This woman had a serious iron deficiency. She needed to see a doctor. Nigel should be administering first aid, not exploring her mouth with his sensuous tongue. Beata tossed the book aside. There was no way she could survive an entire shelf of these. She'd better skip over the romances and move on to non-fiction.

"Ten Days to a Fully Organized Life." 'Raising Teenagers in the Post-Modern World'. 'Train Your Tropical Fish to Sing'. 'Nostradamus, Prophet or Profiteer?' The panoply of titles made Beata feel schizophrenic. She'd hoped focusing on a useful activity would distract her from worrying, but instead, it only seemed to emphasize that she had nothing better to do. Nobody needed her. Nobody cared what she was thinking and feeling. She didn't suppose a tank full of musical fish would change that. If she were willing to do things just for the sake of filling time, she could've called Frank up and tried to wheedle him into giving her another chance, but that wasn't what she was looking for at all. She wanted something to make her inner self more palatable. If she could find that, she wouldn't need anyone else; she could enjoy hanging around with herself. And if she didn't like hanging around with herself, how was she going to find anyone else who did?

Beata's time grew exponentially as she searched for things to occupy it. By the time she was six months into her unemployed life, money was getting tight. She'd spent almost all her savings on the rent and the storage locker. Each month, when the bills came due, she delayed paying them day after day because she dreaded deducting another few dollars from her dwindling bank balance.

She spent a lot of time sleeping. She knew she should get up, make phone calls, put on a suit, mail resumes, search the paper for prospective employment, but she felt frozen with apathy. She'd stopped feeling anything.

She'd shut off her phone after the first couple of months to avoid daily dunning calls from her credit card company. Without the phone, she had little contact with Daphne or Gladys. They never came over. She could've walked three blocks to Albertsons and used the pay phone to invite herself to their places, but she couldn't break through her apathy. What did it matter whether she saw them? She might as well go out on the street and buttonhole passing strangers.

Joshua was the only one that persisted in coming over. Even when she'd had a phone he'd never called beforehand, so it hadn't made any difference when she stopped having one. Every few days she'd find him at the door, sometimes bringing a cup of coffee and a sweet roll, sometimes with nothing but his bright, expectant smile.

She wondered why he bothered. She was miserable company, and most of the time they barely spoke. He seemed to be waiting for something, watching her closely, not asking a lot of questions but exuding comfort, as he always had. He wanted her to confide in him, she supposed. She wasn't going to do that. What could she tell him? She had no words to describe the dullness that lay over the world like a choking cloud of dust, dimming the sun and making even the bright spring grass look dingy and forlorn. How could she explain the dreary stretching of minutes into days into weeks and the constant refrain in her head saying 'what's the point of this'?

She hadn't even gone grocery shopping for over two weeks. Her cupboard was empty of everything but a carton of oatmeal, half a jar of peanut butter and two cans of garbanzo beans. Occasionally she'd get out of bed, wander into the kitchen, open the cupboard and stare at its contents, then, deciding she was neither hungry enough to bother making oatmeal nor interested in eating peanut butter straight out of the jar, she'd shut the cupboard and drift back to her bed pallet on the living room floor.

At last the oatmeal ran out and she realized she would have to drag herself to the grocery store or face starvation. She started to write a list, but kept writing things down and then crossing them off again as she saw the dollar total mount in her mind's eye. After an hour of work, she had produced the following:

> ~~oatmeal~~
> rice
> black beans
> ~~chicken~~
> ice cream
> ~~bread~~
> ~~hamburger~~
> ~~spaghetti~~
> cookies

Then she sat and tapped the pencil on the table, staring at the list and wondering what she would do when she ran completely out of money. The doorbell interrupted her reverie. She sighed, dropped the pencil and shuffled to the door.

"Hi," Joshua said, peering at her over the flaps of a large carton. "I thought maybe you could use this."

Beata stared dully into the carton. "What is it?"

"Food," he said.

"Food," she repeated stupidly. "You brought me food?" Sure enough, the carton was half-full of boxes of macaroni, sacks of rice, loaves of bread, spaghetti sauce, and various canned goods.

"Sure. You're not rolling in money right now…I thought you could use this."

Beata was suddenly furious. What was she – another one of Joshua's charity cases? Okay, she was jobless, but she wasn't a bum. She could handle it. She was surviving. She didn't need handouts from someone who didn't even have a place to live.

She took two quick steps out of the house, drew her arm back and slapped his face with all her strength…she'd never slapped anyone like that before. The box went flying, the food spilled all over the lawn and a red mark rose on Joshua's face, a mark in the accusing shape of a handprint.

He stood quietly, not seeming to notice the slap or the welt. Beata whirled and dashed into the house, slamming the door. She paced angrily around the tiny apartment, glancing out the window every now and then to see him still standing motionless on the front walk. Was he going to stand there all day? Didn't he know he wasn't wanted? The man was infuriating. She stalked into the bathroom and splashed cold water on her face. When she emerged a few minutes later, she again glanced out the window – this time, Joshua was gone, and the box and the food also.

Now she felt twinges of regret, of fear. He was pretty much the only friend she had left in the world – was she so sure she could afford to get rid of him? She stuck her head out the door and scanned the courtyard for a sign of him… nothing.

"Joshua?" she called tentatively. "Um, are you there?"

He was not there, she realized. She'd run him off and he wouldn't be back. Too late for regrets. Move on.

Move on to what, was the question. It wasn't like she had anything pressing to do. She'd lost interest in the groceries. It didn't really matter whether she ate or not. Maybe she'd go for a hike, find some peaceful place in the mountains where she could sooth her lacerated feelings with the balm of natural beauty. She'd hardly taken the car out in weeks. She'd been trying to save money by not driving anywhere. Suddenly she felt reckless. Did it really matter whether she ran out of money today vs. next week? It wasn't like she was going to find a job in the next two days. She got in the car and struck out aimlessly eastward, into the Cascades. She left the freeway and explored a network of National Forest Service roads, looking for a spot where, on this weekday afternoon, there was no one else hiking. She didn't want to see another soul.

It wasn't easy, this close to the city, to find a place that didn't already have someone parked at the trailhead. The popular beauty spots were already claimed by several cars each. People were busily unloading their day packs, water bottles and baby-carriers as they prepared to follow the early-birds up the trail. Beata drove further and further down the unpaved roads, choosing, at each fork, the direction that seemed least traveled.

Finally, she pulled off the road, which had become little more than a rutted track hacked out of the landscape with a single pass of a bulldozer blade, and parked in a wide spot beside a reed-choked lake. There were no other cars in sight, she noted with relief. A trail took off from here and scrambled up the steep hillside rising from the lake in a series of switchbacks. She pitted herself against the slope, taking rhythmic, measured strides, two per breath in, two per breath out. The trail was narrow and ill-defined, and people had short-cut the switch-backs and made their way straight up (or down) the hill, creating new trailets that deceived the eye and led off into dead-ends among the trees. She had to back-track several times to rejoin the trail after missing a switch-back.

She barely noticed the strenuous climb. She was busy brooding. What did Joshua think he was doing, bringing her a box of groceries like she was one of his pet bums? Was she reduced to begging for food now? She knew she was being unreasonable, but insisted on taking insult at his proffered charity. And his was not the only offense. What about Frank, who'd dumped her summarily over a man she wasn't even romantically involved with? What about Gladys, who'd abandoned her for some Johnny-come-lately who sucked his teeth after he ate? Worst of all, what about Daphne, who couldn't stand to have her own mother at her wedding. What kind of daughter did that?

Her resentment quickly turned to self-loathing. It was no wonder all these people treated her like she didn't matter. After all, what had she ever done to make them think she *did*? Selfish, cynical, resentful, melancholy…her life was like a never-ending dirge. Who wanted to listen to all that negativity? Who wanted to be around Beata the Perpetual Downer?

On the heels of loathing came self-pity…how could she help being a downer? Hadn't she tried to change? It wasn't like there was a magic anti-downer-light-switch inside that she could turn on and off at will. How many hours of counseling, how many self-help books, how many different kinds of therapy were required to fix a person like her? She saw the collective consciousness of humanity flowing under the ground like two enormous blood vessels. Some people walked through life with hope, seeing the bright side, enjoying what they could in every situation. These people were tapped into the vein of happiness. Other people drank pain like a river; they were tapped into the sorrow vein. She was one of those.

As she meditated upon this, she climbed higher, finally reaching, at the trail's end, a logging road, which stretched away in both directions. She picked a direction at random and trudged along the road. She wasn't sure where she was. She couldn't see the lake, so she must have come around to the other side of the mountain. Both sides of the road were obscured with tall trees and heavy underbrush, and she couldn't make out the geography she was walking through.

213

Presently, the road twisted around a sharp bend. She entered an area where the ground fell steeply away on one side of the road and, on the other, sloped as steeply upward. Then, it ended abruptly in a rutted turn-around half obscured by encroaching brush. A mound of dirt sat at the end of the turn-around, plowed up and dumped there when the road was scraped out of the mountainside. She felt vaguely cheated. She'd been hoping it would loop back and meet the trail again, or take her to another route back down the hill so she wouldn't have to retrace her steps, or at the very least continue on to the top of the mountain. She walked across the turn-around, climbed over the mound and found herself perched on a cluster of sandy boulders, a high precipice leaning over the wooded valley a thousand feet below.

She scrambled up to the domed crown of the highest boulder and surveyed the view. Across the deepening shadows in the valley, carpeted with a rich blanket of trees, another ridge of mountains glowed in the late sun, an unearthly glow as if illuminated from within. Beneath her boots, the rock undercut the point she stood upon and plunged invisibly to the valley below...she felt suspended in the air.

It's beautiful, she thought, but the shadow on her heart was untouched by it. What good is beauty, what good peace, if you're tapped into the sorrow vein? The gushing out of darkness from that vein smothers your heart in suffocating gloom. There's light for the eyes to see, but no lightness in your heart. Sorrow soaks into your very core. Happiness is ephemeral, fleeting, snatched in infinitesimal moments amid the evil and pain the whole world is writhing in. What was the point in going on and on? If she turned down this mountain, back to the dismal monotony of her worthless life, who would be enriched by it? Not her child. Not her friend. Not her parents.

Even her attempts to reach out she now saw as efforts to pollute everyone else's world with her own bitterness.

No, not *her* bitterness only. She was a conduit for the amassed bitterness of the ages. For some reason, she'd ennobled this, raising herself to the status of a martyr. She'd harangued her friends and family, insisting that happiness was false and naïve in a world where children are abused and people drop dead of starvation every day. Why had she thought that spewing pessimism all over others was a service? Why had she insisted that they 'see the truth'? What value could there possibly be in telling over the suffering of the world (a flimsy disguise for her own suffering) like a Satanic rosary?

She'd thought herself too wise to stick her head in the sand. She'd criticized them for pretending all was well. She'd sneered at their insistence that the world was a good place and that love brings meaning to human existence.

There it was…the 'L' word, the word upon which, more than any other word, Beata poured out her dark sewer of contempt. As if the frail ties people bind around each other could ward off the ugly reality of hardship and suffering that comprise the human experience. As if one reed can lean on another to escape the suffocating pressure of life's steam-roller.

Did she want love? No. What good was it? What could be fixed by hitching herself to another person? Didn't she still have to live in her own skin? Could another person tell her what the meaning of her life was? To Beata, it seemed no more than a feel-good mechanism, like wrapping oneself in a fuzzy blanket while the bombs fell and the world starved to death. Beata needed a rock. She needed assurance that there was a point to all this suffering. And pondering this, she concluded that there was no assurance to be had. Surely, after seeking it for 52 years, she'd have found it by now if it was there to be found.

She was going to throw herself from this rock. She realized that had been lurking at the bottom of her mind from the moment she began driving into the mountains. Why not snuff out her miserable life and, hopefully, start again in a different skin with different thoughts? And if there was no new skin, if reincarnation was all crap, so what? At least she wouldn't be here, grappling ineffectually with mysteries far beyond her feeble understanding.

Beata didn't believe in hell. She didn't believe that God would impose suffering beyond death. God wouldn't hold it against her that she was too weak to carry on. Hadn't He shoved her brutally into this life and expected her to deal with it as best she could? Well, she wasn't equal to the task. She was weighed down by her character flaws, which were symptoms of a deeper evil that penetrated to her very foundation.

She inched closer to the edge of the rock. Don't look down. Look over at the glowing mountains instead. Imagine yourself melting gradually into the wind like a dissolving mist. Her heart was pounding and her breath came in shallow gasps. The wave she'd once imagined carrying her to the beach of enlightenment seemed to swell around her in a glorious flood.

Suddenly obtruding on this ethereal picture, to Beata's dismay, was a more squalid one of stumbling from the peak like an ungainly bird, flapping and tumbling and finally splattering gruesomely on the rocks like a sack of bloody cement.

She swayed back and forth on the balls of her feet, closed her eyes, opened them again. As she inched closer to the edge, her palms started sweating and her knees trembled. The cement picture became gorier. She could hear the mushy thwuck of her body hitting the ground and see gelatinous gobs of flesh flying through the air. What if she didn't die right away? What if she lay there in excruciating pain for hours and hours? It was no good. She simply didn't have the gumption to get rid of herself. Defeated, she backed away and sat with her back to the precipice, glumly hugging her knees and contemplating her shoes.

I am afraid to die, she realized. Her mind wanted out, but her body was quite determined to carry on, thank you very much. No airy-fairy picture of melting into the great beyond was going to convince it to let go. She'd always thought her mind was the stronger of the two. Apparently, in some things anyway, the body had the last word.

She gradually became aware that the fear of dying that had sucked her away from the cliff's edge was morphing into an obsessive paranoia of looming danger... she had to get down off this mountain before dark. She couldn't allow herself to be caught up here on an unfamiliar trail, with no light, after sunset.

Without stopping to examine the irony of her sudden transformation from an otherworldly suicide into a panic-stricken safety nut, she rose and began to run down the road, stumbling over rocks and roots, her knees jarred and aching at every step as she pounded along the road and then, down the steep grade of the trail. As she neared the bottom, she looked around in panic for the trailhead...this terrain didn't look familiar. How had she gotten off track? She must have taken a different trail from the road. She could see the lake through the trees, but seemed to have come too far around it. Finally, she plunged straight off the side of the trail, sliding down on her butt, making for the shore of the lake. There, back around a point, she could see her car in the parking lot, and she stumbled toward it, now lurching to her knees in the cold water, now teetering dangerously on boulders, falling and crawling on hands and feet as she made her way around the lakeshore.

By the time she reached the car, she was soaked to the waist and it was deep twilight. Her knees and ankles ached, and both hands had been bruised against the rocks. It should have relieved her to be safe, but instead she instantly began worrying about the drive home...she might run out of gas. The car might break down. She might get mugged as she paused by the road to change a flat tire. In fact, where were her keys? What if she'd dropped them in her mad scramble down the mountain? Her hands shook as she reached into her pocket, and her heart skipped a few beats when her hand came out empty. Then she reached into the other side, the zipper pocket, and sure enough, pulled out the car keys.

She drove home in a daze, reliving again and again the moment when she'd stood just an inch from eternal deliverance and then lost the courage to claim it. Her newly-revealed fear of death changed nothing. There was no release, no recognition that life wasn't so bad after all. Life *was* so bad, but for her, there wasn't any alternative. She would simply have to slog through her remaining years like a beast of burden under a load of bricks, not questioning, not rebelling, but just putting one foot before the other until she couldn't walk any more.

When she reached her apartment complex, there were no parking spots near her unit, as usual. She parked in a distant spot and trudged toward the little courtyard in her door bordered on. She stood in the middle of it for a moment, within reach of a neighbor's porch light, and fumbled for her house key. As she sorted through her key ring, she sensed a moving figure in the darkness near her own porch...was somebody there? Fear overwhelmed her once again.

Someone had detached himself from the shadows and was now walking up the sidewalk toward Beata.

"Joshua!" she squeaked as he stepped into the light. "What on earth are you doing here? I thought – I thought you'd surely give up on me."

Joshua didn't speak. He came closer. His eyes looked deep into hers. They seemed bottomless, and yet solid, secure. Maybe even safe, she thought. Suddenly, tears spilled over and began running down Beata's cheeks.

"I – I almost killed myself today," she cried, "but I couldn't go through with it. I wish I could've. I hate myself. I'm useless and tiresome. I can't ever seem to be happy. The things that matter to other people don't matter to me." She leaned against Joshua's chest and clung to him, pouring out her bitterness and self-hatred in gusty, incoherent sobs.

Slowly, with infinite tenderness, his hand came up to clasp her shoulder.

"Beata," he whispered, and his voice, though almost inaudible, echoed in her mind like the velvety purr of a lion-sized cat. "Let me in. Let me carry it for you." She looked up then, and saw that his face was illuminated with radiance that seemed to seep from the pores of his flesh. "Will you let me in?" he said again.

She held her breath for a moment. Let him in? All the way to the sordid, ugly bottom of her heart? She didn't want anyone to know just how bad she really was. She would prefer to gloss over the details. But he seemed to know already, and didn't care. She'd slapped him with all the force in her body, driven him away, rejected his help, and here he was again, still asking to come in. She was willing to kill herself (almost). If she'd go that far, what difference did it make whether anyone knew the depths of her depravity. Why struggle? Why hide? What did she have to lose?

Almost, but not quite, habit was too strong. Then, finally making up her mind, she surrendered to him limply. "Yes," she whispered. "Yes, yes. Come in. I will."

Her body relaxed against him. A smile crept across his face, now glowing like an inferno. "Let's dance," he suggested.

"Dance?"

"Yes, dance with me."

"I don't know how," she said.

"I'll show you," he said, and taking one hand in his, putting his arm around her waist, arranging her other hand on his shoulder, began slowly moving in a circle. She closed her eyes. His brightness intensified, and turned the insides of her eyelids warm and red as if lit by the midday sun. They danced.

Was he still there? Was he real? Her arms embraced nothing, and yet she felt him there still as she abandoned herself to the dance. Her body took on a graceful assurance it'd never had before. She wanted to open her eyes to see where he'd gone, if he'd gone, but the light was too blinding. Her heart lifted, soared, and words began tumbling unbidden through her mind: "I will never leave you nor forsake you. Surely I am with you always, to the very end of the age. Come to me, you who are weary and heavy-laden, and I will give you rest."

"He is the rock," she thought. "Love isn't what I thought it was. This is love."

She laughed and tipped back her head, and twirled on the grass like a mad dervish. But more beautiful than the words, or the grace of the dance, or even the laughter pouring from her lips, was the light, the light that rose in her heart like a sweet, piercing star ascending over the horizon. The light.

ALSO BY IMOGEN ALDRIDGE

The Dream Weaver

www.ingramcontent.com/pod-product-compliance
Lightning Source LLC
Chambersburg PA
CBHW070822180626
46818CB00001B/362